John Irving published his first novel, *Setting Free the Bears*, in 1968. He has been nominated for a National Book Award three times – winning once, in 1980, for the novel *The World According to Garp*. He also received an O. Henry Award, in 1981, for the short story 'Interior Space'. In 1992, he was inducted into the National Wrestling Hall of Fame in Stillwater, Oklahoma. In 2000, he won the Oscar for Best Adapted Screenplay for *The Cider House Rules* – a film with seven Academy Award nominations. In 2001, he was elected to the American Academy of Arts and Letters. His most recent novel is *Last Night in Twisted River*.

www.randomhouse.co.uk

THE NOVELS

Setting Free the Bears (1968)

'The most nourishing, satisfying novel I have read for years.
I admire the hell out of it'
Kurt Vonnegut Jr.

The Water-Method Man (1972)

'Three or four times as funny as most novels'
The New Yorker

The 158-Pound Marriage (1973)

'Deft and hard-hitting'
New York Times

The World According to Garp (1978)

'Absolutely extraordinary...A rollercoaster ride that leaves
one breathless'
Los Angeles Times

The Hotel New Hampshire (1981)

'A startlingly original family saga that combines
macabre humour with Dickensian sentiment'
Time

The Cider House Rules (1985)

'Difficult to define, impossible not to admire'
Daily Telegraph

A Prayer for Owen Meany (1989)

'A work of genius'
Independent

A Son of the Circus (1994)

'A wide-ranging fiction of massive design that
encapsulates our world'
Mail on Sunday

A Widow for One Year (1998)

'Grand farce, comic gusto and a deeply poetic sense
of human vulnerability'
Time Out

The Fourth Hand (2001)

'A rich and deeply moving tale...Vintage Irving'
Washington Post

Until I Find You (2006)

'Superbly original...To be read and remembered'
The Times

Last Night in Twisted River (2009)

'A stately, sophisticated rumination on the nature of
storytelling – and love'
Marie Claire

The Short Stories

Trying to Save Piggy Snead (1993)

'Supple and energetic'
New York Times Book Review

The Non-Fiction

The Imaginary Girlfriend (1996)

'Rich, wonderful and diverse'
Denver Post

My Movie Business (1999)

'Instructive, delightful and riveting'
Boston Globe

THE WORLD ACCORDING TO GARP

John Irving

BLACK SWAN

TRANSWORLD PUBLISHERS
61–63 Uxbridge Road, London W5 5SA
A Random House Group Company
www.randomhouse.co.uk

THE WORLD ACCORDING TO GARP
A BLACK SWAN BOOK: 9780552776783

First published in Great Britain
in 1978 by Victor Gollancz Ltd
Corgi edition published 1979
Black Swan edition published 1986
Black Swan edition reissued 2010

Addresses for Random House Group Ltd companies outside the UK
can be found at: www.randomhouse.co.uk
The Random House Group Ltd Reg. No. 954009

Typeset in Giovanni Book by
Kestrel Data, Exeter, Devon.

7

Penguin Random House is committed to a sustainable future for
our business, our readers and our planet. This book is made from
Forest Stewardship Council® certified paper.

Printed and bound in Great Britain by Clays Ltd, St Ives plc

For Colin and Brendan

The author wishes to express his gratitude to the Guggenheim Foundation.

Grateful acknowledgement is made for permission to reprint 'The Plot against the Giant.' Copyright 1923, 1951 by Wallace Stevens. Reprinted from *The Collected Poems of Wallace Stevens*, by permission of Alfred A. Knopf, Inc.

Portions of this book have appeared in different form in the following magazines: *Antaeus, Esquire, Gallery, Penthouse, Playboy, Ploughshares* and *Swank*.

CONTENTS

THE WORLD
ACCORDING
TO GARP

1

Boston Mercy

Garp's mother, Jenny Fields, was arrested in Boston in 1942 for wounding a man in a movie theater. This was shortly after the Japanese had bombed Pearl Harbor and people were being tolerant of soldiers, because suddenly everyone *was* a soldier, but Jenny Fields was quite firm in her intolerance of the behavior of men in general and soldiers in particular. In the movie theater she had to move three times, but each time the soldier moved closer to her until she was sitting against the musty wall, her view of the newsreel almost blocked by some silly colonnade, and she resolved she would not get up and move again. The soldier moved once more and sat beside her.

Jenny was twenty-two. She had dropped out of college almost as soon as she'd begun, but she had finished her nursing-school program at the head of her class and she enjoyed being a nurse. She was an athletic-looking young woman who always had high color in her cheeks; she had dark, glossy hair and what her mother called a mannish way of walking (she swung her arms), and her rump and hips were so slender and hard that, from behind, she resembled a young boy. In Jenny's opinion, her breasts were too large; she thought the ostentation of her bust made her look 'cheap and easy.'

She was nothing of the kind. In fact, she had dropped out of college when she suspected that the chief purpose of her parents' sending her to Wellesley had been to have

her dated by and eventually mated to some well-bred man.
The recommendation of Wellesley had come from her older
brothers, who had assured her parents that Wellesley women
were not thought of loosely and were considered high in
marriage potential. Jenny felt that her education was merely
a polite way to bide time, as if she were really a cow, being
prepared only for the insertion of the device for artificial
insemination.

Her declared major had been English literature, but when
it seemed to her that her classmates were chiefly concerned
with acquiring the sophistication and the poise to deal with
men, she had no trouble leaving literature for nursing. She
saw nursing as something that could be put into immediate
practice, and its study had no ulterior motive that Jenny
could see (later she wrote, in her famous autobiography,
that too many nurses put themselves on display for too
many doctors; but then her nursing days were over).

She liked the simple, no-nonsense uniform; the blouse
of the dress made less of her breasts; the shoes were comfortable, and suited to her fast pace of walking. When she
was at the night desk, she could still read. She did not miss
the young college men, who were sulky and disappointed
if you wouldn't compromise yourself, and superior and
aloof if you would. At the hospital she saw more soldiers
and working boys than college men, and they were
franker and less pretentious in their expectations; if you
compromised yourself a little, they seemed at least grateful
to see you again. Then, suddenly, everyone was a soldier –
and full of the self-importance of college boys – and Jenny
Fields stopped having anything to do with men.

'My mother,' Garp wrote, 'was a lone wolf.'

The Fields' family fortune was in shoes, though Mrs Fields,
a former Boston Weeks, had brought some money of her
own to the marriage. The Fields family had managed well
enough with footwear to have removed themselves from
the shoe factories years ago. They lived in a large, shingled

house on the New Hampshire shore at Dog's Head Harbor. Jenny went home for her days and nights off – mainly to please her mother, and to convince the grande dame that although Jenny was 'slumming her life away as a nurse,' as her mother remarked, she was not developing slovenly habits in her speech or in her moral person.

Jenny frequently met her brothers at the North Station and rode home on the train with them. As all members of the Fields family were bidden to do, they rode on the right-hand side of the Boston and Maine when the train left Boston and sat on the left when they returned. This complied with the wishes of the senior Mr Fields, who admitted that the ugliest scenery lay out that side of the train, but he felt that all Fieldses should be forced to face the grimy source of their independence and higher life. On the right-hand side of the train, leaving Boston, and on the left as you returned, you passed the main Fields Factory Outlet in Haverhill, and the vast billboard with the huge work shoe taking a firm step toward you. The billboard towered above the railroad yard and was reflected in countless miniatures in the windows of the shoe plant. Beneath this menacing, advancing foot were the words:

> *FIELDS* FOR YOUR FEET
> IN THE FACTORY OR IN
> THE FIELDS!

There was a Fields line of nursing shoe, and Mr Fields gave his daughter a free pair whenever she came home; Jenny must have had a dozen pairs. Mrs Fields, who insisted on equating her daughter's leaving Wellesley with a sordid future, also gave Jenny a present every time she came home. Mrs Fields gave her daughter a hot-water bottle, or so she said – and so Jenny assumed; she never opened the packages. Her mother would say, 'Dear, do you still have that hot-water bottle I gave you?' And Jenny would think a minute, believing she had left it on the train or thrown

it away, and she'd say, 'I *may* have lost it, Mother, but I'm
sure I don't need another one.' And Mrs Fields, bringing the
package out from hiding, would press it on her daughter; it
was still concealed in the drugstore paper. Mrs Fields would
say, '*Please,* Jennifer, be more careful. And *use* it, please!'

As a nurse, Jenny saw little use for the hot-water bottle;
she assumed it to be a touching, odd device of old-fashioned
and largely psychological comfort. But some of the packages
made it back to her small room near Boston Mercy Hospital.
She kept them in a closet, which was nearly full of boxes of
nursing shoes – also unopened.

She felt detached from her family, and thought it strange
how they had lavished so much attention on her, as a child,
and then at some appointed, prearranged time they seemed
to stop the flow of affection and begin the expectations – as
if, for a brief phase, you were expected to absorb love (and
get enough), and then, for a much longer and more serious
phase, you were expected to fulfill certain obligations. When
Jenny had broken the chain, had left Wellesley for something
as common as nursing, she had dropped her family –
and they, as if they couldn't help themselves, were in the
process of dropping her. In the Fields family, for example,
it would have been more appropriate if Jenny had become
a doctor, or if she'd stayed in college until she *married* one.
Each time she saw her brothers, her mother, and her father,
they were more uncomfortable in one another's presence.
They were involved in that awkward procedure of getting to
unknow each other.

That must be how families are, thought Jenny Fields.
She felt if she ever had children she would love them no
less when they were twenty than when they were two; they
might need you more at twenty, she thought. What do you
really need when you're two? In the hospital, the babies
were the easiest patients. The older they got, the more they
needed; and the less anyone wanted or loved them.

Jenny felt she had grown up on a large ship without
having seen, much less understood, the engine room. She

liked how the hospital reduced everything to what one ate, if it helped one to have eaten it, and where it went. As a child she had never seen the dirty dishes; in fact, when the maids cleared the table, Jenny was sure they were throwing the dishes away (it was some time before she was even allowed in the kitchen). And when the milk truck brought the bottles every morning, for a while Jenny thought that the truck brought the day's dishes, too – the sound, that glassy clatter and bang, being so like the sound of the maids in the closed kitchen, doing whatever they did to the dishes.

Jenny Fields was five before she saw her father's bathroom. She tracked it down one morning by following the scent of her father's cologne. She found a steamy shower stall – quite modern, for 1925 – a private toilet, a row of bottles so unlike her mother's bottles that Jenny thought she had discovered the lair of a secret man living undetected in their house for years. In fact, she *had*.

In the hospital, Jenny knew where everything went – and she was learning the unmagical answers to where almost everything came from. At Dog's Head Harbor, when Jenny had been a girl, the family members had their own baths, their own rooms, their own doors with their own mirrors on the backs. In the hospital, privacy was not sacred; nothing was a secret; if you wanted a mirror, you had to ask a nurse.

The most mysterious thing she had been allowed to investigate on her own, when Jenny was a child, had been the cellar and the great pottery crock which every Monday was filled with clams. Jenny's mother sprinkled cornmeal on the clams at night, and every morning they were rinsed in fresh sea water from a long pipe that ran into the basement from the sea itself. By the weekend the clams were fat and free of sand, they were growing too big for their shells, and their great, obscene necks lolled on the salt water. Jenny would help the cook sort through them on Fridays; the dead ones did not retract their necks when touched.

Jenny asked for a book about clams. She read all about them: how they ate, how they bred, how they grew. It was the first live thing she understood completely – its life, its sex, its death. At Dog's Head Harbor, human beings were not that accessible. In the hospital, Jenny Fields felt she was making up for lost time; she was discovering that people weren't much more mysterious, or much more attractive, than clams.

'My mother,' Garp wrote, 'was not one for making fine distinctions.'

One striking difference she might have seen between clams and people was that most people had some sense of humor, but Jenny was not inclined toward humor. There was a popular joke among the nurses in Boston at that time, but it was not funny to Jenny Fields. The joke involved one of the other hospitals in Boston. The hospital Jenny worked in was Boston Mercy Hospital, which was called Boston Mercy; there was also Massachusetts General Hospital, which was called the Mass General. And another hospital was the Peter Bent Brigham, which was called the Peter Bent.

One day, the joke goes, a Boston cab driver had his taxi hailed by a man who staggered off the curb toward him, almost dropping to his knees in the street. The man was purple in the face with pain; he was either strangling or holding his breath, so that talking was clearly difficult for him, and the cabby opened the door and helped him inside, where the man lay face down on the floor alongside the back seat, tucking his knees up to his chest.

'Hospital! Hospital!' he cried.

'The Peter Bent?' the cabby asked. That was the closest hospital.

'It's worse than *bent*,' the man moaned. 'I think Molly bit it *off!*'

Few jokes were funny to Jenny Fields, and certainly not this one; no peter jokes for Jenny, who was staying clear of the issue. She had seen the trouble peters could get into; babies were not the worst of it. Of course she saw people who didn't want to have babies, and they were sad that they were pregnant; they shouldn't *have* to have babies, Jenny thought – though she mainly felt sorry for the babies who were born. She saw people who wanted to have their babies, too, and they made *her* want to have one. One day, Jenny Fields thought, she would like to have a baby – just one. But the trouble was that she wanted as little to do with a peter as possible, and nothing whatsoever to do with a man.

Most peter treatment that Jenny saw was done to soldiers. The U.S. Army would not begin to benefit from the discovery of penicillin until 1943, and there were many soldiers who didn't get penicillin until 1945. At Boston Mercy, in the early days of 1942, peters were usually treated with sulfa and arsenic. Sulfathiazole was for the clap – with lots of water recommended. For syphilis, in the days before penicillin, they used neoarsphenamine; Jenny Fields thought that this was the epitome of all that sex could lead to – to introduce *arsenic* into the human chemistry, to try to clean the chemistry up.

The other peter treatment was local and also required a lot of fluid. Jenny frequently assisted with this method of disinfecting, because the patient required lots of attention at the time; sometimes, in fact, he needed to be held. It was a simple procedure that could force as much as one hundred cc's of fluid up the penis and through the surprised urethra before it all came back, but the procedure left everyone feeling a bit raw. The man who invented a device for this method of treatment was named Valentine, and his device was called the Valentine irrigator. Long after Dr Valentine's irrigator was improved, or replaced with another irrigation device, the nurses at Boston Mercy still referred to the procedure as the Valentine treatment – an appropriate punishment for a lover, thought Jenny Fields.

'My mother,' Garp wrote, 'was not romantically inclined.'

When the soldier in the movie theater first started changing seats – when he made his first move for her – Jenny Fields felt that the Valentine treatment would be just the thing for him. But she didn't have an irrigator with her; it was much too large for her purse. It also required the considerable cooperation of the patient. What she *did* have with her was a scalpel; she carried it with her all the time. She had not stolen it from surgery, either; it was a castaway scalpel with a deep nick taken out of the point (it had probably been dropped on the floor, or in a sink) – it was no good for fine work, but it was not for fine work that Jenny wanted it.

At first it had slashed up the little silk pockets of her purse. Then she found part of an old thermometer container that slipped over the head of the scalpel, capping it like a fountain pen. It was this cap she removed when the soldier moved into the seat beside her and stretched his arm along the armrest they were (absurdly) meant to share. His long hand dangled off the end of the armrest; it twitched like the flank of a horse shuddering the flies away. Jenny kept her hand on the scalpel inside her purse; with her other hand, she held the purse tightly in her white lap. She was imagining that her nurse's uniform shone like a holy shield, and for some perverse reason this vermin beside her had been attracted by her light.

'My mother,' Garp wrote, 'went through her life on the lookout for purse-snatchers and snatch-snatchers.'

In the theater, it was not her purse that the soldier wanted. He touched her knee. Jenny spoke up fairly clearly. 'Get your stinking hand off me,' she said. Several people turned around.

'Oh, come on,' the soldier moaned, and his hand shot quickly under her uniform; he found her thighs locked tightly together – he found his whole arm, from his shoulder to his wrist, suddenly sliced open like a soft melon. Jenny had cut cleanly through his insignia and his shirt, cleanly through his skin and muscles, baring his bones at the joint of his elbow. ('If I'd wanted to kill him,' she told the police, later, 'I'd have slit his wrist. I'm a nurse. I know how people bleed.')

The soldier screamed. On his feet and falling back, he swiped at Jenny's head with his uncut arm, boxing her ear so sharply that her head sang. She pawed at him with the scalpel, removing a piece of his upper lip the approximate shape and thinness of a thumbnail. ('I was *not* trying to slash his throat,' she told the police, later. 'I was trying to cut his nose off, but I missed.')

Crying, on all fours, the soldier groped his way to the theater aisle and headed toward the safety of the light in the lobby. Someone else in the theater was whimpering, in fright.

Jenny wiped her scalpel on the movie seat, returned it to her purse, and covered the blade with the thermometer cap. Then she went to the lobby, where keen wailings could be heard and the manager was calling through the lobby doors over the dark audience, 'Is there a doctor here? Please! Is someone a doctor?'

Someone *was* a nurse, and she went to lend what assistance she could. When the soldier saw her, he fainted; it was not really from loss of blood. Jenny knew how facial wounds bled; they were deceptive. The deeper gash on his arm was of course in need of immediate attention, but the soldier was not bleeding to death. No one but Jenny seemed to know that – there was so much blood, and so much of it was on her white nurse's uniform. They quickly realized she had done it. The theater lackeys would not let her touch the fainted soldier, and someone took her purse from her. The mad nurse! The crazed slasher! Jenny Fields was calm. She thought it was only a matter of waiting for the true authorities to comprehend the situation. But the police were not very nice to her, either.

'You been dating this guy long?' the first one asked her, en route to the precinct station.

And another one asked her, later, 'But how did you know he was going to *attack* you? He says he was just trying to introduce himself.'

'That's a real mean little weapon, honey,' a third told her. 'You shouldn't carry something like that around with you. That's asking for trouble.'

So Jenny waited for her brothers to clear things up. They

were law-school men from Cambridge, across the river. One was a law student, the other one taught in the law school.

'Both,' Garp wrote, 'were of the opinion that the *practice* of law was vulgar, but the *study* of it was sublime.'

They were not so comforting when they came.

'Break your mother's heart,' said one.

'If you'd only stayed at Wellesley,' said the other.

'A girl alone has to protect herself,' Jenny said. 'What could be more proper?'

But one of her brothers asked her if she could prove that she had not had previous relations with the man.

'Confidentially,' whispered the other one, 'have you been dating this guy long?'

Finally, things were cleared up when the police discovered that the soldier was from New York, where he had a wife and child. He had taken a leave in Boston and, more than anything else, he feared the story would get back to his wife. Everyone seemed to agree that *would* be awful – for everyone – so Jenny was released without charges. When she made a fuss that the police had not given her back her scalpel, one of her brothers said, 'For God's sake, Jennifer, you can steal another one, can't you?'

'I didn't *steal* it,' Jenny said.

'You should have some friends,' a brother told her.

'At Wellesley,' they repeated.

'Thank you for coming when I called you,' Jenny said.

'What's a family for?' one said.

'Blood runs thick,' said the other. Then he paled, embarrassed at the association – her uniform was so besmirched.

'I'm a good girl,' Jenny told them.

'Jennifer,' said the older one, and her life's earliest model – for wisdom, for all that was right. He was rather solemn. He said, 'It's best not to get involved with married men.'

'We won't tell Mother,' the other one said.

'And certainly not Father!' said the first. In an awkward attempt at some natural warmth, he winked at her – a gesture that contorted his face and for a moment convinced Jenny that her life's earliest model had developed a facial tic.

Beside the brothers was a mailbox with a poster of Uncle Sam. A tiny soldier, all in brown, was climbing down from Uncle Sam's big hands. The soldier was going to land on a map of Europe. The words under the poster said: SUPPORT OUR BOYS! Jenny's oldest brother looked at Jenny looking at the poster.

'And don't get involved with soldiers,' he added, though in a very few months he would be a soldier himself. He would be one of the soldiers who wouldn't come home from the war. He would break his mother's heart, an act he once spoke of with distaste.

Jenny's only other brother would be killed in a sailboat accident long after the war was over. He would be drowned several miles offshore from the Fields' family estate at Dog's Head Harbor. Of his grieving wife, Jenny's mother would say, 'She's still young and attractive, and the children aren't obnoxious. At least not yet. After a decent time, I'm sure she'll be able to find someone else.' It was to Jenny that her brother's widow eventually spoke, almost a year after the drowning. She asked Jenny if she thought a 'decent time' had passed and she could begin whatever had to be begun 'to find someone else.' She was anxious about offending Jenny's mother. She wondered if Jenny thought it would be all right to emerge from mourning.

'If you don't *feel* like mourning, what are you mourning for?' Jenny asked her. In her autobiography, Jenny wrote: 'That poor woman needed to be told what to *feel*.'

'That was the stupidest woman my mother said she ever met,' Garp wrote. 'And she had gone to Wellesley.'

But Jenny Fields, when she said good night to her brothers at her small rooming house near Boston Mercy, was too confused to be properly outraged. She was also sore – her ear, where the soldier had cuffed her, hurt her; and there was a deep muscle cramp between her shoulder blades, which made it hard for her to sleep. She thought she must have wrenched something in there when the theater lackeys had grabbed her in the lobby and pulled her arms behind her back. She remembered that hot-water bottles were supposed to be good for sore muscles and she got out of bed and went to her closet and opened one of her mother's gift packages.

It was not a hot-water bottle. That had been her mother's euphemism for something her mother couldn't bring herself to discuss. In the package was a douche bag. Jenny's mother knew what they were for, and so did Jenny. She had helped many patients at the hospital use them, though at the hospital they were not much used to prevent pregnancies after lovemaking; they were used for general feminine hygiene, and in venereal cases. To Jenny Fields a douche bag was a gentler, more commodious version of the Valentine irrigator.

Jenny opened all her mother's packages. In each one was a douche bag. 'Please *use* it, dear!' her mother had begged her. Jenny knew that her mother, though she meant well, assumed that Jenny's sexual activity was considerable and irresponsible. No doubt, as her mother would put it, 'since Wellesley.' Since Wellesley, Jenny's mother thought that Jenny was fornicating (as she would also put it) 'to beat the band.'

Jenny Fields crawled back to bed with the douche bag filled with hot water and snuggled between her shoulder blades; she hoped the clamps that kept the water from running down the hose would not allow a leak, but to be sure she held the hose in her hands, a little like a rubber rosary, and she dropped the nozzle with the tiny holes into her empty water glass. All night long Jenny lay listening to the douche bag leak.

In this dirty-minded world, she thought, you are either somebody's wife or somebody's whore – or fast on your way to becoming one or the other. If you don't fit either category, then everyone tries to make you think there is something wrong with you. But, she thought, there is nothing wrong with me.

That was the beginning, of course, of the book that many years later would make Jenny Fields famous. However crudely put, her autobiography was said to bridge the usual gap between literary merit and popularity, although Garp claimed that his mother's work had 'the same literary merit as the Sears, Roebuck catalog.'

But what made Jenny Fields vulgar? Not her legal brothers, not the man in the movie theater who stained her uniform. Not her mother's douche bags, though these were responsible for Jenny's eventual eviction. Her landlady (a fretful woman who for obscure reasons of her own suspected that every woman was on the verge of an explosion of lasciviousness) discovered that there were nine douche bags in Jenny's tiny room and bath. A matter of guilt by association: in the mind of the troubled landlady, such a sign indicated a fear of contamination beyond even the landlady's fear. Or worse, this profusion of douche bags represented an actual and awesome *need* for douching, the conceivable reasons for which penetrated the worst of the landlady's dreams.

Whatever she made of the twelve pairs of nursing shoes cannot even be hinted. Jenny thought the matter so absurd – and found her own feelings toward her parents' provisions so ambiguous – that she hardly protested. She moved.

But this did not make her vulgar. Since her brothers, her parents, and her landlady assumed a life of lewdness for her – regardless of her own, private example – Jenny decided that all manifestations of her innocence were futile and appeared defensive. She took a small apartment, which prompted a new assault of packaged douche bags from her mother and a stack of nursing shoes from her father. It struck her that they were thinking: If she is to be a whore, let her at least be clean and well shod.

In part, the war kept Jenny from dwelling on how badly her family misread her – and kept her from any bitterness and self-pity, too; Jenny was not a 'dweller.' She was a good nurse, and she was increasingly busy. Many nurses were joining up, but Jenny had no desire for a change of uniform, or for travel; she was a solitary girl and she didn't want to have to meet a lot of new people. Also, she found the system of *rank* irritating enough at Boston Mercy; in an army field hospital, she assumed, it could only be worse.

First of all, she would have missed the babies. That was really why she stayed, when so many were leaving. She was at her best as a nurse, she felt, to mothers and their babies – and there were suddenly so many babies whose fathers were away, or dead or missing; Jenny wanted most of all to encourage these mothers. In fact, she envied them. It was, to her, the ideal situation: a mother alone with a new baby, the husband blown out of the sky over France. A young woman with her own child, with a life ahead of them – just the two of them. A baby with no strings attached, thought Jenny Fields. An almost virgin birth. At least, no *future* peter treatment would be necessary.

These women, of course, were not always as happy with their lot as Jenny thought she would have been. They were grieving, many of them, or abandoned (many others); they resented their children, some of them; they wanted a husband and a father for their babies (many others). But Jenny Fields was their encourager – she spoke up for solitude, she told them how lucky they were.

'Don't you believe you're a good woman?' she'd ask them. Most of them thought they were.

'And isn't your baby beautiful?' Most of them thought their babies were.

'And the father? What was he like?' A bum, many thought. A swine, a lout, a liar – a no-good run-out fuck-around of a man! But he's *dead!* sobbed a few.

'Then you're better off, aren't you?' Jenny asked.

Some of them came around to seeing it her way, but Jenny's reputation at the hospital suffered for her crusade. The hospital policy toward unwed mothers was not generally so encouraging.

'Old Virgin Mary Jenny,' the other nurses said. 'Doesn't want a baby the easy way. Why not ask God for one?'

In her autobiography, Jenny wrote: 'I wanted a job and I wanted to live alone. That made me a sexual suspect. Then I wanted a baby, but I didn't want to have to share my body or my life to have one. That made me a sexual suspect, too.'

And that was what made her vulgar, too. (And that was where she got her famous title: A Sexual Suspect, the autobiography of Jenny Fields.)

Jenny Fields discovered that you got more respect from shocking other people than you got from trying to live your own life with a little privacy. Jenny told the other nurses that she would one day find a man to make her pregnant – just that, and nothing more. She did not entertain the possibility that the man would need to try more than once, she told them. They, of course, couldn't wait to tell everyone they knew. It was not long before Jenny had several proposals. She had to make a sudden decision: she could retreat, ashamed that her secret was out; or she could be brazen.

A young medical student told her he would volunteer on the condition that he could have at least six chances over a three-day weekend. Jenny told him that he obviously lacked confidence; she wanted a child who would be more secure than that.

An anesthesiologist told her he would even pay for the baby's education – through college – but Jenny told him that his eyes were too close together and his teeth were poorly formed; she would not saddle her would-be child with such handicaps.

One of the other nurses' boyfriends treated her most cruelly; he frightened her in the hospital cafeteria by handing her a milk glass nearly full of a cloudy, viscous substance.

'Sperm,' he said, nodding at the glass. 'All that's one shot – I don't mess around. If one chance is all anyone gets, I'm your man.' Jenny held up the horrid glass and inspected it coolly. God knows what was actually in the glass. The nurse's boyfriend said, 'That's just an indication of what kind of stuff I've got. Lots of seeds,' he added, grinning. Jenny dumped the contents of the glass into a potted plant.

'I want a baby,' she said. 'I don't want to start a sperm farm.'

Jenny knew this was going to be hard. She learned to take a ribbing, and she learned to respond in kind.

So they decided Jenny Fields was crude, that she was going too far. A joke was a joke, but Jenny seemed too determined about it. Either she was sticking to her guns, just to be stubborn – or worse, she really meant it. Her hospital colleagues couldn't make her laugh, and they couldn't get her to bed. As Garp wrote of his mother's dilemma: 'Her colleagues detected that she felt herself to be superior to them. Nobody's colleagues appreciate this.'

So they initiated a get-tough policy with Jenny Fields. It was a staff decision – 'for her own good,' of course. They decided to get Jenny away from the babies and the mothers. She's got babies on her brain, they said. No more obstetrics for Jenny Fields. Keep her away from the incubators – she's got too soft a heart, or a head.

Thus they separated Jenny Fields from the mothers and their babies. She's a good nurse, they all said; let her try some intensive care. It was their experience that a nurse in Boston Mercy's intensive care quickly lost interest in her own problems. Of course Jenny knew why they had sent her away from the babies; she only resented that they thought so little of her self-control. Because what she wanted was strange to them, they assumed that she also had slim restraint. There is no logic to people, Jenny thought. There was lots of time to get pregnant, she knew. She was in no hurry. It was just part of an eventual plan.

Now there was a war. In intensive care, she saw a little more of it. The service hospitals sent them their special patients, and there were always the terminal cases. There were the usual elderly patients, hanging by the usual threads; there were the usual industrial accidents, and automobile accidents, and the terrible accidents to children. But mainly there were soldiers. What happened to them was no accident.

Jenny made her own divisions among the non-accidents that happened to the soldiers; she came up with her own categories for them.

1. There were the men who'd been burned; for the most part, they'd been burned on board ship (the most complicated cases came from Chelsea Naval Hospital), but they'd also been burned in airplanes and on the ground. Jenny called them the Externals.

2. There were the men who'd been shot or damaged in bad places; internally, they were in trouble, and Jenny called them the Vital Organs.

3. There were the men whose injuries seemed almost mystical, to Jenny; they were men who weren't 'there' anymore, whose heads or spines had been tampered with. Sometimes they were paralyzed, sometimes they were merely vague. Jenny called them the Absentees. Occasionally, one of the Absentees had External or Vital Organ damage as well; all the hospital had a name for them.

4. They were Goners.

'My father,' Garp wrote, 'was a Goner. From my mother's point of view, that must have made him very attractive. No strings attached.'

Garp's father was a ball turret gunner who had a non-accident in the air over France.

'The ball turret gunner,' Garp wrote, 'was a member of the bomber's crew who was among the most vulnerable to anti-aircraft fire from the ground. That was called flak; flak often looked to the gunner like fast-moving ink flung upward and spread on the sky as if the sky were a blotter. The little man (for in order to fit in the ball turret, a man was better off if he was small) crouched with his machine guns in his cramped nest – a cocoon in which he resembled one of those insects trapped in glass. This ball turret was a metal sphere with a glass porthole; it was set into the fuselage of a B-17 like a distended navel – like a nipple on the bomber's belly. In this tiny dome were two fifty-caliber machine guns and a short, small man whose chore was to track in his gunsights a fighter plane attacking his bomber. When the turret moved, the gunner revolved with it. There were wooden handles with buttons on the tops to fire the guns; gripping these trigger sticks, the ball turret gunner looked like some dangerous fetus suspended in the bomber's absurdly exposed amniotic sac, intent on protecting his mother. These handles also steered the turret – to a cut-off point, so that the ball turret gunner would not shoot off the props forward.

'With the sky *under* him, the gunner must have felt especially cold, appended to the plane like an afterthought. Upon landing, the ball turret was retracted – usually. Upon landing, an *un*retracted ball turret would send up sparks – as long and violent as automobiles – off the old tarmac.'

Technical Sergeant Garp, the late gunner whose familiarity with violent death cannot be exaggerated, served with the Eighth Air Force – the air force that bombed the Continent from England. Sergeant Garp had experience as a nose gunner in the B-17C and a waist gunner in the B-17E before they made him a ball turret gunner.

Garp did not like the waist gun arrangements on the B-17E. There were two waist gunners tucked into the rib cage of the plane, their gunports opposite each other, and Garp was always getting clouted in the ears when his mate swiveled his gun at the same time Garp was moving with his. In later models, precisely because of this interference between the waist gunners, the gunports would be staggered. But this innovation would happen too late for Sergeant Garp.

His first combat mission was a daylight sortie by B-17Es against Rouen, France, on August 17, 1942, which was accomplished without losses. Technical Sergeant Garp, at his waist gun position, was clouted once on the left ear by his gunner mate and twice on the right. A part of the problem was that the other gunner, compared to Garp, was so large; the man's elbows were level with Garp's ears.

In the ball turret that first day over Rouen was a man

named Fowler who was even smaller than Garp. Fowler had been a jockey before the war. He was a better shot than Garp, but the ball turret was where Garp wished he could be. He was an orphan but he must have liked being alone, and he sought some escape from the crowding and elbowing of his fellow waist gunner. Of course, like a great many gunners, Garp dreamed of his fiftieth mission or so, whereafter he hoped to be transferred to the Second Air Force – the bomber training command – where he could retire safely as a gunnery instructor. But until Fowler was killed, Garp envied Fowler his private place, his jockey's sense of isolation.

'It's a foul spot to be in if you fart a lot,' Fowler maintained. He was a cynical man with a dry, irritating tickle of a cough and a vile reputation among the nurses at the field hospital.

Fowler was killed during a crash landing on an unpaved road. The landing struts were shorn off in a pothole and the whole landing gear collapsed, dropping the bomber into a hard belly slide that burst the ball turret with all the disproportionate force of a falling tree hitting a grape. Fowler, who'd always said he had more faith in machines than he had in horses or in human beings, was crouched in the unretracted ball turret when the plane landed on him. The waist gunners, including Sergeant Garp, saw the debris skid away from under the belly of the bomber. The squadron adjutant, who was the closest ground observer of the landing, threw up in a Jeep. The squadron commander did not have to wait for Fowler's death to become official in order to replace him with the squadron's next-smallest gunner. Tiny Technical Sergeant Garp had always wanted to be a ball turret gunner. In September of 1942, he became one.

'My mother was a stickler for detail,' Garp wrote. When they would bring in a new casualty, Jenny Fields was the first to ask the doctor how it happened. And Jenny classified them,

silently: the Externals, the Vital Organs, the Absentees, and
the Goners. And she found little gimmicks to help her
remember their names and their disasters. Thus: Private
Jones fell off his bones, Ensign Potter stopped a whopper,
Corporal Estes lost his testes, Captain Flynn has no skin,
Major Longfellow is short on answers.

Sergeant Garp was a mystery. On his thirty-fifth flight over
France, the little ball turret gunner stopped shooting. The
pilot noticed the absence of machine-gun fire from the ball
turret and thought that Garp had taken a hit. If Garp had, the
pilot had not felt it in the belly of his plane. He hoped Garp
hadn't felt it much, either. After the plane landed, the pilot
hurried to have Garp transferred to the sidecar of a medic's
motorcycle; all the ambulances were in use. Once seated in
the sidecar, the tiny technical sergeant began to play with
himself. There was a canvas canopy that covered the sidecar
in foul weather; the pilot snapped this covering in place.
The canopy had a porthole, through which the medic, the
pilot, and the gathering men could observe Sergeant Garp.
For such a small man, he seemed to have an especially large
erection, but he fumbled with it only a little more expertly
than a child – not nearly so expertly as a monkey in the zoo.
Like the monkey, however, Garp looked out of his cage and
stared frankly into the faces of the human beings who were
watching him.

'Garp?' the pilot said. Garp's forehead was freckled with
blood, which was mostly dry, but his flight hat was plastered
to the top of his head and dripping; there didn't seem to
be a mark on him. 'Garp!' the pilot shouted at him. There
had been a gash in the metal sphere where the fifty-caliber
machine guns had been; it appeared that some flak had hit
the barrels of the guns, cracking the gun housing and even
loosening the trigger handles, though there was nothing
wrong with Garp's hands – they just seemed to be clumsy
at masturbation.

'Garp!' cried the pilot.

'Garp?' said Garp. He was mimicking the pilot, like a

smart parrot or a crow. 'Garp,' said Garp, as if he had just learned the word. The pilot nodded to Garp, encouraging him to remember his name. Garp smiled. 'Garp,' he said. He seemed to think this was how people greeted each other. Not hello, hello! – but Garp, Garp!

'Jesus, Garp,' the pilot said. Some holes and glass cracks had been visible in the porthole of the ball turret. The medic now unzipped the porthole of the sidecar's canopy and peered into Garp's eyes. Something was wrong with Garp's eyes, because they rolled around independently of each other; the medic thought that the world, for Garp, was probably looming up, then going by, then looming up again – if Garp could see at all. What the pilot and the medic couldn't know, at the time, was that some sharp and slender shards from the flak blast had damaged one of the oculomotor nerves in Garp's brain – and other parts of his brain as well. The oculomotor nerve consists chiefly of motor fibers that innervate most of the muscles of the eyeball. As for the rest of Garp's brain, he had received some cuts and slashes a lot like a prefrontal lobotomy – though it was rather careless surgery.

The medic had a great fear of *how* carelessly a lobotomy had been performed on Sergeant Garp, and for that reason he thought against taking off the blood-sodden flight hat which was stuck to Garp and yanked down to where it touched a taut, shiny knob that appeared, now, to be growing on his forehead. Everyone looked around for the medic's motorcyclist, but he was off vomiting somewhere and the medic supposed he would have to find someone to sit in the sidecar with Garp while he drove the motorcycle himself.

'Garp?' Garp said to the medic, trying his new word.

'Garp,' the medic confirmed. Garp seemed pleased. He had both his small hands on his impressive erection when he successfully masturbated.

'Garp!' he barked. There was joy in his voice, but also surprise. He rolled his eyes at his audience, begging the world to loom up and hold still. He was unsure of what he'd done. 'Garp?' he asked, doubtfully.

The pilot patted his arm and nodded to the others of the flight and landing crew, as if to say: Let's give a bit of support to the sergeant, men. Please, let's make him feel at home. And the men, respectfully dumbstruck by Garp's ejaculation, all said, 'Garp! Garp! Garp!' to him – a reassuring, seallike chorus intent on putting Garp at ease.

Garp nodded his head, happily, but the medic held his arm and whispered anxiously to him, 'No! Don't move your head, okay? Garp? Please don't move your head.' Garp's eyes roamed past the pilot and the medic, who waited for them to come around again. 'Easy does it, Garp,' the pilot whispered. 'Just sit tight, okay?'

Garp's face radiated pure peace. With both hands holding his dying erection, the little sergeant looked as if he had done just the thing that the situation called for.

They could do nothing for Sergeant Garp in England. He was lucky to have been brought home to Boston long before the end of the war. Some senator was actually responsible. An editorial in a Boston newspaper had accused the U.S. Navy of transporting wounded servicemen back home only if the wounded came from wealthy and important American families. In an effort to quell such a vile rumor, a U.S. senator claimed that if *any* of the severely wounded were lucky enough to get back to America, 'even an *orphan* would get to make the trip – just like anyone else.' There was then some scurrying around to come up with a wounded orphan, to prove the senator's point, but they came up with a perfect person.

Not only was Technical Sergeant Garp an orphan; he was an idiot with a one-word vocabulary, so he was not complaining to the press. And in all the photographs they took, Gunner Garp was smiling.

When the drooling sergeant was brought to Boston Mercy, Jenny Fields had trouble categorizing him. He was clearly an Absentee, more docile than a child, but she wasn't sure how much else was wrong with him.

'Hello. How are you?' she asked him, when they wheeled him – grinning – into the ward.

'Garp!' he barked. The oculomotor nerve had been partially restored, and his eyes now leapt, rather than rolled, but his hands were wrapped in gauze mittens, the result of Garp's playing in an accidental fire that broke out in the hospital compound aboard his transport ship. He'd seen the flames and had reached out his hands to them, spreading some of the flames up to his face; he'd singed off his eyebrows. He looked a lot like a shaved owl, to Jenny.

With the burns, Garp was an External and an Absentee all at once. Also, with his hands so heavily bandaged, he had lost the ability to masturbate, an activity that his papers said he pursued frequently and successfully – and without any self-consciousness. Those who'd observed him closely, since his accident with the ship's fire, feared that the childish gunner was becoming depressed – his one adult pleasure taken from him, at least until his hands healed.

It was possible, of course, that Garp had Vital Organ damage as well. Many fragments had entered his head; many of them were too delicately located to be removed. Sergeant Garp's brain damage might not stop with his crude lobotomy; his internal destruction could be progressing. 'Our general deterioration is complicated enough,' Garp wrote, 'without the introduction of flak to our systems.'

There'd been a patient before Sergeant Garp whose head had been similarly penetrated. He'd been fine for months, just talking to himself and occasionally peeing in his bed. Then he started to lose his hair; he had trouble completing his sentences. Just before he died, he began to develop breasts.

Given the evidence, the shadows, and the white needles in the X-rays, Gunner Garp was probably a Goner. But to Jenny Fields he looked very nice. A small, neat man, the former ball turret gunner was as innocent and straightforward in his demands as a two-year-old. He cried 'Garp!' when he was hungry and 'Garp!' when he was glad; he asked 'Garp?' when something puzzled him, or when addressing strangers, and he said 'Garp' without the question mark when he recognized you. He usually did what he was told, but he couldn't be trusted; he forgot easily, and if one time he was as obedient as a six-year-old, another time he was as mindlessly curious as if he were one and a half.

His depressions, which were well documented in his transport papers, seemed to occur simultaneously with his erections. At these moments he would clamp his poor, grown-up peter between his gauzy, mittened hands and weep. He wept because the gauze didn't feel as good as his short memory of his hands, and also because it hurt his hands to touch anything. It was then that Jenny Fields would come sit with him. She would rub his back between his shoulder blades until he tipped back his head like a cat, and she'd talk to him all the while, her voice friendly and full of exciting shifts of accent. Most nurses droned to their patients – a steady, changeless voice intent on producing sleep, but Jenny knew that it wasn't sleep Garp needed. She knew he was only a baby, and he was bored – he needed some distraction. So Jenny entertained him. She played the radio for him, but some of the programs upset Garp; no one knew why. Other programs gave him terrific erections, which led to his depressions, and so forth. One program, just once, gave Garp a wet dream, which so surprised and pleased him that he was always eager to *see* the radio. But Jenny couldn't find that program again, she couldn't repeat the performance. She knew that if she could plug poor Garp into the wet-dream program, her job and his life would be much happier. But it wasn't that easy.

She gave up trying to teach him a new word. When she fed him and she saw that he liked what he was eating, she'd say, 'Good! That's *good*.'

'Garp!' he'd agree.

And when he spat out food on his bib and made a terrible

face, she'd say, 'Bad! That stuff's *bad*, right?'

'Garp!' he'd gag.

The first sign Jenny had of his deterioration was when he seemed to lose the G. One morning he greeted her with an 'Arp.'

'Garp,' she said firmly to him. 'G-arp.'

'Arp,' he said. She knew she was losing him.

Daily he seemed to grow younger. When he slept, he kneaded the air with his wriggling fists, his lips puckering, his cheeks sucking, his eyelids trembling. Jenny had spent a lot of time around babies; she knew that the ball turret gunner was nursing in his dreams. For a while she contemplated stealing a pacifier from maternity, but she stayed away from that place now; the jokes irritated her ('Here's Virgin Mary Jenny, swiping a phony nipple for her child. Who's the lucky father, Jenny?'). She watched Sergeant Garp suckle in his sleep and tried to imagine that his ultimate regression would be peaceful, that he would turn into his fetus phase and no longer breathe through his lungs; that his personality would blissfully separate, half of him turning to dreams of an egg, half of him to dreams of sperm. Finally, he simply wouldn't *be* anymore.

It was almost like that. Garp's nursing phase became so severe that he seemed to wake up like a child on a four-hour feeding schedule; he even cried like a baby, his face scarlet, his eyes springing tears in an instant, and in an instant being pacified – by the radio, by Jenny's voice. Once, when she rubbed his back, he burped. Jenny burst into tears. She sat at his bedside wishing him a swift, painless journey back into the womb and beyond.

If only his hands would heal, she thought. Then he could suck his thumb. When he woke from his suckling dreams, hungry to nurse, or so he imagined, Jenny would put her own finger to his mouth and let his lips tug at her. Though he had real, grown-up teeth, in his *mind* he was toothless and he never bit her. It was this observation that led Jenny, one night, to offer him her breast, where he sucked inexhaustibly and didn't seem to mind that there was nothing to be had there. Jenny thought that if he kept nursing at her, she *would* have milk; she felt such a firm tug in her womb, both maternal and sexual. Her feelings were so vivid – she believed for a while that she could possibly *conceive* a child simply by suckling the baby ball turret gunner.

It was almost like that. But Gunner Garp was not *all* baby. One night, when he nursed at her, Jenny noticed he had an erection that lifted the sheet; with his clumsy, bandaged hands he fanned himself, yelping frustration while he wolfed at her breast. And so one night she helped him; with her cool, powdered hand she took hold of him. At her breast he stopped nursing, he just nuzzled her.

'Ar,' he moaned. He had lost the *p*.

Once a Garp, then an Arp, now only an Ar; she knew he was dying. He had just one vowel and one consonant left.

When he came, she felt his shot wet and hot in her hand. Under the sheet it smelled like a greenhouse in summer, absurdly fertile, growth gotten out of hand. You could plant *anything* there and it would blossom. Garp's sperm struck Jenny Fields that way: if you spilled a little in a greenhouse, *babies* would sprout out of the dirt.

Jenny gave the matter twenty-four hours of thought.

'Garp?' Jenny whispered.

She unbuttoned the blouse of her dress and brought forth the breasts she had always considered too large. 'Garp?' she whispered in his ear; his eyelids fluttered, his lips reached. Around them was a white shroud, a curtain on runners, which enclosed them in the ward. On one side of Garp was an External – a flame-thrower victim, slippery with salve, swaddled in gauze. He had no eyelids, so it appeared he was always watching, but he was blind. Jenny took off her sturdy nurse's shoes, unfastened her white stockings, stepped out of her dress. She touched her finger to Garp's lips.

On the other side of Garp's white-shrouded bed was a

Vital Organ patient on his way to becoming an Absentee. He had lost most of his lower intestine and his rectum; now a kidney was giving him trouble and his liver was driving him crazy. He had terrible nightmares that he was being forced to urinate and defecate, though this was ancient history for him. He was actually quite unaware when he did those things, and he did them through tubes into rubber bags. He groaned frequently and, unlike Garp, he groaned in whole words.

'Shit,' he groaned.

'Garp?' Jenny whispered. She stepped out of her slip and her panties; she took off her bra and pulled back the sheet.

'Christ,' said the External, softly; his lips were blistered with burns.

'Goddamn shit!' cried the Vital Organ man.

'Garp,' said Jenny Fields. She took hold of his erection and straddled him.

'Aaa,' said Garp. Even the *r* was gone. He was reduced to a vowel sound to express his joy or his sadness. 'Aaa,' he said, as Jenny drew him inside her and sat on him with all her weight.

'Garp?' she asked. 'Okay? Is that good, Garp?'

'*Good*,' he agreed, distinctly. But it was only a word from his wrecked memory, thrown clear for a moment when he came inside her. It was the first and last true word that Jenny Fields heard him speak: good. As he shrank and his vital stuff seeped from her, he was once again reduced to Aaa's; he closed his eyes and slept. When Jenny offered him her breast, he wasn't hungry.

'God!' called the External, being very gentle with the *d*; his tongue had been burned, too.

'Piss!' snarled the Vital Organ man.

Jenny Fields washed Garp and herself with warm water and soap in a white enamel hospital bowl. She wasn't going to douche, of course, and she had no doubt that the magic had worked. She felt more receptive than prepared soil – the nourished earth – and she had felt Garp shoot up inside her as generously as a hose in summer (as if he could water a lawn).

She never did it with him again. There was no reason. She didn't enjoy it. From time to time she helped him with her hand, and when he cried for it, she gave him her breast, but in a few weeks he had no more erections. When they took the bandages off his hands, they noticed that even the healing process seemed to be working in reverse; they wrapped him back up again. He lost all interest in nursing. His dreams struck Jenny as the dreams a fish might have. He was back in the womb, Jenny knew; he resumed a fetal position, tucked up small in the center of the bed. He made no sound at all. One morning Jenny watched him kick with his small, weak feet; she imagined she felt a kick *inside*. Though it was too soon for the real thing, she knew the real thing was on its way.

Soon Garp stopped kicking. He still got his oxygen by breathing air with his lungs, but Jenny knew this was simply an example of human adaptability. He wouldn't eat; they had to feed him intravenously, so once again he was attached to a kind of umbilical cord. Jenny anticipated his last phase with some anxiousness. Would there be a struggle at the end, like the sperm's frantic struggle? Would the sperm shield be lifted and the naked egg wait, expectantly, for death? In little Garp's return trip, how would his *soul* at last divide? But the phase passed without Jenny's observation. One day, when she was off duty, Technical Sergeant Garp died.

'When *else* could he have died?' Garp has written. 'With my mother off duty was the only way he could escape.'

'Of course I *felt* something when he died,' Jenny Fields wrote in her famous autobiography. 'But the best of him was inside me. That was the best thing for both of us, the only way he could go on living, the only way I wanted to have a child. That the rest of the world finds this an immoral act only shows me that the rest of the world doesn't respect the rights of an individual.'

It was 1943. When Jenny's pregnancy was apparent, she lost her job. Of course, it was all that her parents and brothers had expected; they weren't surprised. Jenny had long ago stopped trying to convince them of her purity. She moved through the big corridors in the parental estate at Dog's Head Harbor like a satisfied ghost. Her composure alarmed her family, and they left her alone. Secretly, Jenny was quite happy, but with all the musing she must have done about this expected child, it's a wonder she never gave a thought to names.

Because, when Jenny Fields gave birth to a nine-pound baby boy, she had no name in mind. Jenny's mother asked her what she wanted to name him, but Jenny had just delivered and had just received her sedative; she was not cooperative.

'Garp,' she said.

Her father, the footwear king, thought she had burped, but her mother whispered to him, 'The name is *Garp*.'

'Garp?' he said. They knew they might find out who this baby's father was, this way. Jenny, of course, had not admitted a thing.

'Find out if that's the son of a bitch's first name or last name,' Jenny's father whispered to Jenny's mother.

'Is that a first name or a last name, dear?' Jenny's mother asked her.

Jenny was very sleepy. 'It's Garp,' she said. 'Just Garp. That's the whole thing.'

'I think it's a last name,' Jenny's mother told Jenny's father.

'What's his *first* name?' Jenny's father asked crossly.

'I never knew,' Jenny mumbled. This is true; she never did.

'She never knew his first name!' her father roared.

'Please, dear,' her mother said. 'He *must* have a first name.'

'Technical Sergeant Garp,' said Jenny Fields.

'A goddamn soldier, I knew it!' her father said.

'Technical Sergeant?' Jenny's mother asked her.

'T. S.,' Jenny Fields said. 'T. S. Garp. That's my baby's name.' She fell asleep.

Her father was furious. 'T. S. Garp!' he hollered. 'What kind of a name for a baby is *that*?'

'All his own,' Jenny told him, later. 'It's his *own* goddamn name, all his own.'

'It was great fun going to school with a name like that,' Garp has written. 'The teachers would ask you what the initials stood for. First I used to say that they were *just* initials, but they never believed me. So I'd have to say, "Call my mom. She'll tell you." And they would. And old Jenny would give them a piece of her mind.'

Thus was the world given T. S. Garp: born from a good nurse with a will of her own, and the seed of a ball turret gunner – his last shot.

2

Blood and Blue

T. S. Garp always suspected he would die young. 'Like my father,' Garp wrote, 'I believe I have a knack for brevity. I'm a one-shot man.'

Garp narrowly escaped growing up on the grounds of an all-girls' school, where his mother was offered the position of school nurse. But Jenny Fields saw the possibly harrowing future that would have been involved in this decision: her little Garp surrounded by women (Jenny and Garp were offered an apartment in one of the dorms). She imagined her son's first sexual experience: a fantasy inspired by the sight and feel of the all-girls' laundry room, where, as a game, the girls would bury the child in soft mountains of young women's underwear. Jenny would have liked the job, but it was for Garp's sake that she turned down the offer. She was hired instead by the vast and famous Steering School, where she would be simply one more school nurse among many, and where the apartment offered her and Garp was in the cold, prison-windowed wing of the school's infirmary annex.

'Never mind,' her father told her. He was irritated with her that she chose to work at all; there was money enough, and he'd have been happier if she'd gone into hiding at the family estate in Dog's Head Harbor until her bastard son had grown up and moved away. 'If the child has any native intelligence,' Jenny's father told her, 'he should eventually *attend* Steering, but in the meantime, I suppose, there's no better atmosphere for a boy to be raised in.'

'Native intelligence' was one of the ways her father had of referring to Garp's dubious genetic background. The Steering School, where Jenny's father and brothers had gone, was at that time an all-boys' school. Jenny believed that if she could endure her confinement there – through young Garp's prep school years – she would be doing her best for her son. 'To make up for denying him a father,' as her father put it to her.

'It's odd,' Garp wrote, 'that my mother, who perceived herself well enough to know that she wanted nothing to do with living with a man, ended up living with eight hundred boys.'

So young Garp grew up with his mother in the infirmary annex of the Steering School. He was not exactly treated as a 'faculty brat' – the students' term for all the underage children of the faculty and staff. A school nurse was not considered in quite the same class or category as a faculty member. Moreover, Jenny made no attempt to invent a mythology for Garp's father – to make up a marriage story for herself, to legitimize her son. She was a Fields, she made a point of telling you her name. Her son was a Garp. She made a point of telling you *his* name. 'It's his own name,' she said.

Everyone got the picture. Not only were certain kinds of arrogance tolerated by the society of the Steering School, certain kinds were encouraged; but acceptable arrogance was a matter of taste and style. *What* you were arrogant about had to appear worthy – of higher purpose – and the manner in which you were arrogant was supposed to be charming. Wit did not come naturally to Jenny Fields. Garp wrote that his mother 'never chose to be arrogant but was only arrogant under duress.' Pride was well loved in the community of the Steering School, but Jenny Fields appeared to be proud of an illegitimate child. Nothing to hang her head about, perhaps; however, she might show a *little* humility.

But Jenny was not only proud of Garp, she was especially

pleased with the manner in which she had gotten him. The world did not know that manner, yet; Jenny had not brought out her autobiography – she hadn't begun to write it, in fact. She was waiting for Garp to be old enough to appreciate the story.

The story Garp knew was all that Jenny would tell anyone who was bold enough to ask. Jenny's story was a sober three sentences long.

1. The father of Garp was a soldier.

2. The war killed him.

3. Who took the time for weddings when there was a war?

Both the precision and mystery of this story might have been interpreted romantically. After all, given the mere facts, the father might have been a war hero. A doomed love affair could be imagined. Nurse Fields might have been a field nurse. She might have fallen in love 'at the front.' And the father of Garp might have felt he owed one last mission 'to the men.' But Jenny Fields did not inspire the imagination of such a melodrama. For one thing, she seemed too pleased with her aloneness; she didn't appear in the least misty about the past. She was never distracted, she was simply all for little Garp – and for being a good nurse.

Of course, the Fields name was known at the Steering School. The famous footwear king of New England was a generous alumnus, and whether or not it was suspected at the time, he would even become a trustee. His was not the oldest but not the newest of New England money, and his wife, Jenny's mother – a former Boston Weeks – was perhaps still better known at Steering. Among the older faculty there were those who could remember years and years, without interruption, when there had always been a graduating Weeks. Yet, to the Steering School, Jenny Fields didn't seem to have inherited all the credentials. She was handsome, they would admit, but she was plain; she wore her nurse's uniform when she could have dressed in something smarter. In fact, this whole business of being a nurse – of which she also appeared too proud – was curious. Considering her family. Nursing was not enough of a profession for a Fields or a Weeks.

Socially, Jenny had that kind of graceless seriousness which makes more frivolous people uncomfortable. She read a lot and was a great ransacker of the Steering library; the book someone wanted was always discovered to be checked out to Nurse Fields. Phone calls were politely answered; Jenny frequently offered to deliver the book directly to the party who wanted it, as soon as she finished it. She finished such books promptly, but she had nothing to say about them. In a school community, someone who reads a book for some secretive purpose, other than discussing it, is strange. What was she reading for?

That she attended classes in her off-duty hours was stranger still. It was written in the constitution of the Steering School that faculty and staff and/or their spouses could attend, free of charge, any course offered at Steering, simply by securing the permission of the instructor. Who would turn away a nurse? – from the Elizabethans, from the Victorian Novel, from the History of Russia until 1917, from an Introduction to Genetics, from Western Civilization I and II. Over the years Jenny Fields would march from Caesar to Eisenhower – past Luther and Lenin, Erasmus and mitosis, osmosis and Freud, Rembrandt and chromosomes and van Gogh – from the Styx to the Thames, from Homer to Virginia Woolf. From Athens to Auschwitz, she never said a word. She was the only woman in the classes. In her white uniform she listened so quietly that the boys and finally the teacher forgot her and relaxed; they went on with the learning process while she sat keenly white and still among them, a witness to everything – maybe determining nothing, possibly judging it all.

Jenny Fields was getting the education she had waited for; now the time seemed ripe. But her motives were not wholly selfish; she was screening the Steering School for her son. When Garp was old enough to attend, she'd be able to give him lots of advice – she'd know the deadweights in every department, those courses that meandered and those that sang.

Her books spilled out of the tiny wing apartment in the infirmary annex. She spent ten years at the Steering School before discovering that the bookstore offered a 10 percent discount to the faculty and staff (which the bookstore had never offered her). This made her angry. She was generous with her books, too – eventually shelving them in every room of the bleak infirmary annex. But they outgrew the shelf space and slid into the main infirmary, into the waiting room, and into X-ray, first covering and then replacing the newspapers and the magazines. Slowly, the sick of the Steering School learned what a serious place Steering was – not your ordinary hospital, crammed with light reading and the media trash. While you waited to see the doctor, you could browse through *The Waning of the Middle Ages*; waiting for your lab results, you could ask the nurse to bring you that invaluable genetics manual, *The Fruit Fly Handbook*. If you were seriously ill, or might be visiting the infirmary for a long time, there was sure to be a copy of *The Magic Mountain*. For the boy with the broken leg, and all the athletically wounded, there were the good heroes and their meaty adventures – there were Conrad and Melville instead of *Sports Illustrated*; instead of *Time* and *Newsweek*, there were Dickens and Hemingway and Twain. What a wet dream for the lovers of literature, to lie sick at Steering! At last, a hospital with something good to read.

When Jenny Fields had spent twelve years at Steering, it was a habit among the school librarians, upon recognizing that they didn't have a book which someone sought, to say, 'Perhaps the infirmary has it.'

And at the bookstore, when something was out of stock or out of print, they might recommend that you 'find Nurse Fields over at the infirmary; *she* might have it.'

And Jenny would frown upon hearing the request, and say, 'I believe that's in twenty-six, at the annex, but McCarty is reading it. He has the flu. Perhaps when he's through, he'll be glad to let you have it.' Or she might respond, 'I last saw that one down at the whirlpool bath. It might be a little wet, in the beginning.'

It is impossible to judge Jenny's influence on the quality of education at Steering, but she never got over her anger at being cheated out of the 10 percent discount for ten years. 'My mother supported that bookstore,' Garp wrote. 'By comparison, nobody else at Steering ever read anything.'

When Garp was two, the Steering School offered Jenny a three-year contract; she was a good nurse, everyone agreed, and the slight distaste that everyone felt toward her had not increased in those first two years. The baby, after all, was like *any* baby; perhaps a little darker-skinned in summer than most, and a little sallow-skinned in winter – and a little fat. There was something rounded about him, like a bundled Eskimo, even when he wasn't actually bundled. And those younger faculty who had just gotten over the last war remarked that the shape of the child was as blunt as a bomb. But illegitimate children are still children, after all. The irritation at Jenny's oddness was acceptably mild.

She accepted the three-year contract. She was learning, improving herself but also preparing the way through Steering for her Garp. 'A superior education' is what the Steering School could offer, her father had said. Jenny thought she'd better make sure.

When Garp was five, Jenny Fields was made head nurse. It was hard to find young, active nurses who could tolerate the freshness and wild behavior of the boys; it was hard to find anyone willing to live in, and Jenny seemed quite content to stay in her wing of the infirmary annex. In this sense she became a mother to many: up in the night when one of the boys threw up, or buzzed her, or smashed his water glass. Or when the occasionally bad boys fooled around in the dark aisles, raced their hospital beds, engaged in gladiatorial combat in wheelchairs, stole conversations with girls from the town through the iron-grate windows, attempted to climb down, or up, the thick rungs of ivy that laced the old brick buildings of the infirmary and its annex.

The infirmary was connected to the annex by an underground tunnel, wide enough for a bed-on-wheels with a slim nurse on either side of it. The bad boys occasionally *bowled* in the tunnel, the sound reaching Jenny and Garp in their faraway wing – as if the test rats and rabbits in the basement laboratory had overnight grown terribly large and were rolling the rubbish barrels deeper underground with their powerful snouts.

But when Garp was five – when his mother was made head nurse – the Steering School community noticed something strange about him. What could be exactly different about a five-year-old boy is not clear, but there was a certain sleek, dark, wet look to his head (like the head of a seal), and the exaggerated compactness of his body brought back the old speculations about his genes. Temperamentally, the child appeared to resemble his mother: determined, possibly dull, aloof but eternally watchful. Although he was small for his age, he seemed unnaturally mature in other ways; he had a discomforting calmness. Close to the ground, like a well-balanced animal, he seemed unusually well coordinated. Other mothers noted, with occasional alarm, that the child could *climb* anything. Look at jungle gyms, swing sets, high slides, bleacher seats, the most dangerous trees: Garp would be at the top of them.

One night after supper, Jenny could not find him. Garp was free to wander through the infirmary and the annex, talking to the boys, and Jenny normally paged him on the intercom when she wanted him back in the apartment. 'GARP HOME,' she'd say. He had his instructions: which rooms he was not to visit, the contagious cases, the boys who felt really rotten and would prefer to be left alone. Garp liked the athletic injuries best; he liked looking at casts and slings and big bandages, and he liked listening to the cause of the injury, over and over again. Like his mother, perhaps – a nurse at heart – he was happy to run errands for the patients, deliver messages, sneak food. But one night, when he was five, Garp did not respond to the GARP HOME call. The intercom was broadcast through every room of the infirmary and the annex, even those rooms Garp was under strict orders not to be in – the lab, surgery, and X-ray. If Garp couldn't hear the GARP HOME message, Jenny knew that he was either in trouble or not in the buildings. She quickly organized a search party among the healthier and more mobile patients.

It was a foggy night in the early spring; some boys went outside and called through the damp forsythia and the parking lot. Others poked through the dark, empty nooks and the forbidden equipment rooms. Jenny indulged her first fears first. She checked the laundry chute, a slick cylinder that for four floors dropped straight down to the basement (Garp was not allowed even to put laundry down the chute). But beneath where the chute shot through the ceiling, and spewed its contents on the basement floor, there was only laundry on the cold cement. She checked the boiler room and the scalding, huge, hot-water furnace, but Garp had not been cooked there. She checked the stairwells, but Garp was instructed not to play on the stairs and he wasn't lying broken at the bottom of any of the four-story wells. Then she started in on her unexpressed fears that little Garp would fall victim to a secret sex violator among the Steering School boys. But in the early spring there were too many boys in the infirmary for Jenny to keep track of them all – much less know them well enough to suspect their sexual tastes. There were the fools who went swimming on that first sunny day, even before the snow was off the ground. There were the last victims of drag-on winter colds, their various resistances worn down. There were the culminating winter-sports injuries and the first to be injured in spring-sports practice.

One such person was Hathaway, who, Jenny heard, was buzzing her now from his room on the fourth floor of the annex. Hathaway was a lacrosse player who had done ligament damage to his knee; two days after they put him in a cast and turned him loose on crutches, Hathaway had gone out in the rain and his crutch tips had slipped at the top of the long marble stairs of Hyle Hall. In the fall, he had broken his other leg. Now Hathaway, with both his long legs in casts, sprawled in his bed on the fourth floor of the infirmary annex, a lacrosse stick held fondly in his large-knuckled hands. He had been put out of the way, almost all by himself on the fourth floor of the annex, because of his irritating habit of flinging a lacrosse ball across his room and letting it carom off the wall. Then he snared the hard, bouncy ball in the looping basket on the end of his lacrosse stick and flicked it back against the wall. Jenny could have put a stop to this, but she had a son of her own, after all, and she recognized the need in boys to devote themselves, mindlessly, to a repetitious physical act. It seemed to relax them, Jenny had noticed – whether they were five, like Garp, or seventeen, like Hathaway.

But it made her furious that Hathaway was so clumsy with his lacrosse stick that he was always losing his ball! She had gone out of her way to put him where other patients would not complain about the thumping, but whenever Hathaway lost his ball, he buzzed for someone to fetch it for him; although there was an elevator, the fourth floor of the annex was out of everyone's way. When Jenny saw the elevator was in use, she went up the four flights of stairs too quickly, and was out of breath, as well as angry, when she got to Hathaway's room.

'I *know* how much your game means to you, Hathaway,' Jenny said, 'but right now Garp is lost and I don't really have time to retrieve your ball.'

Hathaway was an ever-pleasant, slow-thinking boy with a slack, hairless face and a forward-falling flop of reddish-blond hair, which partially hid one of his pale eyes. He had a habit of tipping his head back, perhaps so that he could see out from under his hair, and for this reason, and the fact that he was tall, everyone who looked at Hathaway looked up his wide nostrils.

'Miss Fields?' he said. Jenny noticed he was not holding his lacrosse stick.

'What *is* it, Hathaway?' Jenny asked. 'I'm sorry I'm in a rush, but Garp is lost. I'm looking for *Garp.*'

'Oh,' Hathaway said. He looked around his room – perhaps for Garp – as if someone had just asked him for an ashtray. 'I'm sorry,' Hathaway said. 'I wish I could help you look for him.' He stared helplessly at both his casts.

Jenny rapped lightly on one of his plastered knees, as if she were knocking on a door behind which someone might be asleep. 'Don't worry, please,' she said; she waited for him to tell her what he wanted, but Hathaway seemed to have forgotten that he'd buzzed her. 'Hathaway?' she asked, again knocking on his leg to see if anyone was home. 'What did you *want*? Did you lose your ball?'

'No,' Hathaway said. 'I've lost my *stick.*' Mechanically, they both took a moment to look around Hathaway's room for the missing lacrosse stick. 'I was asleep,' he explained, 'and when I woke up, it was gone.'

Jenny first thought of Meckler, the menace of the second-floor annex. Meckler was a sarcastically brilliant boy who was in the infirmary at least four days out of every month. He was a chain smoker at sixteen, he edited most of the school's student publications, and he had twice won the annual Classics Cup. Meckler scorned dining-hall food and lived on coffee and fried-egg sandwiches from Buster's Snack and Grill, where he actually wrote most of his long and long-overdue, but brilliant, term papers. Collapsing in the infirmary each month to recover from his physical self-abuse, and his brilliance, Meckler's mind turned to hideous pranks that Jenny could never quite prove him guilty of. Once there were boiled polliwogs in the teapot sent down to the lab technicians, who complained of the fishiness of the tea; once, Jenny was sure, Meckler had filled a prophylactic with egg whites and slipped its snug neck over the doorknob to her apartment. She knew the filling had been egg whites only because she later found the shells. In her purse. And it had been Meckler, Jenny was sure, who had organized the third floor of the infirmary during the chicken pox epidemic of a few years ago: the boys were beating off, in turn, and rushing with their hot spunk in their hands to the microscopes in the infirmary lab – to see if they were sterile.

But Meckler's style, Jenny thought, would have been to cut a hole in the netting of the lacrosse stick – and to have left the useless stick in the sleeping Hathaway's hands.

'I'll bet Garp has it,' Jenny told Hathaway. 'When we find Garp, we'll find your stick.' She resisted, for the hundredth time, the impulse to take her hand and brush back the flop of hair that nearly hid one of Hathaway's eyes; instead, she gently squeezed Hathaway's big toes where they thrust out of his casts.

If Garp was going to play lacrosse, Jenny thought, where would he go? Not out, because it's dark; he'd lose the ball. And the only place he might not have heard the intercom was in the underground tunnel between the annex and the infirmary – a perfect place for flinging that ball, Jenny knew. It had been done before; once Jenny had broken up an after-midnight scrimmage. She took the elevator directly to the basement. Hathaway is a sweet boy, she was thinking; Garp could do worse than grow up to be like that. But he could do better, too.

However slowly, Hathaway was thinking. He hoped little Garp was all right; he sincerely wished he could get up to help find the child. Garp was a frequent visitor to Hathaway's room. A crippled athlete with two casts was better than average. Hathaway had allowed Garp to draw all over his plastered legs; over and through the signatures of friends were the looping, crayoned faces and monsters of Garp's imagination. Hathaway now looked at the child's drawings on his casts and worried about Garp. That was why he saw the lacrosse ball, between his thighs; he had not felt it, through the plaster. It lay there as if it were Hathaway's own egg, keeping warm. How could Garp play lacrosse without a ball?

When he heard the pigeons, Hathaway knew Garp wasn't playing lacrosse. The pigeons! he remembered. He had complained about them to the boy. The pigeons kept Hathaway awake at night with their damn cooing, their cluckish fussing under the eaves and in the rain gutter beneath the steep slate roof. That was a problem with the sleeping conditions on the fourth and topmost floor; that was a problem for every top-floor sleeper at the Steering School – *pigeons* seemed to rule the campus. The maintenance men had caged off most of the eaves and perches with chicken wire, but the pigeons roosted in the rain gutters, in dry weather, and found niches under the roofs, and perches on the old gnarled ivy. There was no way to keep them off the buildings. And how they could coo! Hathaway hated them. He'd told Garp that if he had even *one* good leg, he would get them.

'How?' Garp asked.

'They don't like to fly at night,' Hathaway told the boy. It was in Bio. II that Hathaway had learned about the habits of pigeons; Jenny Fields had taken the same course. 'I could get up on the roof,' Hathaway told Garp, 'at night – when it wasn't raining – and trap them in the rain gutter. That's all they do, just sit in the rain gutter and coo and crap all night.'

'But *how* would you trap them?' Garp asked.

And Hathaway twirled his lacrosse stick, cradling the ball. He rolled the ball between his legs, he dropped the net of the stick gently over Garp's little head. 'Like that,' he said. 'With this, I'd get them easy – with my lacrosse stick. One by one, until I got them all.'

Hathaway remembered how Garp had smiled at him – this big friendly boy with his two heroic casts. Hathaway looked out the window, saw that it was indeed dark and not raining. Hathaway rang his buzzer. 'Garp!' he cried out.

'Oh, God.' He held his thumb on the buzzer button and did not let up.

When Jenny Fields saw it was the fourth-floor light that was flashing, she could only think that Garp had brought Hathaway's lacrosse equipment back to him. What a good boy, she thought, and rode the elevator, up again, to the fourth floor. She ran squeakily on her good nurse's shoes to Hathaway's room. She saw the lacrosse ball in Hathaway's hand. His one eye, which was clearly in view, looked frightened.

'He's on the roof,' Hathaway told her.

'On the roof!' Jenny said.

'He's trying to capture pigeons with my lacrosse stick,' Hathaway said.

A full-grown man, if he stood on the fourth-floor fire-escape landing, could reach over the rim of the rain gutter with his hands. When the Steering School cleaned its rain gutters, only after all the leaves were fallen and before the heavy spring rains, only *tall* men were sent to do the job because the shorter men complained of reaching into the rain gutters and touching things they couldn't see – dead pigeons and well-rotted squirrels and unidentifiable glop. Only the tall men could stand on the fire-escape landings and peek into the rain gutters before they reached. The gutters were as wide and nearly as deep as pig troughs, but they were not as strong – and they were old. In those days, *everything* at the Steering School was old.

When Jenny Fields went out the fourth-floor fire door and stood on the fire escape, she could barely reach the rain gutter with her fingertips; she could not see over the rain gutter to the steep slate roof – and in the darkness and fog, she could not even see the underside of the rain gutter as far down as either corner of the building. She could not see Garp at all.

'Garp?' she whispered. Four stories below, among the shrubbery and the occasional glint from the hood or roof of a parked car, she could hear some of the boys calling him, too. 'Garp?' she whispered, a little louder.

'Mom?' he asked, startling her – although his whisper was softer than hers. His voice came from somewhere close, almost within her reach, she thought, but she couldn't see him. Then she saw the netted basket end of the lacrosse stick silhouetted against the foggy moon like the strange, webbed paw of some unknown, nocturnal animal; it jutted out from the rain gutter, almost directly above her. Now, when she reached up, she was frightened to feel Garp's leg, broken through the corroded gutter, which had torn his pants and cut him, wedging him there, one leg through the gutter up to his hip, the other leg sprawled out in the gutter behind him, along the edge of the steep slate roof. Garp lay on his belly in the creaky rain gutter.

When he had broken through the gutter, he'd been too scared to cry out; he could feel that the whole flimsy trough was rotted through and ready to tear apart. His *voice*, he thought, could make the roof fall down. He lay with his cheek in the gutter, and through a tiny rusted hole he watched the boys in the parking lot and bushes, four stories below him, looking for him. The lacrosse stick, which had indeed held a surprised pigeon, had swung out over the edge of the gutter, releasing the bird.

The pigeon, despite being captured and freed, had not moved. It squatted in the gutter, making its small, stupid sounds. Jenny realized that Garp could never have reached the rain gutter from the fire escape, and she shuddered to think of him climbing up the ivy to the roof with the lacrosse stick in one hand. She held his leg very tightly; his bare, warm calf was slightly sticky with blood, but he had not cut himself badly on the rusty gutter. A tetanus shot, she was thinking; the blood was almost dry and Jenny did not think he would need stitches – though, in the darkness, she could not clearly make out the wound. She was trying to think how she could get him down. Below her, the forsythia bushes winked in the light from the downstairs windows;

from so far away, the yellow flowers looked (to her) like the tips of small gas flames.

'Mom?' Garp asked.

'Yes,' she whispered. 'I've got you.'

'Don't let go,' he said.

'Okay,' she told him. As if triggered by her voice, a little more of the gutter gave way.

'Mom!' Garp said.

'It's okay,' Jenny said. She wondered if the best way would be to yank him down, hard, and hope that she could pull him right through the rotten gutter. But then the whole gutter could possibly rip free of the roof – and *then* what? she thought. She saw them both swept off the fire escape and falling. But she knew no one could actually go up *on* the rain gutter and pull the child out of the hole, and then lower him to her over the edge. The gutter could barely support a five-year-old; it certainly couldn't support a grown-up. And Jenny knew that she would not let go of Garp's leg long enough to let someone try.

It was the new nurse, Miss Creen, who saw them from the ground and ran inside to call Dean Bodger. Nurse Creen was thinking of Dean Bodger's spotlight, fastened to the dean's dark car (which cruised the campus each night in search of boys out after curfew). Despite the complaints of the grounds crew, Bodger drove down the footpaths and over the soft lawns, flashing his spotlight into the deep shrubs alongside the buildings, making the campus an unsafe place for lurkers – or for lovers, with no indoor place to go.

Nurse Creen also called Dr Pell, because her mind, in a crisis, always ran to people who were supposed to take charge. She did not think of the fire department, a thought that was crossing Jenny's mind; but Jenny feared they would take too long and the gutter would collapse before they arrived; worse, she imagined, they would insist she let *them* handle everything and make her let go of Garp's leg.

Surprised, Jenny looked up at Garp's small, soggy sneaker, which now dangled in the sudden and ghastly glare of Dean

Bodger's spotlight. The light was disturbing and confusing the pigeons, whose perception of dawn was probably not the best and who appeared almost ready to come to some decision in the rain gutter; their cooing and the scrabbling sounds of their claws grew more frantic.

Down on the lawn, running around Dean Bodger's car, the boys in their white hospital smocks appeared to have been bedlamized by the experience – or by Dean Bodger's sharp orders to run here or run there, fetch this or fetch that. Bodger called all the boys 'men.' As in 'Let's have a line of mattresses under the fire escape, men! Double-quick!' he barked. Bodger had taught German for twenty years at Steering before being appointed dean; his commands sounded like the rapid-fire conjugating of German verbs.

The 'men' piled mattresses and oogled through the skeletal fire escape at Jenny's marvelous white uniform in the spotlight. One of the boys stood flush to the building, well under the fire escape, and his view up Jenny's skirt and her spotlit legs must have dazzled him because he appeared to forget the crisis and he just *stood* there. 'Schwarz!' Dean Bodger yelled at him, but his name was Warner and he did not respond. Dean Bodger had to shove him to make him stop staring. 'More mattresses, Schmidt!' Bodger told him.

A piece of the gutter, or a particle of leaf, stuck in Jenny's eye and she had to spread her legs wider apart, for balance. When the gutter gave way, the pigeon Garp had caught was launched out of the broken end of the trough and forced into brief and frenzied flight. Jenny gagged at her first thought: that the pigeon blurring past her vision was the falling body of her son; but she reassured herself with her grip on Garp's leg. She was first knocked into a deep squat, and then thrown to one hip on the fire-escape landing, by the weight of a substantial chunk of the rain gutter that still contained Garp. Only when she realized that they were both safe on the landing, and sitting down, did Jenny let go of Garp's leg. An elaborate bruise, in the near-perfect form of her fingerprints, would be on his calf for a week.

From the ground, the scene was confusing. Dean Bodger saw a sudden movement of bodies above him, he heard the sound of the rain gutter ripping, he saw Nurse Fields fall. He saw a three-foot hunk of the rain gutter drop into the darkness, but he never saw the child. He saw what looked like a pigeon dart into and through the beam of his spotlight, but he did not follow the flight of the bird – blinded by the light, then lost in the night. The pigeon struck the iron edge of the fire escape and broke its neck. The pigeon wrapped its wings around itself and spiraled straight down, like a slightly soft football falling well out of the line of mattresses Bodger had ordered for the ultimate emergency. Bodger saw the bird falling and mistook its small, fast-moving body for the child.

Dean Bodger was a basically brave and tenacious man, the father of four rigorously raised children. His devotion to campus police work was not so much motivated by his desire to prevent people from having fun as stemming from his conviction that almost every accident was unnecessary and could, with cunning and industry, be avoided. Thus Bodger believed he could catch the falling child, because in his ever-anxious heart he was prepared for just such a situation as plucking a plummeting body out of the dark sky. The dean was as short-haired and muscular and curiously proportioned as a pit bull, and shared with that breed of dog a similar smallness of the eyes, which were always inflamed, as red-lidded and squinty as a pig's. Like a pit bull, too, Bodger was good at digging in and lunging forward, which he now did, his fierce arms outstretched, his piggy eyes never leaving the descending pigeon. 'I've got you, son!' Bodger cried, which terrified the boys in their hospital smocks. They were unprepared for anything like this.

Dean Bodger, on the run, dove for the bird, which struck his chest with an impact even Bodger was not wholly prepared for. The pigeon sent the dean reeling, rolled him over on his back, where he felt the wind socked out of him and he lay gasping. The battered bird was hugged in his arms;

its beak poked Bodger's bristly chin. One of the frightened boys cranked the spotlight down from the fourth floor and shone the beam directly on the dean. When Bodger saw that he clutched a pigeon to his breast, he threw the dead bird over the heads of the gaping boys and into the parking lot.

There was much fussing in the admittance room of the infirmary. Dr Pell had arrived and he treated little Garp's leg – it was a ragged but superficial wound that needed a lot of trimming and cleaning, but no stitches. Nurse Creen gave the boy a tetanus shot while Dr Pell removed a small, rusty particle from Jenny's eye; Jenny had strained her back supporting the weight of Garp and the rain gutter, but was otherwise fine. The aura of the admittance room was hearty and jocular, except when Jenny was able to catch her son's eye; in public, Garp was a kind of heroic survivor, but he must have been anxious about how Jenny would deal with him back in their apartment.

Dean Bodger became one of the few people at the Steering School to endear himself to Jenny. He beckoned her aside and confided to her that, if she thought it useful, he would be glad to reprimand the boy – if Jenny thought that, coming from Bodger, it would make a more lasting impression than any reprimand she could deliver. Jenny was grateful for the offer, and she and Bodger agreed upon a threat that would impress the boy. Bodger then brushed the feathers off his chest and tucked in his shirt, which was escaping, like a cream filling, from under his tight vest. He announced rather suddenly to the chattering admittance room that he would appreciate a moment alone with young Garp. There was a hush. Garp tried to leave with Jenny, who said, 'No. The *dean* would like to speak to you.' Then they were alone. Garp didn't know what a dean was.

'Your mother runs a tight ship over here, doesn't she, boy?' Bodger asked. Garp didn't understand, but he nodded. 'She runs things very well, if you ask me,' Dean Bodger said. 'She should have a son whom she can *trust*. Do you know what *trust* means, boy?'

'No,' Garp said.

'It means: Can she believe you'll be where you *say* you'll be? Can she believe you'll never do what you're not supposed to do? *That's* trust, boy,' Bodger said. 'Do you believe your mother can trust you?'

'Yes,' Garp said.

'Do you like living here?' Bodger asked him. He knew perfectly well that the boy loved it; Jenny had suggested that this be the point Bodger touch.

'Yes,' Garp said.

'What do you hear the boys call me?' the dean asked.

'"Mad Dog"?' asked Garp. He *had* heard the boys in the infirmary call *someone* 'Mad Dog,' and Dean Bodger looked like a mad dog to Garp. But the dean was surprised; he had many nicknames, but he had never heard that one.

'I meant that the boys call me sir,' Bodger said, and was grateful that Garp was a sensitive child – he caught the injured tone in the dean's voice.

'Yes, sir,' Garp said.

'And you *do* like living here?' the dean repeated.

'Yes, sir,' Garp said.

'Well, if you *ever* go out on that fire escape, or anywhere near that roof again,' Bodger said, 'you won't be *allowed* to live here anymore. Do you understand?'

'Yes, sir,' Garp said.

'Then be a good boy for your mother,' Bodger told him, 'or you'll have to move to some place strange and far away.'

Garp felt a darkness surround him, akin to the darkness and sense of being far away that he must have felt while lying in the rain gutter, four stories above where the world was safe. He started to cry, but Bodger took his chin between one stumpish, deanly thumb and forefinger; he waggled the boy's head. 'Don't *ever* disappoint your mother, boy,' Bodger told him. 'If you do, you'll feel as bad as this all your life.'

'Poor Bodger meant well,' Garp wrote. 'I *have* felt bad most of my life, and I *did* disappoint my mother. But Bodger's sense of what *really* happens in the world is as suspect as anyone's sense of that.'

Garp was referring to the illusion poor Bodger embraced in his later life: that it had been little Garp he caught falling from the annex roof, and not a pigeon. No doubt, in his advancing years, the moment of catching the bird had meant as much to the good-hearted Bodger as if he *had* caught Garp.

Dean Bodger's grasp of reality was often warped. Upon leaving the infirmary, the dean discovered that someone had removed the spotlight from his car. He went raging through every patient's room – even the contagious cases. 'That light will one day shine on him who took it!' Bodger claimed, but no one came forward. Jenny was sure it had been Meckler, but she couldn't prove it. Dean Bodger drove home without his light. Two days later he came down with someone's flu and was treated as an outpatient at the infirmary. Jenny was especially sympathetic.

It was another four days before Bodger had reason to look in his glove compartment. The sneezing dean was out cruising the nighttime campus, with a new spotlight mounted on his car, when he was halted by a freshly recruited patrolman from campus security.

'For God's sake, I'm the dean,' Bodger told the trembling youth.

'I don't know that for sure, sir,' the patrolman said. 'They told me not to let anyone drive on the footpaths.'

'They should have told you not to tangle with Dean Bodger!' Bodger said.

'They told me that, too, sir,' the patrolman said, 'but I don't *know* that you're Dean Bodger.'

'Well,' said Bodger, who was secretly very pleased with the young patrolman's humorless devotion to his duty, 'I can certainly prove who I *am*.' Dean Bodger then remembered that his driver's license had expired, and he decided to show the patrolman his automobile registration instead.

When Bodger opened the glove compartment, there was the deceased pigeon.

Meckler had struck again; and, again, there was no proof. The pigeon was not excessively ripe, not writhing with maggots (yet), but Dean Bodger's glove compartment was infested with lice. The pigeon was so dead that the lice were looking for a new home. The dean found his automobile registration as quickly as possible, but the young patrolman could not take his eyes off the pigeon.

'They told me they were a real problem around here,' the patrolman said. 'They told me how they got into everything.'

'The *boys* get into everything,' Bodger crooned. 'The pigeons are relatively harmless, but the *boys* bear watching.'

For what seemed to Garp like a long and unfair time, Jenny kept a very close watch on *him*. She really had always watched him closely, but she had learned to trust him, too. Now she made Garp prove to her that he could be trusted again.

In a community as small as Steering, news spread more easily than ringworm. The story of how little Garp climbed to the roof of the infirmary annex, and how his mother didn't know he was there, cast suspicion on them both – on Garp as a child who could ill influence other children, on Jenny as a mother who did not look after her son. Of course, Garp sensed no discrimination for a while, but Jenny, who was quick to recognize discrimination (and quick to anticipate it, too), felt once again that people were making unfair assumptions. Her five-year-old had gotten loose on the roof; therefore, she never looked after him properly. And, therefore, he was clearly an *odd* child.

A boy without a father, some said, has dangerous mischief forever on his mind.

'It's odd,' Garp wrote, 'that the family who would convince *me* of my own uniqueness was never close to my mother's heart. Mother was practical, she believed in evidence and in results. She believed in Bodger, for example, for what a dean did was at least clear. She believed in *specific* jobs: teachers of history, coaches of wrestling – nurses, of course. But the family who convinced me of my own uniqueness was never a family my mother respected. Mother believed that the Percy family *did* nothing.'

Jenny Fields was not entirely alone in her belief. Stewart Percy, although he did have a title, did not have a real job. He was called the Secretary of Steering School, but no one ever saw him typing. In fact, he had his own secretary, and no one was very sure *what* she could have to type. For a while Stewart Percy appeared to have some connection with the Steering Alumni Association, a body of Steering graduates so powerful with wealth and sentimental with nostalgia that they were highly esteemed by the administration of the school. But the Director of Alumni Affairs claimed that Stewart Percy was too unpopular with the young alumni to be of use. The young alumni remembered Percy from the days when they had been students.

Stewart Percy was not popular with students, who themselves suspected Percy of doing nothing.

He was a large, florid man with the kind of false barrel chest that at any moment can reveal itself to be merely a stomach – the kind of bravely upheld chest that can drop suddenly and forcefully burst open the tweed jacket containing it, lifting the regimental-striped tie with the Steering School colors. 'Blood and blue,' Garp always called them.

Stewart Percy, whom his wife called Stewie – although a generation of Steering schoolboys called him Paunch – had a flat-top head of hair the color of Distinguished Silver. The boys said that Stewart's flat-top was meant to resemble an aircraft carrier, because Stewart had been in the Navy in World War II. His contribution to the curriculum at Steering was a single course he taught for fifteen years – which was as long as it took the History Department to develop the nerve and necessary disrespect to forbid him to teach it. For fifteen years it was an embarrassment to them all. Only the most unsuspecting freshmen at Steering were ever suckered into taking it. The course was called 'My Part of the Pacific,' and it concerned only those naval battles of World War II which Stewart Percy had personally fought in. There had been two. There were no texts for the course; there were only Stewart's lectures and Stewart's personal slide collection. The slides had been created from old black-and-white photographs – an interestingly blurred process. At least one memorable class week of slides concerned Stewart's shore leave in Hawaii, where he met and married his wife, Midge.

'Mind you, boys, she was not a *native*,' he would faithfully tell his class (although, in the gray slide, it was hard to tell *what* she was). 'She was just *visiting* there, she didn't *come* from there,' Stewart would say. And there would follow an endless number of slides of Midge's gray-blond hair.

All the Percy children were blond, too, and one suspected they would one day become Distinguished Silver, like Stewie, whom the Steering students of Garp's day named after a dish served them in the school dining halls at least once every week: Fat Stew. Fat Stew was made from another of the weekly Steering dining-hall dishes: Mystery Meat. But Jenny Fields used to say that Stewart Percy was made entirely of Distinguished Silver hair.

And whether they called him Paunch or Fat Stew, the boys who took Stewart Percy's 'My Part of the Pacific' course were supposed to know already that Midge was not a Hawaiian native, though some of them really did have to be told. What the smarter boys knew, and what every member of the Steering community was nearly born knowing – and committed thereafter to silent scorn – was that Stewart Percy had married Midge *Steering*. She was the last Steering. The unclaimed princess of the Steering School – no headmaster had yet come her way. Stewart Percy married into so much money that he didn't *have* to be able to do anything, except stay married.

Jenny Fields' father, the footwear king, used to think of Midge Steering's money and shake in his shoes.

'Midge was such a dingbat,' Jenny Fields wrote in her autobiography, 'that she went to Hawaii for a *vacation* during World War II. And she was such a *total* dingbat,' Jenny wrote, 'that she actually fell in love with Stewart Percy, and she began to have his empty, Distinguished Silver children almost immediately – even before the war was over. And when the war *was* over, she brought him and her growing family back to the Steering School. And she told the school to give her Stewie a job.'

'When I was a boy,' Garp wrote, 'there were already three or four little Percys, and more – seemingly always more – on the way.'

Of Midge Percy's many pregnancies, Jenny Fields made up a nasty rhyme.

> What lies in Midge Percy's belly,
> so round and exceedingly fair?
> In fact, it is really nothing
> but a ball of Distinguished Silver hair.

'My mother was a bad writer,' Garp wrote, referring to Jenny's autobiography. 'But she was an even worse poet.' When Garp was five, however, he was too young to be told such poems. And what made Jenny Fields so unkind concerning Stewart and Midge?

Jenny knew that Fat Stew looked down on her. But Jenny said nothing, she was just wary of the situation. Garp was a playmate of the Percy children, who were not allowed to visit Garp in the infirmary annex. 'Our house is really better for children,' Midge told Jenny once, on the phone. 'I mean' – she laughed – 'I don't think there's anything they can *catch*.'

Except a little stupidity, Jenny thought, but all she said was, 'I know who's contagious and who isn't. And nobody plays on the roof.'

To be fair: Jenny knew that the Percy house, which had been the Steering family house, was a comforting

house to children. It was carpeted and spacious and full
of generations of tasteful toys. It was rich. And because it
was cared for by servants, it was also casual. Jenny resented
the casualness that the Percy family could afford. Jenny
thought that neither Midge nor Stewie had the brains to
worry about their children as much as they should; they
also had so *many* children. Maybe when you have a *lot* of
children, Jenny pondered, you aren't so anxious about each
of them?

Jenny was actually worried for her Garp when he was
off playing with the Percy children. Jenny had grown up
in an upper-class home, too, and she knew perfectly well
that upper-class children were not magically protected
from danger just because they were somehow born safer,
with hardier metabolisms and charmed genes. Around the
Steering School, however, there were many who seemed
to believe this – because, superficially, it often *looked* true.
There *was* something special about the aristocratic children
of those families: their hair seemed to stay in place, their
skin did not break out. Perhaps they did not appear to be
under any stress because there was nothing they wanted,
Jenny thought. But then she wondered how she'd escaped
being like them.

Her concern for Garp was truly based on her specific
observations of the Percys. The children ran free, as if their
own mother believed them to be charmed. Almost albino-
like, almost translucent-skinned, the Percy kids really *did*
seem more magical, if not actually healthier, than other
children. And despite the feeling most faculty families had
toward Fat Stew, they felt that the Percy children, and even
Midge, had obvious 'class.' Strong, protective genes were at
work, they thought.

'My mother,' Garp wrote, 'was at *war* with people who
took genes this seriously.'

And one day Jenny watched her small, dark Garp go running
across the infirmary lawn, off toward the more elegant

faculty houses, white and green-shuttered, where the Percy house sat like the oldest church in a town full of churches. Jenny watched this tribe of children running across the safe, charted footpaths of the school – Garp the fleetest. A string of clumsy, flopping Percys was in pursuit of him – and the other children who ran with this mob.

There was Clarence DuGard, whose father taught French and smelled as if he never washed; he never opened a window all winter. There was Talbot Mayer-Jones, whose father knew more about all of America's history than Stewart Percy knew about his small part of the Pacific. There was Emily Hamilton, who had eight brothers and would graduate from an inferior all-girls' school just a year before Steering would vote to admit women; her mother would commit suicide, not necessarily as a result of this vote but simultaneously with its announcement (causing Stewart Percy to remark that *this* was what would come of admitting girls to Steering: more suicide). And there were the Grove brothers, Ira and Buddy, 'from the town'; their father was with the maintenance department of the school, and it was a delicate case – whether the boys should even be encouraged to attend Steering, and how well it could be expected they would do.

Down through the quadrangles of bright green grass and fresh tar paths, boxed in by buildings of a brick so worn and soft it resembled pink marble, Jenny watched the children run. With them, she was sorry to note, ran the Percy family dog – to Jenny's mind, a mindless oaf of an animal who for years would defy the town leash law the way the Percys would flaunt their casualness. The dog, a giant Newfoundland, had grown from a puppy who spilled garbage cans, and the witless thief of baseballs, to being *mean*.

One day when the kids had been playing, the dog had mangled a volleyball – not an act of viciousness, usually. A mere bumble. But when the boy who owned the deflated ball had tried to remove it from the great dog's mouth, the dog bit him – deep puncture wounds in the forearm: not the type of bite, a nurse knew, that was only an accident, a case of 'Bonkers getting a little excited, because he loves playing with the children so much.' Or so said Midge Percy, who had named the dog Bonkers. She told Jenny that she'd gotten the dog shortly after the birth of her fourth child. The word *bonkers* meant 'a little crazy,' she told Jenny, and that's how Midge said she still felt about Stewie after their first four children together. 'I was just *bonkers* about him,' Midge said to Jenny, 'so I named the poor dog Bonkers to prove my feelings for Stew.'

'Midge Percy was bonkers, all right,' wrote Jenny Fields. 'That dog was a killer, protected by one of the many thin and senseless bits of logic that the upper classes in America are famous for: namely, that the children and pets of the aristocracy couldn't possibly be *too* free, or hurt anybody. That *other* people should not overpopulate the world, or be allowed to release *their* dogs, but that the dogs and children of rich people have a right to run free.'

'The curs of the upper class,' Garp would call them, always – both the dogs and the children.

He would have agreed with his mother that the Percys' dog, Bonkers, the Newfoundland retriever, was dangerous. A Newfoundland is a breed of oily-coated dog resembling an all-black Saint Bernard with webbed feet; they are generally slothful and friendly. But on the Percys' lawn, Bonkers broke up a touch football game by hurling his one hundred and seventy pounds on five-year-old Garp's back and biting off the child's left earlobe – and part of the rest of Garp's ear, as well. Bonkers would probably have taken *all* the ear, but he was a dog notably lacking concentration. The other children fled in all directions.

'Bonkie bit someone,' said a younger Percy, pulling Midge away from the phone. It was a Percy family habit to put a *-y* or an *-ie* at the end of almost every family member's name. Thus the children – Stewart (Jr.), Randolph, William, Cushman (a girl), and Bainbridge (another girl) – were called, within the family, Stewie Two, Dopey, Shrill Willy,

Cushie, and Pooh. Poor Bainbridge, whose name did not convert easily to a -*y* or an -*ie* ending, was also the last in the family to be in diapers; thus, in a cute attempt to be both descriptive and literary, *she* was Pooh.

It was Cushie at Midge's arm, telling her mother that 'Bonkie bit someone.'

'Who'd he get this time?' said Fat Stew; he seized a squash racket, as if he were going to take charge of the matter, but he was completely undressed; it was Midge who drew her dressing gown together and prepared to be the first grown-up to run outside to inspect the damage.

Stewart Percy was frequently undressed at home. No one knows why. Perhaps it was to relieve himself of the strain of how *very* dressed he was when he strolled the Steering campus with nothing to do, Distinguished Silver on display, and perhaps it was out of necessity – for all the procreation he was responsible for, he *must* have been frequently undressed at home.

'Bonkie bit Garp,' said little Cushie Percy. Neither Stewart nor Midge noticed that Garp was there, in the doorway, the whole side of his head bloody and chewed.

'Mrs Percy?' Garp whispered, not loud enough to be heard.

'So it was Garp?' Fat Stew said. Bending to return the squash racket to the closet, he farted. Midge looked at him. 'So Bonkie bit Garp,' Stewart mused. 'Well, at least the dog's got good taste, doesn't he?'

'Oh, Stewie,' Midge said; a laughter light as spit escaped her. 'Garp's still just a little boy.' And there he was, in fact, near-to-fainting and bleeding on the costly hall carpet, which actually spread, without a tuck or a ripple, through four of the monstrous first-floor rooms.

Cushie Percy, whose young life would terminate in childbirth while she tried to deliver what would have been only her first child, saw Garp bleeding on the Steering family heirloom: the remarkable rug. 'Oh, gross!' she cried, running out the door.

'Oh, I'll have to call your mother,' Midge told Garp, who felt dizzy with the great dog's growl and slobber still singing in his partial ear.

For years Garp would mistakenly interpret Cushie Percy's outcry of 'Oh, gross!' He thought she was *not* referring to his gnawed and messy ear but to her father's great gray nakedness, which filled the hall. *That* was what was gross to Garp: the silver, barrel-bellied navy man approaching him in the nude from the well of the Percys' towering spiral staircase.

Stewart Percy knelt down in front of Garp and peered curiously into the boy's bloody face; Fat Stew did not appear to be directing his attention to the mauled ear, and Garp wondered if he should advise the enormous, naked man concerning the whereabouts of his injury. But Stewart Percy was not looking for where Garp was hurt. He was looking at Garp's shining brown eyes, at their color and at their shape, and he seemed to convince himself of something, because he nodded austerely and said to his foolish blond Midge, 'Jap.'

It would be years before Garp would fully comprehend this, too. But Stewie Percy said to Midge, 'I spent enough time in the Pacific to recognize Jap eyes when I see them. I *told* you it was a Jap.' The *it* Stewart Percy referred to was whoever he had decided was Garp's father. That was a frequent, speculative game around the Steering community: guessing who Garp's father was. And Stewart Percy, from his experience in his part of the Pacific, had decided that Garp's father was Japanese.

'At that moment,' Garp wrote, 'I thought "Jap" was a word that meant my ear was all gone.'

'No sense in calling his mother,' Stewie said to Midge. 'Just take him over to the infirmary. She's a nurse, isn't she? *She'll* know what to do.'

Jenny knew, all right. 'Why not bring the dog over here?' she asked Midge, while she gingerly washed around what was left of Garp's little ear.

'Bonkers?' Midge asked.

'Bring him here,' Jenny said, 'and I'll give him a shot.'

'An injection?' Midge asked. She laughed. 'Do you mean there's actually a *shot* to make him so he won't bite any more people?'

'No,' Jenny said. 'I mean you could save your money – instead of taking him to a vet. I mean there's a shot to make him *dead*. *That* kind of an injection. *Then* he won't bite any more people.'

'Thus,' Garp wrote, 'was the Percy War begun. For my mother, I think, it was a class war, which she later said all wars were. For me, I just knew to watch out for Bonkers. And for the rest of the Percys.'

Stewart Percy sent Jenny Fields a memo on the stationery of the Secretary of the Steering School: 'I cannot believe you actually want us to have Bonkers put to sleep,' Stewart wrote.

'You bet your fat ass I do,' Jenny said to him, on the phone. 'Or at least tie him up, forever.'

'There's no point in having a dog if the dog can't run free,' Stewart said.

'Then kill him,' Jenny said.

'Bonkers has had all his shots, thank you just the same,' Stewart said. 'He's a gentle dog, really. Only if he's provoked.'

'Obviously,' Garp wrote, 'Fat Stew felt that Bonkers had been provoked by my *Jap*ness.'

'What's "good taste" mean?' little Garp asked Jenny. At the infirmary, Dr Pell sewed up his ear; Jenny reminded the doctor that Garp had recently had a tetanus shot.

'Good taste?' Jenny asked. The odd-looking amputation of the ear forced Garp always to wear his hair long, a style he often complained about.

'Fat Stew said that Bonkers has got "good taste,"' Garp said.

'To bite you?' Jenny asked.

'I guess so,' Garp said. 'What's it mean?'

Jenny knew, all right. But she said, 'It means that Bonkers must have known you were the best-tasting kid in the whole pile of kids.'

'Am I?' Garp asked.

'Sure,' Jenny said.

'How did Bonkers know?' Garp asked.

'*I* don't know,' Jenny said.

'What's "Jap" mean?' Garp asked.

'Did Fat Stew say that to you?' Jenny asked him.

'No,' Garp said. 'I think he said it about my ear.'

'Oh yes, your ear,' Jenny said. 'It means you have *special* ears.' But she was wondering whether to tell him what she felt about the Percys, *now,* or whether he was enough like her to profit at some later, more important time from the experience of anger. Perhaps, she thought, I should save this morsel for him, for a time when he could *use* it. In her mind, Jenny Fields saw always more and larger battles ahead.

'My mother seemed to need an enemy,' Garp wrote. 'Real or imagined, my mother's enemy helped her see the way *she* should behave, and how she should instruct me. She was no natural at motherhood; in fact, I think my mother doubted that *any*thing happened naturally. She was self-conscious and deliberate to the end.'

It was the world according to Fat Stew that became Jenny's enemy in those early years for Garp. That phase might be called 'Getting Garp Ready for Steering.'

She watched his hair grow and cover the missing parts of his ear. She was surprised at his handsomeness, because handsomeness had not been a factor in her relationship with Technical Sergeant Garp. If the sergeant had been handsome, Jenny Fields hadn't really noticed. But young Garp was handsome, she could see, though he remained small – as if he were born to fit in the ball turret installation.

The band of children (who coursed the Steering footpaths

and grassy quadrangles and playing fields) grew more awkward and self-conscious as Jenny watched them grow. Clarence DuGard soon needed glasses, which he was always smashing; over the years Jenny would treat him many times for ear infections and once for a broken nose. Talbot Mayer-Jones developed a lisp; he had a bottle-shaped body, though a lovely disposition, and low-grade chronic sinusitis. Emily Hamilton grew so tall that her knees and elbows were forever raw and bleeding from all her stumbling falls, and the way her small breasts asserted themselves made Jenny wince – occasionally wishing she had a daughter. Ira and Buddy Grove, 'from the town,' were thick in the ankles and wrists and necks, their fingers smudged and mashed from messing around in their father's maintenance department. And up grew the Percy children, blond and metallically clean, their eyes the color of the dull ice on the brackish Steering River that seeped through the salt marshes to the nearby sea.

Stewart, Jr., who was called Stewie Two, graduated from Steering before Garp was even of age to enter the school; Jenny treated Stewie Two twice for a sprained ankle and once for gonorrhea. He later went through Harvard Business School, a staph infection, and a divorce.

Randolph Percy was called Dopey until his dying day (of a heart attack, when he was only thirty-five; he was a procreator after his fat father's heart, himself the father of five). Dopey never managed to graduate from Steering, but successfully transferred to some other prep school and graduated after a while. Once Midge cried out in the Sunday dining room, 'Our Dopey's dead!' His nickname sounded so awful in that context that the family, after his death, finally spoke of him as Randolph.

William Percy, Shrill Willy, was embarrassed by his stupid nickname, to his credit, and although he was three years older than Garp, he befriended Garp in a very decent fashion while he was an upperclassman at Steering and Garp was just starting out. Jenny always liked William, whom she called William. She treated him many times for bronchitis and was moved enough by the news of his death (in a war, immediately following his graduation from Yale) that she even wrote a long letter of commiseration to Midge and Fat Stew.

As for the Percy girls, Cushie would get hers (and Garp would even get to play a small part; they were near the same age). And poor Bainbridge, the youngest Percy, who was cursed to be called Pooh, would be spared *her* encounter with Garp until Garp was in his prime.

All these children, and her Garp, Jenny watched grow. While Jenny waited for Garp to get ready for Steering, the black beast Bonkers grew very old, and slower – but not toothless, Jenny noticed. And always Garp watched out for him, even after Bonkers stopped running with the crowd; when he lurked, hulking by the Percys' white front pillars – as matted and tangled and nasty as a thorn bush in the dark – Garp still kept his eye on him. An occasional younger child, or someone new in the neighborhood, would get too close and be chomped. Jenny kept track of the stitches and missing bits of flesh for which the great slathering dog was accountable, but Fat Stew endured all Jenny's criticisms and Bonkers lived.

'I believe my mother grew fond of that animal's presence, although she would never have admitted it,' Garp wrote. 'Bonkers was the Percy Enemy come alive – made into muscle and fur and halitosis. It must have pleased my mother to watch the old dog slowing down while I was growing up.'

By the time Garp was ready for Steering, black Bonkers was fourteen years old. By the time Garp entered the Steering School, Jenny Fields had a few Distinguished Silver hairs of her own. By the time Garp started Steering, Jenny had taken all the courses that were worth taking and had listed them in order of universal value and entertainment. By the time Garp was a Steering student, Jenny Fields had been awarded the traditional gift for faculty and staff enduring fifteen years of service: the famous Steering dinner plates. The stern brick buildings of the school, including the infirmary annex, were baked into the big-eating surfaces of the plates, vividly rendered in the Steering School colors. Good old blood and blue.

3

What He Wanted to Be When He Grew Up

In 1781 the widow and children of Everett Steering founded Steering Academy, as it was first called, because Everett Steering had announced to his family, while carving his last Christmas goose, that his only disappointment with *his* town was that he had not provided his boys with an academy capable of preparing them for a higher education. He did not mention his girls. He was a shipbuilder in a village whose life-link to the sea was a doomed river; Everett knew the river was doomed. He was a smart man, and not usually playful, but after Christmas dinner he indulged in a snowball fight with both his boys and his girls. He died of apoplexy before nightfall. Everett Steering was seventy-two; even his boys and his girls were too old for snowball fights, but he had a right to call the town of Steering *his* town.

It had been named after him in a glut of enthusiasm for the town's independence following the Revolutionary War. Everett Steering had organized the installation of mounted cannons at strategic points along the river shore; these cannons were meant to discourage an attack that never came – from the British, who were expected to sail up the river from the sea at Great Bay. The river was called Great River then, but after the war it was called the Steering River; and the town, which had no proper name – but had always been called The Meadows, because it lay in the salt- and freshwater marshes only a few miles inland from Great Bay – was also called Steering.

Many families in Steering were dependent on ship-building, or on other business that came up the river from the sea; since it was first called The Meadows, the village had been a backup port to Great Bay. But along with his wishes to found a boys' academy, Everett Steering told his family that Steering would *not* be a port for very long. The river, he noticed, was choking with silt.

In all his life, Everett Steering was known to tell only one joke, and only to his family. The joke was that the only river to have been named after him was full of mud; and it was getting fuller by the minute. The land was all marsh and meadow, from Steering to the sea, and unless people decided that Steering was worth maintaining as a port, and gouged a deeper channel for the river, Everett knew that even a rowboat would eventually have trouble making it from Steering to Great Bay (unless there was a very high tide). Everett knew that the tide would one day fill in the riverbed from his hometown to the Atlantic.

In the next century, the Steering family was wise to stake its life-support system on the textile mills they constructed to span the waterfall on the freshwater part of the Steering River. By the time of the Civil War the *only* business in the town of Steering, on the Steering River, was the Steering Mills. The family got out of boats and into textiles when the time was ripe.

Another shipbuilding family in Steering was not so lucky; this family's last ship made it only half the way from Steering to the sea. In a once-notorious part of the river, called The Gut, the last ship made in Steering settled into the mud forever, and for years it could be seen from the road, half out of the water at high tide and completely dry at low tide. Kids played in it until it listed to its side and crushed someone's dog. A pig farmer named Gilmore salvaged the ship's masts to raise his barn. And by the time young Garp attended Steering, the varsity crew could row their shells on the river only at high tide. At low tide the Steering River is one wet mudflat from Steering to the sea.

It was, therefore, due to Everett Steering's instincts about water that a boys' academy was founded in 1781. After a century or so, it flourished.

'Over all those years,' Garp wrote, 'the shrewd Steering genes must have suffered some dilution; the family instincts regarding water went from good to very bad.' Garp enjoyed referring to Midge Steering Percy in this way. 'A Steering whose water instincts had run their course,' he said. Garp thought it wonderfully ironic 'that the Steering genes for water sense ran out of chromosomes when they got to Midge. *Her* sense of water was so perverse,' Garp wrote, 'that it attracted her first to Hawaii and then to the United States Navy – in the form of Fat Stew.'

Midge Steering Percy was the end of the bloodline. The Steering School itself would become the last Steering after her, and perhaps old Everett foresaw that, too; many families have left less, or worse, behind. In Garp's day, at least, the Steering School was still relentless and definite in its purpose: 'the preparing of young men for a higher education.' And in Garp's case, he had a mother who also took that purpose seriously. Garp himself took the school so seriously that even Everett Steering, with his one joke in a lifetime, would have been pleased.

Garp knew what to take for courses and whom to have for teachers. That is often the difference between doing well or poorly in a school. He was not really a gifted student, but he had direction; many of his courses were still fresh in Jenny's mind, and she was a good drillmaster. Garp was probably no more of a natural at intellectual pursuits than his mother, but he had Jenny's powerful discipline; a nurse *is* a natural at establishing a routine, and Garp believed in his mother.

If Jenny was remiss in her advice, it was in only one area. She had never paid any attention to the sports at Steering; she could offer Garp no suggestions as to what games he might like to play. She could tell him that he would like

East Asian Civilization with Mr Merrill more than he would like Tudor England with Mr Langdell. But, for example, Jenny did not know the differences in pleasure and pain between football and soccer. She had observed only that her son was small, strong, well balanced, quick, and solitary; she assumed he already knew what games he liked to play. He did not.

Crew, he thought, was stupid. Rowing a boat in unison, a galley slave dipping your oar in foul water – and the Steering River was indeed foul. The river was afloat with factory scum and human turds – and always the after-tide, saltwater slime was on the mudflats (a muck the texture of refrigerated bacon fat). Everett Steering's river was full of more than mud, but even if it had been sparkling clean, Garp was no oarsman. And no tennis player, either. In one of his earliest essays – his freshman year at Steering – Garp wrote: 'I do not care for balls. The ball stands between the athlete and his exercise. So do hockey pucks and badminton birdies – and skates, like skis, intrude between the body and the ground. And when one further removes one's body from the contest by an extension device – such as a racket, a bat, or a stick – all purity of movement, strength, and focus is lost.' Even at fifteen, one could sense his instinct for a personal aesthetic.

Since he was too small for football, and soccer certainly involved a ball, he ran long distance, which was called cross-country, but he stepped in too many puddles and suffered all fall from a perpetual cold.

When the winter sports season opened, Jenny was distressed at how much restlessness her son exhibited; she criticized him for making too much of a mere athletic decision – why didn't he know what form of exercise he might prefer? But sports did not feel like recreation to Garp. *Nothing* felt like recreation to Garp. From the beginning, he appeared to believe there was something strenuous to achieve. ('Writers do not read for fun,' Garp would write, later, speaking for himself.) Even before young Garp knew he was going to be a writer, or knew *what* he wanted to be, it appears he did nothing 'for fun.'

Garp was confined to the infirmary on the day he was supposed to sign up for a winter sport. Jenny would not let him get out of bed. 'You don't know what you want to sign up for, anyway,' she told him. All Garp could do was cough.

'This is silly beyond mortal belief,' Jenny told him. 'Fifteen years in this snotty, rude community and you fall to pieces trying to decide what *game* you're going to play to occupy your afternoons.'

'I haven't found my sport, Mom,' Garp croaked. 'I've *got* to have a sport.'

'Why?' Jenny asked.

'I don't know,' he moaned. He coughed and coughed.

'God, listen to you,' Jenny complained. '*I'll* find you a sport,' she said. 'I'll go over to the gym and sign you up for something.'

'No!' Garp begged.

And Jenny pronounced what was for Garp, in his four years at Steering, her litany. 'I know more than you do, don't I?' she said. Garp fell back on his sweaty pillow.

'Not about *this*, Mom,' he said. 'You took all the courses but you never played on any of the *teams*.'

If Jenny Fields recognized this as a rare oversight, she did not admit it. It was a typical Steering December day, the ground glassy with frozen slush and the snow gray and muddy from the boots of eight hundred boys. Jenny Fields bundled up and trudged across the winter-grim campus like the convinced and determined mother she was. She looked like a nurse resigned to bring what slim hope she could to the bitter Russian front. In such a manner Jenny Fields approached the Steering gym. In her fifteen years at Steering, Jenny had never been there; she had not known it was important. At the far end of the Steering campus, ringed by the acres of playing fields, the hockey rinks, the tennis courts like the cross section of a huge, human hive, Jenny saw the giant gymnasium loom out of the dirty snow like a battle she had not anticipated, and her heart filled with worry and with gloom.

The Seabrook Gymnasium and Field House – and the Seabrook Stadium, and the Seabrook Ice Hockey Rinks – were named after the superb athlete and World War I flying ace Miles Seabrook, whose face and massive torso greeted Jenny in a triptych of photographs enshrined in the display case in the gym's vast entranceway. Miles Seabrook, '09, his head in a leather football helmet, his shoulder pads probably unnecessary. Beneath the photo of old No. 32 was the near-demolished jersey itself: faded and frequently under the attack of moths, the jersey lay in a heap in the locked trophy case under the first third of Miles Seabrook's triptych photograph. A sign said: HIS ACTUAL SHIRT.

The center shot in the triptych showed Miles Seabrook as a hockey goalie – in those old days the goalies wore pads, but the brave face was naked, the eyes clear and challenging, the scar tissue everywhere. Miles Seabrook's bulk filled the dwarfed net. How could anyone have scored on Miles Seabrook, his cat-quick and bear-sized leather paws, his clublike stick and swollen chest protector, his skates like the long claws of a giant anteater? Beneath the football and the hockey pictures were the scores of the annual *big* games: in every Steering sport, the season ended in the traditional contest with Bath Academy, nearly as old and famous as Steering, and every Steering schoolboy's hated rival. The vile Bath boys in their gold and green (in Garp's day, these colors were called puke and babyshit). STEERING 7, BATH 6; STEERING 3, BATH 0. Nobody scored on Miles.

Captain Miles Seabrook, as he was called in the third photo in the triptych, stared back at Jenny Fields in a uniform all too familiar to her. It was a flyboy's suit, she saw in an instant; although the costumes changed between world wars, they did not change so much that Jenny failed to recognize the fleece-lined collar of the flight jacket, turned up at a cocky angle, and the confident, untied chin strap of the flight cap, the tipped-up earmuffs (Miles Seabrook's ears could never get cold!), and the goggles pushed carelessly up off the forehead. At his throat, the pure white scarf. No score was cited beneath this portrait, but if anyone in the Steering Athletic Department had possessed a sense of humor, Jenny might have read: UNITED STATES 16, GERMANY 1. Sixteen was the number of planes Miles Seabrook shot down before the Germans scored on him.

Ribbons and medals lay dusty in the locked trophy case, like offerings at an altar to Miles Seabrook. There was a battered wooden thing, which Jenny mistook for part of Miles Seabrook's shot-down plane; she was prepared for *any* tastelessness, but the wood was only all that remained of his last hockey stick. Why not his jock? thought Jenny Fields. Or, like a keepsake of a dead baby, a lock of his hair? Which was, in all three photos, covered by a helmet or a cap or a big striped sock. Perhaps, Jenny thought – with characteristic scorn – Miles Seabrook was hairless.

Jenny resented the implications lying honored in that dusty case. The warrior-athlete, merely undergoing another change of uniform. Each time the body was offered only a pretense of protection: as a Steering School nurse, Jenny had seen fifteen years of football and hockey injuries, in spite of helmets, masks, straps, buckles, hinges, and pads. And Sergeant Garp, and the others, had shown Jenny that men at war had the most illusory protection of all.

Wearily, Jenny moved on; when she passed the display cases, she felt she was moving toward the engine of a dangerous machine. She avoided the arena-sized spaces in the gymnasium, where she could hear the shouts and grunts of contest. She sought the dark corridors, where, she supposed, the offices were. Have I spent fifteen years, she thought, to lose my child to *this*?

She recognized a part of the smell. Disinfectant. Years of strenuous scrubbing. No doubt that a gym was a place where germs of monstrous potential lay waiting for a chance to breed. That part of the smell reminded her of hospitals, and of the Steering infirmary – bottled, postoperative air. But here in the huge house built to the memory of Miles Seabrook there was *another* smell, as distasteful to Jenny Fields as the smell of sex. The complex of gym and field house had been erected in 1919, less than a year before she was born: what Jenny smelled was almost forty years of the forced farts and the sweat of boys under stress and strain. What Jenny smelled was *competition*, fierce and full of disappointment. She was such an outsider, it had never been part of *her* growing up.

In a corridor that seemed separated from the central areas of the gym's various energies, Jenny stood still and listened. Somewhere near her was a weight-lifting room; she heard the iron bashing and the terrible heaves of hernias in progress – a nurse's view of such exertion. In fact, it seemed to Jenny that the whole building groaned and pushed, as if every schoolboy at Steering suffered constipation and sought relievement in the horrid gym.

Jenny Fields felt undone, the way only a person who has been careful can feel when confronted by a mistake.

The bleeding wrestler was at that instant upon her. Jenny was not sure how the groggy, dripping boy had surprised her, but a door opened off this corridor of small, innocuous-appearing rooms, and the matted face of the wrestler was smack in front of her with his ear guards pulled so askew on his head that the chin strap had slipped to his mouth, where it tugged his upper lip into a fishlike sneer. The little bowl of the strap, which had once cupped his chin, now brimmed with blood from his streaming nose.

As a nurse, Jenny was not overimpressed with blood, but she cringed at her anticipated collision with the thick, wet, hard-looking boy, who somehow dodged her, lunging sideways. With admirable trajectory and volume, he vomited on his fellow wrestler who was struggling to support him. 'Excuse me,' he burbled, for most of the boys at Steering were well brought up.

His fellow wrestler did him the favor of pulling his

headgear off, so that the hapless puker would not choke or strangle; quite unmindful of his own bespattering, he called loudly back into the open door of the wrestling room, 'Carlisle didn't make it!'

From the door of that room, whose heat beckoned Jenny in the way a tropical greenhouse might be alluring in midwinter, a man's clear tenor voice responded. 'Carlisle! You had *two* helpings of that dining-hall slop for lunch, Carlisle! *One* helping and you deserve to lose it! *No sympathy*, Carlisle!'

Carlisle, for whom there was no sympathy, continued his lurching progress down the corridor; he bled and barfed his way to a door, through which he made his smeared escape. His fellow wrestler, who in Jenny's opinion had also withheld his sympathy, dropped Carlisle's headgear in the corridor with the rest of Carlisle's muck; then he followed Carlisle to the lockers. Jenny hoped that he was going somewhere to change his clothes.

She looked at the wrestling room's open door; she breathed deeply and stepped inside. Immediately, she felt off-balance. Underfoot was a soft fleshy feel, and the wall sank under her touch when she leaned against it; she was inside a padded cell, the floor and the wall mats warm and yielding, the air so stifling hot and stench-full of sweat that she hardly dared to breathe.

'Shut the door!' said the man's tenor voice – because wrestlers, Jenny would later know, *love* the heat and their own sweat, especially when they're cutting weight, and they *thrive* when the walls and floors are as hot and giving as the buttocks of sleeping girls.

Jenny shut the door. Even the door had a mat on it, and she slumped against it, imagining someone might open the door from the outside and mercifully release her. The man with the tenor voice was the coach and Jenny, through the shimmering heat, watched him pace against the long room's wall, unable to stand still while he squinted at his struggling wrestlers. 'Thirty seconds!' he screamed to them.

The couples on the mat bucked as if they were electrically stimulated. The batches of twosomes around the wrestling room were each locked in some violent tangle, the intent of each wrestler, in Jenny's eye, as deliberate and as desperate as rape.

'Fifteen seconds!' the coach screamed. '*Push* it!'

The twisted pair nearest Jenny suddenly came apart, their limbs unknotting, the veins on their arms and necks popping. A breathless cry and a string of saliva broke from one boy's mouth as his opponent broke free of him and they uncoupled, bashing into the padded wall.

'Time's up!' the coach screamed. He did not use a whistle. The wrestlers went suddenly limp, untying each other from each other with great slowness. A half dozen of them now lumbered toward Jenny at the door; they had the water fountain and fresh air on their minds, though Jenny assumed they were all heading for the hall in order to throw up, or bleed in peace – or both.

Jenny and the coach were the only standing bodies left in the wrestling room. Jenny observed that the coach was a neat, small man, as compact as a spring; she also observed he was nearly blind, because the coach now squinted in her direction, recognizing that her whiteness and her shape were foreign to the wrestling room. He began to grope for his glasses, which he usually stashed above the wall mats, at about head level – where they would not be so easily crushed by a wrestler who was flung upon them. Jenny observed that the coach was about her age, and that she had never seen him on or about the Steering campus before – with or without his glasses.

The coach was new at Steering. His name was Ernie Holm, and so far he had found the Steering community to be just as snotty as Jenny had found it. Ernie Holm had been a two-time Big Ten wrestling champion at the University of Iowa, but he had never won a national title and he had coached in high schools all over Iowa for fifteen years while trying to raise his only child, a daughter, all by himself. He was bone-tired of the Midwest, as he would have said it himself, and he had come East to assure his daughter of a classy education – as he would also have said it. She was the brains of the family, he was fond of saying – and she had her mother's fine looks, which he never mentioned.

Helen Holm, at fifteen, had spent a lifetime of three-hour afternoons sitting in wrestling rooms, from Iowa to Steering, watching boys of many sizes sweat and throw each other around. Helen would remark, years later, that spending her childhood as the only girl in a wrestling room had made her a reader. 'I was brought up to be a spectator,' Helen said. 'I was raised to be a voyeur.'

She was such a good and nonstop reader, in fact, that Ernie Holm had moved East just for her. He took the job at Steering for Helen's sake, because he had read in his contract that the children of the faculty and staff could attend the Steering School for free – or they could receive a comparable sum of money toward their tuition at another private school. Ernie Holm was a bad reader, himself; he had somehow overlooked the fact that Steering admitted only boys.

He found himself moving into the chilly Steering community in the fall, with his brainy daughter once more enrolled in a small, bad public school. In fact, the public school in the town of Steering was probably worse than most public schools because the smart boys in the town went to Steering, and the smart girls went away. Ernie Holm hadn't figured he'd have to send his daughter away from him – that had been why he'd moved: to stay with her. So while Ernie Holm was getting used to his new duties at Steering, Helen Holm wandered the fringes of the great school, devouring its bookstore and its library (hearing stories, no doubt, of the community's *other* great reader: Jenny Fields); and Helen continued to be bored, as she had been bored in Iowa, by her boring classmates in her boring public school.

Ernie Holm was sensitive to people who were bored. He had married a nurse sixteen years earlier; when Helen had been born, the nurse gave up her nursing to be a full-time mother. After six months she wanted to be a nurse again, but there were no day-care centers in Iowa in those years, and Ernie Holm's new wife grew gradually more distant under the strain of being a full-time mother and an ex-nurse. One day she left him. She left him with a full-time daughter and no explanation.

So Helen Holm grew up in wrestling rooms, which are very safe for children – being padded everywhere, and always warm. Books had kept Helen from being bored, although Ernie Holm worried how long his daughter's studiousness could continue to be nourished in a vacuum. Ernie was sure that the *genes* for being bored were in his daughter.

Thus he came to Steering. Thus Helen, who also wore glasses – as needfully as her father – was with him that day Jenny Fields walked into the wrestling room. Jenny didn't notice Helen; few people noticed Helen, when Helen was fifteen. Helen, however, noticed Jenny right away; Helen was unlike her father in that she didn't wrestle with the boys, or demonstrate moves and holds, and so she kept her glasses *on*.

Helen Holm was forever on the lookout for nurses because she was forever on the lookout for her disappeared mother, whom Ernie had made no attempt to find. With women, Ernie Holm had some experience at taking no for an answer. But when Helen had been small, Ernie had indulged her with a speculative fable he no doubt liked to imagine himself – it was a story that had always intrigued Helen, too. 'One day,' went the story, 'you might see a pretty nurse, sort of looking like she doesn't know where she *is* anymore, and she might look at you like she doesn't know who *you* are, either – but she might look curious to find out.'

'And that will be my mom?' Helen used to ask her father.

'And that will be your mom!' Ernie used to say.

So when Helen Holm looked up from her book in the Steering wrestling room, she thought she saw her mother.

Jenny Fields in her white uniform was forever appearing out of place; there on the crimson mats of the Steering School, she looked dark and healthy, strong-boned and handsome if not exactly pretty, and Helen Holm must have thought that no other woman would have ventured into this soft-floored inferno where her father worked. Helen's glasses fogged, she closed her book; in her anonymous gray sweat suit, which hid her gawky fifteen-year-old frame – her hard hips and her small breasts – she stood up awkwardly against the wrestling-room wall and waited for her father's sign of recognition.

But Ernie Holm was still groping for his glasses; in a blur he saw the white figure – vaguely womanly, perhaps a nurse – and his heart paused at the possibility he had never really believed in: his wife's return, her saying, 'Oh, how I've missed you and our daughter!' What *other* nurse would enter his place of employment?

Helen saw her father's fumbling, she took this to be the necessary sign. She stepped toward Jenny across the blood-warm mats, and Jenny thought: My God, that's a *girl*! A pretty girl with glasses. What's a pretty girl doing in a place like this?

'Mom?' the girl said to Jenny. 'It's *me*, Mom! It's *Helen*,' she said, bursting into tears; she flung her slim arms around Jenny's shoulders and pressed her wet face to Jenny's throat.

'Jesus Christ!' said Jenny Fields, who was never a woman who liked to be touched. Still, she was a nurse and she must have felt Helen's need; she did not shove the girl away from her, though she knew very well she was not Helen's mother. Jenny Fields thought that having been a mother *once* was enough. She coolly patted the weeping girl's back and looked imploringly at the wrestling coach, who had just found his glasses. 'I'm not *your* mother, either,' Jenny said politely to him, because he was looking at her with the same brief relief in his face that Jenny had seen in the face of the pretty girl.

What Ernie Holm thought was that the resemblance went deeper than the uniform and the coincidence of a wrestling room in two nurses' lives; but Jenny stopped short of being as pretty as Ernie's runaway wife, and Ernie was reflecting that even fifteen years would not have made his wife as plain and merely handsome as Jenny. Still, Jenny looked all right to Ernie Holm, who smiled an unclear, apologetic smile that his wrestlers were familiar with, when they lost.

'My daughter thought you were her mother,' Ernie Holm said to Jenny. 'She hasn't seen her mother in quite a while.'

Obviously, thought Jenny Fields. She felt the girl tense and spring out of her arms.

'That's not your mom, darlin',' Ernie Holm said to Helen, who retreated to the wrestling-room wall; she was a tough-minded girl, not at all in the habit of emotionally displaying herself – not even to her father.

'And did you think I was your *wife?*' Jenny asked Ernie, because it had looked to her, for a moment, that Ernie had mistaken her, too. She wondered how long a 'while' Mrs Holm had been missing.

'You fooled me, for a minute,' Ernie said, politely; he had a shy grin, which he used sparingly.

Helen crouched in a corner of the wrestling room, fiercely eyeing Jenny as if Jenny were deliberately responsible for her embarrassment. Jenny felt moved by the girl; it had been years since Garp had hugged her like that, and it was a feeling that even a very selective mother, like Jenny, remembered missing.

'What's your name?' she asked Helen. 'My name is Jenny Fields.'

It was a name Helen Holm knew, of course. She was the other mystery reader around the Steering School. Also, Helen had not previously given to anyone the feelings she reserved for a mother; even though it had been an accident that she'd flung those feelings around Jenny, Helen found it hard to call them back entirely. She had her father's shy smile and she looked thankfully at Jenny; oddly, Helen felt she would like to hug Jenny again, but she restrained herself. There were wrestlers shuffling back into the room, gasping from the drinking fountain, where those who were cutting weight had only rinsed their mouths.

'No more practice,' Ernie Holm told them, waving them out of the room. 'That's it for today. Go run your laps!' Obediently, even relieved, they bobbed in the doorway of the crimson room; they picked up their headgear, their rubber sweat suits, their spools of tape. Ernie Holm waited for the room to clear, while his daughter and Jenny Fields waited for him to explain; at the very least, an explanation was in order, he felt, and there was nowhere Ernie felt as comfortable as he felt in a wrestling room. For him it was the natural place to tell someone a story, even a difficult story with no ending – and even to a stranger. So when his wrestlers had left to run their laps, Ernie very patiently began his father-and-daughter tale, the brief history of the nurse who left them, and of the Midwest they only recently had left. It was a story Jenny could appreciate, of course, because Jenny did not know another single parent with a single child. And although she may have felt tempted to tell them *her* story – there being interesting similarities, and differences – Jenny merely repeated her standard version: the father of Garp was a soldier, and so forth. And who takes the time for weddings when there is a war? Though it was not the whole story, it clearly appealed to Helen and Ernie, who had met no one else in the Steering community as receptive and frank as Jenny.

There in the warm red wrestling room, on the soft mats, surrounded by those padded walls – in such an environment, sudden and inexplicable closeness is possible.

Of course Helen would remember that first hug her whole life; however her feelings for Jenny might change, and change back, from that moment in the wrestling room Jenny Fields was more of a mother to Helen than Helen had ever had. Jenny would also remember how it felt to be hugged like a mother, and would even note, in her autobiography, how a daughter's hug was different from a son's. It is at least ironic that her one experience for making such a pronouncement occurred that December day in the giant gymnasium erected to the memory of Miles Seabrook.

It is unfortunate if Ernie Holm felt any desire toward Jenny Fields, and if he imagined, even briefly, that here might be another woman with whom he might live his life. Because Jenny Fields was given to no such feelings; she thought only that Ernie was a nice, good man – perhaps, she hoped, he would be her friend. If he would be, he would be her first.

And it must have perplexed Ernie and Helen when Jenny asked if she could stay a moment, in the wrestling room, just by herself. What for? they must have wondered. Ernie then remembered to ask her why she had come.

'To sign my son up for wrestling,' Jenny said quickly. She hoped Garp would approve.

'Well, sure,' Ernie said. 'And you'll turn out the lights, and the heaters, when you leave? The door locks itself.'

Thus alone, Jenny turned off the lights and heard the great blow heaters hum down to stillness. There in the dark room, the door ajar, she took off her shoes and she paced the mat. Despite the apparent violence of this sport, she was thinking, why do I feel so *safe* here? Is it him? she wondered, but Ernie passed quickly through her mind – simply a small, neat, muscular man with glasses. If Jenny thought of men at all, and she never really did, she thought they were more tolerable when they were small and neat, and she preferred men *and* women to have muscles – to be strong. She enjoyed people with glasses the way only someone who doesn't need to wear glasses can enjoy glasses on other people – can find them 'nice.' But mostly it is this *room*, she thought – the red wrestling room, huge but contained, padded against pain, she imagined. She dropped thud! to her knees, just to hear the way the mats received her. She did a somersault and split her dress; then she sat on the mat and looked at the heavy boy who loomed in the doorway of the blackened room. It was Carlisle, the wrestler who'd lost his lunch; he had changed his equipment and come back for more punishment, and he peered across the dark crimson mats at the glowing white nurse who crouched like a she-bear in her cave.

'Excuse me, ma'am,' he said. 'I was just looking for someone to work out with.'

'Well, don't look at *me*,' Jenny said. 'Go run your laps!'

'Yes, ma'am,' Carlisle said, and he trotted off.

When she closed the door and it locked behind her, she realized she'd left her shoes inside. A janitor did not seem able to find the right key, but he lent her a large boy's basketball shoes that had turned up in Lost and Found. Jenny trudged across the frozen slush to the infirmary, feeling that her first trip to the world of sports had left her more than a little changed.

In the annex, in his bed, Garp still coughed and coughed. 'Wrestling!' he croaked. 'Good God, Mother, are you trying to get me killed?'

'I think you'll like the coach,' Jenny said. 'I met him, and he's a nice man. I met his daughter, too.'

'Oh, Jesus,' Garp groaned. 'His *daughter* wrestles?'

'No, she reads a lot,' Jenny said, approvingly.

'Sounds exciting, Mom,' Garp said. 'You realize that setting me up with the wrestling coach's daughter may cost me my neck? Do you want that?'

But Jenny was innocent of such a scheme. She really had only been thinking about the wrestling room, and Ernie Holm; her feelings for Helen were entirely motherly, and when her crude young son suggested the possibility of matchmaking – of *his* taking an interest in young Helen Holm – Jenny was rather alarmed. She had not previously thought of the possibility of her son's being interested in anyone, in that way – at least, she'd thought, he wouldn't be interested for a long time. It was very disquieting to her and she could only say to him, 'You're only fifteen years old. Remember that.'

'Well, how old is the daughter?' Garp asked. 'And what's her name?'

'Helen,' Jenny answered. 'She's only fifteen, too. And she wears *glasses*,' she added, hypocritically. After all, she knew what *she* thought of glasses; maybe Garp liked them, too. 'They're from *Iowa*,' she added, and felt she was being a more terrible snob than those hated dandies who thrived in the Steering School community.

'God, *wrestling*,' Garp groaned, again, and Jenny felt relieved that he had passed on from the subject of Helen. Jenny was embarrassed at herself for how much she clearly objected to the possibility. The girl *is* pretty, she thought – though not in an obvious way; and don't young boys like only *obvious* girls? And would I prefer it if Garp were interested in one of those?

As for *those* kind of girls, Jenny had her eye on Cushie Percy – a little too saucy with her mouth, a little too slack about her appearance; and should a fifteen-year-old of Cushman Percy's breeding be so *developed* already? Then Jenny hated herself for even thinking of the word *breeding*.

It had been a confusing day for her. She fell asleep, for once untroubled by her son's coughing because it seemed that more serious troubles might lie ahead for him. Just when I was thinking we were home free! Jenny thought. She must discuss *boys* with someone – Ernie Holm, maybe; she hoped she'd been right about him.

She was right about the wrestling room, it turned out – and what intense comfort it gave to her Garp. The boy liked Ernie, too. In that first wrestling season at Steering, Garp worked hard and happily at learning his moves and his holds. Though he was soundly trounced by the varsity boys in his weight class, he never complained. He knew he had found his sport and his pastime; it would take the best of his energy until the writing came along. He loved the singleness of the combat, and the frightening confines of that circle inscribed on the mat; the terrific conditioning; the mental constancy of keeping his weight down. And in that first season at Steering, Jenny was relieved to note, Garp hardly mentioned Helen Holm, who sat in her glasses, in her gray sweat suit, reading. She occasionally looked up, when there was an unusually loud slam on the mat or a cry of pain.

It had been Helen who returned Jenny's shoes to the infirmary annex, and Jenny embarrassed herself by not even asking the girl to come in. For a moment, they had seemed so close. But Garp had been in. Jenny did not want to introduce them. And besides – Garp had a cold.

One day, in the wrestling room, Garp sat beside Helen. He was conscious of a pimple on his neck and how much he was sweating. Her glasses looked so fogged, Garp doubted she could see what she was reading. 'You sure read a lot,' he said to her.

'Not as much as your mother,' Helen said, not looking at him.

Two months later Garp said to Helen, 'Maybe you'll wreck your eyes, reading in a hot place like this.' She looked at him, her glasses very clear this time and magnifying her eyes in a way that startled him.

'I've already got wrecked eyes,' she said. 'I was *born* with ruined eyes.' But to Garp they looked like very nice eyes; so nice, in fact, that he could think of nothing further to say to her.

Then the wrestling season was over. Garp got a junior varsity letter and signed up for track and field events, his listless choice for a spring sport. His condition from the wrestling season was good enough so that he ran the mile; he was the third-best miler on the Steering team, but he would never get any better. At the end of a mile, Garp felt he was just getting started. ('A novelist, even then – though I didn't know it,' Garp would write, years later.) He also threw the javelin, but not far.

The javelin throwers at Steering practiced behind the football stadium, where they spent much of their time spearing frogs. The upper, freshwater reaches of the Steering River ran behind Seabrook Stadium; many javelins were lost there, and many frogs were slain. Spring is no good, thought Garp, who was restless, who missed wrestling; if he couldn't have wrestling, at least let the summer come, he thought, and he would run long-distance on the road to the beach at Dog's Head Harbor.

One day, in the top row of empty Seabrook Stadium, he saw Helen Holm alone with a book. He climbed up the stadium stairs to her, clicking his javelin against the cement so that she wouldn't be startled by seeing him so suddenly beside her. She wasn't startled. She had been watching him and the other javelin throwers for weeks.

'Killed enough little animals for today?' Helen asked him. 'Hunting something else?'

'From the very beginning,' Garp wrote, 'Helen knew how to get the words in.'

'With all the reading you do, I think you're going to be a writer,' Garp told Helen; he was trying to be casual, but he guiltily hid the point of his javelin with his foot.

'No chance,' Helen said. She had no doubt about it.

'Well, maybe you'll *marry* a writer,' Garp said to her. She looked up at him, her face very serious, her new prescription sunglasses better suited to her wide cheekbones than her last pair that always slid down her nose.

'If I marry *anybody*, I'll marry a writer,' Helen said. 'But I doubt I'll marry anybody.'

Garp had been trying to joke; Helen's seriousness made him nervous. He said, 'Well, I'm sure you won't marry a *wrestler.*'

'You can be *very* sure,' Helen said. Perhaps young Garp could not conceal his pain, because Helen added, 'Unless it's a wrestler who's also a writer.'

'But a writer first and foremost,' Garp guessed.

'Yes, a *real* writer,' Helen said, mysteriously – but ready to define what she meant by that. Garp didn't dare ask her. He let her go back to her book.

It was a long walk down the stadium stairs, dragging his javelin behind him. Will she ever wear anything but that gray sweat suit? he wondered. Garp wrote later that he first discovered he had an imagination while trying to imagine Helen Holm's body. 'With her always in that damn sweat suit,' he wrote, 'I *had* to imagine her body; there was no other way to see it.' Garp imagined that Helen had a very good body – and nowhere in his writing does he say he was disappointed when he finally saw the real thing.

It was that afternoon in the empty stadium, with frog gore on the point of his javelin, when Helen Holm provoked his imagination and T. S. Garp decided he was going to be a writer. A *real* writer, as Helen had said.

4

Graduation

T. S. Garp wrote a short story every month he was at Steering, from the end of his freshman year until his graduation, but it wasn't until his junior year that he showed anything he wrote to Helen. After her first year as a spectator at Steering, Helen was sent to Talbot Academy for girls, and Garp saw her only on occasional weekends. She would sometimes attend the home wrestling meets. It was after one such match that Garp saw her and asked her to wait for him until he'd showered; he had something in his locker he wanted to give her.

'Oh boy,' Helen said. 'Your old elbow pads?'

She didn't come to the wrestling room anymore, even if she was home from Talbot on a long vacation. She wore dark green knee socks and a gray flannel skirt, with pleats; often her sweater, always a dark and solid color, matched her knee socks, and always her long dark hair was up, twirled in a braid on top of her head, or complexly pinned. She had a wide mouth with very thin lips and she never wore lipstick. Garp knew that she always smelled nice, but he never touched her. He did not imagine that anyone did; she was as slender and nearly as tall as a young tree – she was taller than Garp by two inches or more – and she had sharp, almost painful-looking bones in her face, although her eyes behind her glasses were always soft and large, and a rich honey-brown.

'Your old wrestling shoes?' Helen asked him, inquiring of

the large-sized, lumpy envelope that was sealed.

'It's something to read,' Garp said.

'I've got plenty to read,' Helen said.

'It's something I wrote,' Garp told her.

'Oh boy,' Helen said.

'You don't have to read it now,' Garp told her. 'You can take it back to school and write me a letter.'

'I've got plenty to write,' Helen said. 'I've got papers due all the time.'

'Then we can talk about it, later,' Garp said. 'Are you going to be here for Easter?'

'Yes, but I have a date,' Helen said.

'Oh boy,' said Garp. But when he reached to take back his story, the knuckles of her long hand were very white and she would not let go of the package.

In the 133-pound class, his junior year, Garp finished the season with a won-lost record of 12–1, losing only in the finals of the New England championships. In his senior year, he would win everything – captain the team, be voted Most Valuable Wrestler, and take the New England title. His team would represent the beginning of an almost twenty-year dominance of New England wrestling by Ernie Holm's Steering teams. In this part of the country, Ernie had what he called an Iowa advantage. When Ernie was gone, Steering wrestling would go downhill. And perhaps because Garp was the first of many Steering stars, he was always special to Ernie Holm.

Helen couldn't have cared less. She was glad when her father's wrestlers won, because that made her father happy. But in Garp's senior year, when he captained the Steering team, Helen never attended a single match. She did return his story, though – in the mail from Talbot, with this letter.

Dear Garp,

This story shows promise, although I do think, at this point, you are more of a wrestler than a writer. There is a care taken with the language, and a feeling for people, but the situation seems

rather contrived and the ending of this story is pretty juvenile. I
do appreciate you showing it to me, though.

Yours,
Helen

There would be other rejection letters in Garp's writing
career, of course, but none would mean as much to him
as this one. Helen had actually been kind. The story Garp
gave her was about two young lovers who are murdered in
a cemetery by the girl's father, who thinks they are grave
robbers. After this unfortunate error, the lovers are buried
side by side; for some completely unknown reason, their
graves are promptly robbed. It is not certain what becomes
of the father – not to mention the grave robber.

Jenny told Garp that his first efforts at writing were rather
unreal, but Garp was encouraged by his English teacher –
the closest thing Steering had to a writer-in-residence, a frail
man with a stutter whose name was Tinch. He had very bad
breath, remindful to Garp of the dog breath of Bonkers – a
closed room of dead geraniums. But what Tinch said, though
odorous, was kind. He applauded Garp's imagination, and
he taught Garp, once and for all, good old grammar and a
love of exact language. Tinch was called Stench by the Steering boys of Garp's day, and messages were constantly left for
him about his halitosis. Mouthwash deposited on his desk.
Toothbrushes in the campus mail.

It was after one such message – a package of spearmint
breath fresheners taped to the map of Literary England –
that Tinch asked his composition class if they thought he
had bad breath. The class sat as still as moss, but Tinch
singled out young Garp, his favorite, his most trusted, and
he asked him directly, 'Would *you* say, Garp, that my b-b-
breath was bad?'

Truth moved in and out of the open windows on this
spring day of Garp's senior year. Garp was known for his
humorless honesty, his wrestling, his English composition.
His other grades were indifferent to poor. From an early age,

Garp later claimed, he sought perfection and did not spread himself thin. His test scores, for general aptitude, showed that he wasn't very apt at anything; he was no natural. This came as no surprise to Garp, who shared with his mother a belief that *nothing* came naturally. But when a reviewer, after Garp's second novel, called Garp 'a born writer,' Garp had a fit of mischief. He sent a copy of the review to the testing people in Princeton, New Jersey, with a note suggesting that they double-check their previous ratings. Then he sent a copy of his test scores to the reviewer, with a note that said: 'Thank you very much, but I wasn't "born" anything.' In Garp's opinion, he was no more a 'born' writer than he was a born nurse or a born ball turret gunner.

'G-G-Garp?' stuttered Mr Tinch, bending close to the boy – who smelled the terrible truth in Senior Honors English Composition. Garp knew he would win the annual creative writing prize. The sole judge was always Tinch. And if he could just pass third-year math, which he was taking for the second time, he would respectably graduate and make his mother very happy.

'Do I have b-b-bad breath, Garp?' Tinch asked.

' "Good" and "bad" are matters of opinion, sir,' Garp said.

'In *your* opinion, G-G-Garp?' Tinch said.

'In *my* opinion,' Garp said, without batting an eye, 'you've got the best breath of any teacher at this school.' And he looked hard across the classroom at Benny Potter from New York – a *born* wise-ass, even Garp would agree – and he stared Benny's grin off Benny's face because Garp's eyes said to Benny that Garp would break Benny's neck if he made a peep.

And Tinch said, 'Thank you, Garp,' who won the writing prize, despite the note submitted with his last paper.

Mr Tinch: I lied in class because I didn't want those other assholes to laugh at you. You should know, however, that your breath is really pretty bad. Sorry.

T. S. Garp

'You know w-w-what?' Tinch asked Garp when they were alone together, talking about Garp's last story.

'What?' Garp said.

'There's nothing I can d-d-do about my breath,' Tinch said. 'I think it's because I'm d-d-dying,' he said, with a twinkle. 'I'm r-r-rotting from the inside out!' But Garp was not amused and he watched for news of Tinch for years after his graduation, relieved that the old gentleman did not appear to have anything terminal.

Tinch would die in the Steering quadrangle one winter night of causes wholly unrelated to his bad breath. He was coming home from a faculty party, where it was admitted that he'd possibly had too much to drink, and he slipped on the ice and knocked himself unconscious on the frozen footpath. The night watchman did not find the body until almost dawn, by which time Tinch had frozen to death.

It is unfortunate that wise-ass Benny Potter was the first to tell Garp the news. Garp ran into Potter in New York, where Potter worked for a magazine. Garp's low opinion of Potter was enhanced by Garp's low opinion of magazines, and by Garp's belief that Potter always envied Garp for Garp's more significant output as a writer. 'Potter is one of those wretches who has a dozen novels hidden in his drawers,' Garp wrote, 'but he wouldn't dare show them to anybody.'

In Garp's Steering years, however, Garp was also not outgoing at showing his work around. Only Jenny and Tinch got to see his progress – and there was the one story he gave Helen Holm. Garp decided he wouldn't give Helen another story until he wrote one that was so good she wouldn't be able to say anything bad about it.

'Did you hear?' Benny Potter asked Garp in New York.

'What?' Garp said.

'Old Stench kicked off,' Benny said. 'He f-f-froze to death.'

'What did you say?' Garp said.

'Old Stench,' Potter said. Garp had never liked that nickname. 'He got drunk and went wobbling home through the quad – fell down and cracked his noggin, and never woke up in the morning.'

'You asshole,' Garp said.

'It's the truth, Garp,' Benny said. 'It was fucking fifteen-below. Although,' he added, dangerously, 'I'd have thought that old furnace of a mouth of his would have kept him w-w-warm.'

They were in the bar of a nice hotel, somewhere in the Fifties, somewhere between Park Avenue and Third; Garp never knew where he was when he was in New York. He was meeting someone else for lunch and had run into Potter, who had brought him here. Garp picked Potter up by his armpits and sat him on the bar.

'You little gnat, Potter,' Garp said.

'You never liked me,' Benny said.

Garp tipped Benny Potter backward on the bar so that the pockets of Potter's open suit jacket were dipped into the bar sink.

'Leave me alone!' Benny said. 'You were always old Stench's favorite ass-wipe!'

Garp shoved Benny so that Benny's rump slouched into the bar sink; the sink was full of soaking glasses, and the water sloshed up on the bar.

'Please don't sit on the bar, sir,' the bartender said to Benny.

'Jesus Christ, I'm being assaulted, you moron!' Benny said. Garp was already leaving and the bartender had to pull Benny Potter out of the sink and set him down, off the bar. 'That son of a bitch, my *ass* is all wet!' Benny cried.

'Would you please watch your language here, sir?' the bartender said.

'My fucking wallet is soaked!' Benny said, wringing out the·seat of his pants and holding up his sodden wallet to the bartender. 'Garp!' Benny hollered, but Garp was gone. 'You always had a lousy sense of humor, Garp!'

It *is* fair to say, especially in Garp's Steering days, that he was at least rather humorless about his wrestling and his writing – his favorite pastime and his would-be career.

'How do you know you're going to be a writer,' Cushie Percy asked him once.

It was Garp's senior year and they were walking out of town along the Steering River to a place Cushie said she knew. She was home for the weekend from Dibbs. The Dibbs School was the fifth prep school for girls that Cushie Percy had attended; she'd started out at Talbot, in Helen's class, but Cushie had disciplinary problems and she'd been asked to leave. The disciplinary problems had repeated themselves at three other schools. Among the boys at Steering, the Dibbs School was famous – and popular – for its girls with disciplinary problems.

It was high tide on the Steering River and Garp watched an eight-oared shell glide out on the water; a seagull followed it. Cushie Percy took Garp's hand. Cushie had many complicated ways of testing a boy's affection for her. Many of the Steering boys were willing to handle Cushie when they were alone with her, but most of them did not like to be *seen* demonstrating any affection for her. Garp, Cushie noticed, didn't care. He held her hand firmly; of course, they had grown up together, but she did not think they were very good or close friends. At least, Cushie thought, if Garp wanted what the others wanted, he was not embarrassed to be seen pursuing it. Cushie liked him for this.

'I thought you were going to be a wrestler,' Cushie said to Garp.

'I *am* a wrestler,' Garp said. 'I'm *going* to be a writer.'

'And you're going to marry Helen Holm,' Cushie teased him.

'Maybe,' Garp said; his hand went a little limp in hers. Cushie knew this was another humorless topic with him – Helen Holm – and she should be careful.

A group of Steering boys came up the river path toward

them; they passed, and one of them called back, 'What are you getting into, Garp?'

Cushie squeezed his hand. 'Don't let them bother you,' she said.

'They don't bother me,' Garp said.

'What are you going to write about?' Cushie asked him.

'I don't know,' Garp said.

He didn't even know if he was going to college. Some schools in the Midwest had been interested in his wrestling, and Ernie Holm had written some letters. Two places had asked to see him and Garp had visited them. In their wrestling rooms, he had not felt so much outclassed as he had felt out*wanted*. The college wrestlers seemed to want to beat him more than he wanted to beat them. But one school had made him a cautious offer – a little money, and no promises beyond the first year. Fair enough, considering he was from New England. But Ernie had told him this already. 'It's a different sport out there, kid. I mean, you've got the ability – and if I do say so myself, you've had the coaching. What you haven't had is the competition. And you've got to be hungry for it, Garp. You've got to really be interested, you know.'

And when he asked Tinch about where he should go to school, for his *writing*, Tinch had appeared at a typical loss. 'Some g-g-good school, I guess,' he said. 'But if you're going to w-w-write,' Tinch said, 'won't you d-d-do it anywhere?'

'You have a nice body,' Cushie Percy whispered to Garp, and he squeezed her hand back.

'So do *you*,' he told her, honestly. She had, in fact, an absurd body. Small but wholly bloomed, a compact blossom. Her name, Garp thought, should not have been Cushman but *Cushion* – and since their childhood together, he had sometimes called her that. 'Hey, Cushion, want to take a walk?' She said she knew a place.

'Where are you taking me?' Garp asked her.

'Ha!' she said. '*You're* taking *me*. I'm just showing you the way. And the place,' she said.

They went off the path by the part of the Steering River that long ago was called The Gut. A ship had been mired there once, but there was no visible evidence. Only the shore betrayed a history. It was at this narrow bend that Everett Steering had imagined obliterating the British – and here were Everett's cannons, three huge iron tubes, rusting into the concrete mountings. Once they had swiveled, of course, but the latter-day town fathers had fixed them forever in place. Beside them was a permanent cluster of cannonballs, grown together in cement. The balls were greenish and red with rust, as if they belonged to a vessel long undersea, and the concrete platform where the cannons were mounted was now littered with youthful trash – beer cans and broken glass. The grassy slope leading down to the still and almost empty river was trampled, as if nibbled by sheep – but Garp knew it was merely pounded by countless Steering schoolboys and their dates. Cushie's choice of a place to go was not very original, though it was like her, Garp thought.

Garp liked Cushie, and William Percy had always treated Garp well. Garp had been too young to know Stewie Two, and Dopey was Dopey. Young Pooh was a strange, scary child, Garp thought, but Cushie's touching brainlessness was straight from her mother, Midge Steering Percy. Garp felt dishonest with Cushie for not mentioning what he took to be the utter assholery of her father, Fat Stew.

'Haven't you ever been here before?' Cushie asked Garp.

'Maybe with my mother,' Garp said, 'but it's been a while.' Of course he knew what 'the cannons' were. The pet phrase at Steering was 'getting banged at the cannons' – as in 'I got banged at the cannons last weekend,' or 'You should have seen old Fenley blasting away at the cannons.' Even the cannons themselves bore these informal inscriptions: 'Paul banged Betty, '58,' and 'M. Overton, '59, shot his wad here.'

Across the languid river Garp watched the golfers from the Steering Country Club. Even far away, their ridiculous clothing looked unnatural against the green fairway and beyond the marsh grass that grew down to the mudflats.

Their madras prints and plaids among the green-brown, gray-brown shoreline made them look like cautious and out-of-place land animals following their hopping white dots across a lake. 'Jesus, golf is silly,' Garp said. His thesis of games with balls and clubs, again; Cushie had heard it before and wasn't interested. She settled down in a soft place – the river below them, bushes around them, and over their shoulders the yawning mouths of the great cannons. Garp looked up into the mouth of the nearest cannon and was startled to see the head of a smashed doll, one glassy eye on him.

Cushie unbuttoned his shirt and lightly bit his nipples.

'I like you,' she said.

'I like *you*, Cushion,' he said.

'Does it spoil it?' Cushie asked him. 'Us being old friends?'

'Oh no,' he said. He hoped they would hurry ahead to 'it' because *it* had never happened to Garp before, and he was counting on Cushie for her experience. They kissed wetly in the well-pounded grass; Cushie was an open-mouthed kisser, artfully jamming her hard little teeth into his.

Honest, even at this age, Garp tried to mumble to her that he thought her father was an idiot.

'Of course he is,' Cushie agreed. 'Your mother's a little strange, too, don't you think?'

Well, yes, Garp supposed she was. 'But I like her anyway,' he said, most faithful of sons. Even then.

'Oh, *I* like her, too,' Cushie said. Thus having said what was necessary, Cushie undressed. Garp undressed, but she asked him, suddenly, 'Come on, where is it?'

Garp panicked. Where was *what*? He'd thought she was holding it.

'Where's your *thing*?' Cushie demanded, tugging what Garp thought *was* his thing.

'What?' Garp said.

'Oh wow, didn't you bring any?' Cushie asked him. Garp wondered what he was supposed to have brought.

'What?' he said.

'Oh, Garp,' Cushie said. 'Don't you have any *rubbers?*'

He looked apologetically at her. He was only a boy who'd lived his whole life with his mother, and the only rubber he'd seen had been slipped over the doorknob of their apartment in the infirmary annex, probably by a fiendish boy named Meckler – long since graduated and gone on to destroy himself.

Still, he should have known: Garp had heard much conversation of rubbers, of course.

'Come here,' Cushie said. She led him to the cannons. 'You've never done this, have you?' she asked him. He shook his head, honest to his sheepish core. 'Oh, Garp,' she said. 'If you weren't such an old friend.' She smiled at him, but he knew she wouldn't let him do it, now. She pointed into the mouth of the middle cannon. 'Look,' she said. He looked. A jewel-like sparkle of ground glass, like pebbles he imagined might make up a tropical beach; and something else – not so pleasant. 'Rubbers,' Cushie told him.

The cannon was crammed with old condoms. Hundreds of prophylactics! A display of arrested reproduction. Like dogs urinating around the borders of their territory, the boys of the Steering School had left their messes in the mouth of the mammoth cannon guarding the Steering River. The modern world had left its stain upon another historical landmark.

Cushie was getting dressed. 'You don't know anything,' she teased him, 'so what are you going to write about?' He had suspected this would pose a problem for a few years – a kink in his career plans.

He was about to get dressed but she made him lie down so that she could look at him. 'You *are* beautiful,' she said. 'And it's all right.' She kissed him.

'I can go *get* some rubbers,' he said. 'It wouldn't take long, would it? And we could come back.'

'My train leaves at five,' Cushie said, but she smiled sympathetically.

'I didn't think you had to be back at any special time,' Garp said.

'Well, even Dibbs has *some* rules, you know,' Cushie said; she sounded hurt by her school's lax reputation. 'And besides,' she said, 'you see Helen. I know you do, don't you?'

'Not like this,' he admitted.

'Garp, you shouldn't tell anybody everything,' Cushie said.

It was a problem with his writing, too; Mr Tinch had told him.

'You're too serious, all the time,' Cushie said, because for once she was in a position where she could lecture him.

On the river below them an eight-oared shell sleeked through the narrow channel of water remaining in The Gut and rowed toward the Steering boathouse before the tide went out and left them without enough water to get home on.

Then Garp and Cushie saw the golfer. He had come down through the marsh grass on the other side of the river; with his violet madras slacks rolled up above his knees, he waded into the mudflats where the tide had already receded. Ahead of him, on the wetter mudflats, lay his golf ball, perhaps six feet from the edge of the remaining water. Gingerly, the golfer stepped forward, but the mud now rose above his calf; using his golf club for balance, he dipped the shiny head into the muck and swore.

'Harry, come back!' someone called to him. It was his golfing partner, a man dressed with equal vividness, knee-length shorts of a green that no grass ever was – and yellow knee socks. The golfer called Harry grimly stepped closer to his ball. He looked like a rare aquatic bird pursuing its egg in an oil slick.

'Harry, you're going to *sink* in that shit!' his friend warned him. It was then that Garp recognized Harry's partner: the man in green and yellow was Cushie's father, Fat Stew.

'It's a new ball!' Harry yelled; then his left leg disappeared, up to the hip; trying to turn back, Harry lost his balance and sat down. Quickly, he was mired to his waist, his frantic face very red above his powder-blue shirt – bluer than any sky. He waved his club but it slipped out of his hand and sailed into the mud, inches from his ball, impossibly white and forever out of Harry's reach.

'Help!' Harry screamed. But on all fours he was able to move a few feet toward Fat Stew and the safety of shore. 'It feels like eels!' he cried. He moved forward on the trunk of his body, using his arms the way a seal on land will use its flippers. An awful *slorp*ing noise pursued him through the mudflats, as if beneath the mud some mouth was gasping to suck him in.

Garp and Cushie stifled their laughter in the bushes. Harry made his last lunge for shore. Stewart Percy, trying to help, stepped on the mudflats with just one foot and promptly lost a golf shoe and a yellow sock to the suction.

'Ssshhh! And lie *still*,' Cushie demanded. They both noticed Garp was erect. 'Oh, that's too bad,' Cushie whispered, looking sadly at his erection, but when he tried to tug her down in the grass with him, she said, 'I don't want babies, Garp. Not even yours. And yours might be a *Jap* baby, you know,' Cushie said. 'And I surely don't want one of those.'

'What?' Garp said. It was one thing not to know about rubbers, but what's this about Jap babies? he wondered.

'Ssshhh,' Cushie whispered. 'I'm going to give you something to write about.'

The furious golfers were already slashing their way through the marsh grass, back to the immaculate fairway, when Cushie's mouth nipped the edge of Garp's tight belly button. Garp was never sure if his actual memory was jolted by that word *Jap*, and if at that moment he truly recalled bleeding in the Percys' house – little Cushie telling her parents that 'Bonkie bit Garp' (and the scrutiny the child Garp had undergone in front of the naked Fat Stew). It may have been then that Garp remembered Fat Stew saying he had Jap eyes, and a view of his personal history clicked into perspective; regardless, at this moment Garp resolved to ask his mother for more details than she had offered him up to now. He felt the need to know more than that his father had been a soldier, and so forth. But he also felt Cushie Percy's soft lips on his belly, and when she took him suddenly into her warm mouth, he was very surprised and his sense of resolve was as quickly blown as the rest of him. There under the triple barrels of the Steering family cannons, T. S. Garp was first treated to sex in this relatively safe and nonreproductive manner. Of course, from Cushie's point of view, it was nonreciprocal, too.

They walked back along the Steering River holding hands.

'I want to see you next weekend,' Garp told her. He resolved he would not forget the rubbers.

'I know you really love Helen,' Cushie said. She probably hated Helen Holm, if she really knew her at all. Helen was such a snob about her brains.

'I still want to see you,' Garp said.

'You're nice,' Cushie told him, squeezing his hand. 'And you're my oldest friend.' But they both must have known that you can know someone all your life and never quite be friends.

'Who told you my father was Japanese?' Garp asked her.

'I don't know,' Cushie said. 'I don't know if he really is, either.'

'I don't either,' Garp admitted.

'I don't know why you don't ask your mother,' Cushie said. But of course he had asked, and Jenny was absolutely unwavering from her first and only version.

When Garp phoned Cushie at Dibbs, she said, 'Wow, it's *you!* My father just called and told me I was not to see you or write to you or talk to you. Or even read your letters – as if you wrote any. I think some golfer saw us leaving the cannons.' She thought it was very funny, but Garp only saw that his future at the cannons had slipped from him. 'I'll be home that weekend you graduate,' Cushie told him. But Garp wondered: If he bought the condoms now, would they still be usable for graduation? Could rubbers go bad? In how many weeks? And should you keep them in the refrigerator? There was no one to ask.

Garp thought of asking Ernie Holm, but he was already fearful that Helen would hear of his being with Cushie Percy, and although he had no real relationship with Helen that he could be unfaithful to, Garp did have his imagination and his plans.

He wrote Helen a long confessional letter about his 'lust,' as he called it – and how it did not compare to his higher feelings for her, as he referred to them. Helen replied promptly that she didn't know why he was telling *her* all this, but that in her opinion he *wrote* about it very well. It was better writing than the story he'd shown her, for example, and she hoped he would continue to show her his writing. She added that her opinion of Cushie Percy, from what little she knew of the girl, was that she was rather *stupid*. 'But pleasant,' Helen wrote. And if Garp was given to this lust, as he called it, wasn't he fortunate to have someone like Cushie around?

Garp wrote back that he would not show her another story until he wrote one that was good enough for her. He also discussed his feelings for not going to college. First, he thought, the only reason to go to college was to wrestle, and he wasn't sure he cared enough about it to wrestle at *that* level. He saw no point in simply continuing to wrestle at some small college where the sport wasn't emphasized. 'It's only worth doing,' Garp wrote to Helen, 'if I'm going to try to be the best.' He thought that trying to be the best at wrestling was not what he wanted; also, he knew, it was not likely he *could* be the best. And whoever heard of going to college to be the best at *writing*?

And where did he get this idea of wanting to be the best?

Helen wrote him that he should go to Europe, and Garp discussed this idea with Jenny.

To his surprise, Jenny had never thought he *would* go to college; she did not accept that this was what prep schools were *for*. 'If the Steering School is supposed to give everyone such a first-rate education,' Jenny said, 'what on earth do you need *more* education for? I mean, if you've been paying attention, now you're educated. Right?' Garp didn't feel educated but he said he supposed he was. He thought he had been paying attention. As for Europe, Jenny was interested. 'Well, I'd certainly like to try that,' she said. 'It beats staying here.'

It was then that Garp realized his mother meant to stay *with* him.

'I'll find out the best place for a writer to go in Europe,' Jenny said to him. 'I was thinking of writing something myself.'

Garp felt so awful he went to bed. When he got up, he wrote Helen that he was doomed to be followed by his mother the rest of his life. 'How can I write,' he wrote to Helen, 'with my mom looking over my shoulder?' Helen had no answers for that one; she said she would mention the problem to her father, and maybe Ernie would give Jenny some advice. Ernie Holm liked Jenny; he occasionally took her to a movie. Jenny had even become something of a wrestling fan, and although there couldn't have been anything more than friendship between them, Ernie was very sensitive to the unwed mother story – he had heard and accepted Jenny's version as all *he* needed to know, and he defended Jenny rather fiercely to those in the Steering community who suggested they were curious to know more.

But Jenny took her advice on cultural matters from Tinch. She asked him where a boy and his mother could go in Europe – which was the most artistic climate, the best place to write. Mr Tinch had last been to Europe in 1913. He had stayed only for the summer. He had gone to England first, where there were several living Tinches, his British ancestry, but his old family frightened him by asking him for money

– they asked for so much, and so rudely, that Tinch quickly fled to the Continent. But people were rude to him in France, and loud to him in Germany. He had a nervous stomach and was afraid of Italian cooking, so Tinch had gone to Austria. 'In Vienna,' Tinch told Jenny, 'I found the *real* Europe. It was c-c-contemplative and artistic,' Tinch said. 'You could sense the sadness and the g-g-grandness.'

A year later, World War I began. In 1918 the Spanish grippe would kill many of the Viennese who had survived the war. The flu would kill old Klimt, and it would kill young Schiele and Schiele's young wife. Forty percent of the remaining male population would not survive World War II. The Vienna that Tinch would send Jenny and Garp to was a city whose life was over. Its tiredness could still be mistaken for a c-c-contemplative nature, but Vienna was hard-put to show much g-g-grandness anymore. Among the half-truths of Tinch, Jenny and Garp would still sense the sadness. 'And *any* place can be artistic,' Garp later wrote, 'if there's an artist working there.'

'Vienna?' Garp said to Jenny. He said it in the way he had said 'Wrestling?' to her, over three years ago, lying on his sickbed and doubtful of her ability to pick out a sport for him. But he remembered she had been right then, and he knew nothing about Europe, and very little about anyplace else. Garp had taken three years of German at Steering, so there was some help, and Jenny (who was not good with languages) had read a book about the strange bedfellows of Austrian history: Maria Theresa and fascism. *From Empire to Anschluss!* was the name of the book. Garp had seen it in the bathroom, for years, but now no one could find it. Perhaps it was lost to the whirlpool bath.

'The last person I saw with it was Ulfelder,' Jenny told Garp.

'Ulfelder graduated three years ago, Mom,' Garp reminded her.

* * *

When Jenny told Dean Bodger that she would be leaving, Bodger said that Steering would miss her and would always be glad to have her back. Jenny did not want to be impolite, but she mumbled that one could be a nurse almost anywhere, she supposed; she did not know, of course, that she would never be a nurse again. Bodger was puzzled by Garp's not going to college. In the dean's opinion, Garp had not been a disciplinary problem at Steering since he had survived the roof of the infirmary annex at the age of five, and Bodger's fondness for the role he played in that rescue had always given him a fondness for Garp. Also, Dean Bodger was a wrestling fan, and one of Jenny's few admirers. But Bodger accepted that the boy seemed convinced by 'the writing business,' as Bodger called it. Jenny did not tell Bodger, of course, that she planned to do some writing of her own.

This part of the plan made Garp the most uncomfortable, but he did not even say a word of it to Helen. Everything was happening very fast and Garp could express his apprehension only to his wrestling coach, Ernie Holm.

'Your mom knows what she's doing, I'm sure,' Ernie told him. 'You just be sure about *you*.'

Even old Tinch was full of optimism for the plan. 'It's a little ec-ec-eccentric,' Tinch told Garp, 'but many good ideas are.' Years later Garp would recall that Tinch's endearing stutter was like a message to Tinch from Tinch's body. Garp wrote that Tinch's body was trying to tell Tinch that he was going to f-f-freeze to death one day.

Jenny was saying that they would leave shortly after graduation, but Garp had hoped to stay around Steering for the summer.

'What on earth for?' Jenny asked him.

For Helen, he wanted to tell her, but he had no stories good enough for Helen; he had already said so. There was nothing to do but go away and write them. And he could never expect Jenny to stay another summer in Steering so that he could keep his appointment at the cannons with Cushie Percy; perhaps that was not meant to be. Still, he was hopeful that he could connect with Cushie on graduation weekend.

For Garp's graduation, it rained. The rain washed over the soggy Steering campus in sheets; the storm sewers bogged and the out-of-state cars plowed through the streets like yachts in a squall. The women looked helpless in their summer dresses; the loading of station wagons was hurried and miserable. A great crimson tent was erected in front of the Miles Seabrook Gymnasium and Field House, and the diplomas were handed out in this stale circus air; the speeches were lost in the rain beating the crimson canvas overhead.

Nobody stayed around. The big boats left town. Helen had not come because Talbot had its graduation the following weekend and she was still taking exams. Cushie Percy had been in attendance at the disappointing ceremony, Garp was sure; but he had not seen her. He knew she would be with her ridiculous family and Garp was wise to keep a safe distance from Fat Stew – an outraged father was still a father, after all, even if Cushman Percy's honor had long ago been lost.

When the late-afternoon sun came out, it hardly mattered. Steering was steamy and the ground – from Seabrook Stadium to the cannons – would be sodden for days. Garp imagined the deep ruts of water that he knew would be coursing through the soft grass at the cannons; even the Steering River would be swollen. The cannons themselves would be overflowing; the barrels were tilted up, and they filled with water every time it rained. In such weather, the cannons dribbled streams of broken glass and left slick puddles of old condoms on the stained concrete. There would be no enticing Cushie to the cannons this weekend, Garp knew.

But the three-pack of prophylactics crackled in his pocket like a tiny, dry fire of hope.

'Look,' said Jenny. 'I bought some beer. Go ahead and get drunk, if you want to.'

'Jesus, Mom,' Garp said, but he drank a few with her. They sat by themselves on his graduation night, the infirmary empty beside them, and every bed in the annex was empty and stripped of linen, too – except for the beds they would sleep in. Garp drank the beer and wondered if *everything* was an anticlimax; he reassured himself by thinking of the few good stories he had read, but though he had a Steering education, he was no reader – no match for Helen, or Jenny, for example. Garp's way with a story was to find one he liked and read it again and again; it would spoil him for reading any other story for a long while. When he was at Steering he read Joseph Conrad's 'The Secret Sharer' thirty-four times. He also read D. H. Lawrence's 'The Man Who Loved Islands' twenty-one times; he felt ready to read it again, now.

Outside the windows of the tiny apartment in the infirmary annex, the Steering campus lay dark and wet and deserted.

'Well, look at it this way,' Jenny said; she could see he was feeling let down. 'It took you only four years to graduate from Steering, but *I've* been going to this damn school for eighteen.' She was not much of a drinker, Jenny: half the way through her second beer, she fell asleep. Garp carried her into her bedroom; she had already taken off her shoes, and Garp removed only her nurse's pin – so that she wouldn't roll over and stick herself with it. It was a warm night, so he didn't cover her.

He drank another beer and then took a walk.

Of course he knew where he was going.

The Percy family house – originally the Steering family house – sat on its damp lawn not far from the infirmary annex. Only one light was on in Stewart Percy's house, and Garp knew whose light it was: little Pooh Percy, now fourteen, could not sleep with her light out. Cushie had also told Garp that Bainbridge was still inclined to wear a diaper – perhaps, Garp thought, because her family still insisted on calling her Pooh.

'Well,' Cushie said, 'I don't see what's *wrong* with it. She doesn't *use* the diapers, you know; I mean, she's *housebroken*, and all that. Pooh just likes to *wear* diapers – occasionally.'

Garp stood on the misty grass beneath Pooh Percy's window and tried to remember which room was Cushie's. Since he couldn't remember, he decided to wake up Pooh; she was sure to recognize him, and she was sure to tell Cushie. But Pooh came to her window like a ghost; she did not immediately appear to recognize Garp, who clung tenaciously to the ivy outside her window. Bainbridge Percy had eyes like a deer paralyzed in a car's headlights, about to be hit.

'For Christ's sake, Pooh, it's *me*,' Garp whispered to her.

'You want Cushie, don't you?' Pooh asked him, sullenly.

'Yes!' Garp grunted. Then the ivy tore and he fell into the hedges below. Cushie, who slept in her bathing suit, helped extricate him.

'Wow, you're going to wake up the whole house,' she said. 'Have you been drinking?'

'I've been *falling*,' Garp said, irritably. 'Your sister is really weird.'

'It's wet outside, all over,' Cushie said to him. 'Where can we go?'

Garp had thought of that. In the infirmary, he knew, were sixty empty beds.

But Garp and Cushie were not even past the Percy porch when Bonkers confronted them. The black beast was already out of breath, from descending the porch stairs, and his iron-gray muzzle was flecked with froth; his breath reached Garp like old sod flung in his face. Bonkers was growling, but even his growl had slowed down.

'Tell him to beat it,' Garp whispered to Cushie.

'He's deaf,' Cushie said. 'He's very old.'

'I know how old he is,' Garp said.

Bonkers barked, a creaky and sharp sound, like the hinge of an unused door being forced open. He was thinner, but he easily weighed one hundred and forty pounds. A victim of ear mites and mange, old dog bite and barbed wire,

Bonkers sniffed his enemy and held Garp cornered against the porch.

'Go *away*, Bonkie!' Cushie hissed.

Garp tried to sidestep the dog and noticed how slowly Bonkers reacted.

'He's half-*blind*,' Garp whispered.

'And his nose doesn't smell much anymore,' Cushie said.

'He ought to be dead,' Garp whispered to himself, but he tried to step around the dog. Dimly, Bonkers followed. His mouth still reminded Garp of a steam shovel's power, and the loose flap of muscle on his black and shaggy chest indicated to Garp how hard the dog could lunge – but long ago.

'Just ig*nore* him,' Cushie suggested, just as Bonkers lunged.

The dog was slow enough so that Garp could spin behind him; he pulled the dog's forepaws from under him and dropped his own weight, from his chest, on the dog's back. Bonkers buckled forward, he slid into the ground nose first – his hind legs still clawing. Garp now controlled the crumpled forepaws but the great dog's head was held down only by the weight of Garp's chest. A terrifying snarling developed as Garp bore down on the animal's spine and drove his chin into the dog's dense neck. In the scuffle, an *ear* appeared – in Garp's mouth – and Garp bit it. He bit as hard as he could, and Bonkers howled. He bit Bonkers' ear in memory of his own missing flesh, he bit him for the four years he'd spent at Steering – and for his mother's eighteen years.

It was only when lights came on in the Percy house that Garp let old Bonkers go.

'Run!' Cushie suggested. Garp grabbed her hand and she came with him. A vile taste was in his mouth. 'Wow, did you have to *bite* him?' Cushie asked.

'He bit me,' Garp reminded her.

'I remember,' Cushie said. She squeezed his hand and he led her where he wanted to go.

'What the hell is going on here?' they heard Stewart Percy yelling.

'It's Bonkie, it's Bonkie!' Pooh Percy called into the night.

'Bonkers!' called Fat Stew. 'Here, Bonkers! Here, Bonkers!' And they all heard the deaf dog's resounding caterwaul.

It was a commotion capable of carrying across an empty campus. It woke Jenny Fields, who peered out her window in the infirmary annex. Fortunately for Garp, he saw her turn on a light. He made Cushie hide behind him, in a corridor of the unoccupied annex, while he sought Jenny's medical advice.

'What happened to you?' Jenny asked him. Garp wanted to know if the blood running down his chin was his own or entirely Bonkers'. At the kitchen table, Jenny washed away a black scablike thing that was stuck to Garp. It fell off Garp's throat and landed on the table – it was the size of a silver dollar. They both stared at it.

'What *is* it?' Jenny asked.

'An ear,' Garp said. 'Or part of one.'

On the white enamel table lay the black leathery remnant of an ear, curling slightly at the edges and cracked like an old, dry glove.

'I ran into Bonkers,' Garp said.

'An ear for an ear,' said Jenny Fields.

There was not a mark on Garp; the blood belonged solely to Bonkers.

When Jenny went back to her bedroom, Garp snuck Cushie into the tunnel that led to the main infirmary. For eighteen years he had learned the way. He took her to the wing farthest from his mother's apartment in the annex; it was over the main admittance room, near the rooms for surgery and anesthesia.

Thus sex for Garp would forever be associated with certain smells and sensations. The experience would remain secretive but relaxed: a final reward in harrowing times. The odor would stay in his mind as deeply personal and yet vaguely *hospital*. The surroundings would forever seem to be deserted. Sex for Garp would remain in his mind as a solitary act committed in an abandoned universe – sometime after it had rained. It was always an act of terrific optimism.

Cushie, of course, evoked for Garp many images of cannons. When the third condom of the three-pack was exhausted, she asked if that was all he had – if he'd bought only one package. A wrestler loves nothing so much as hard-earned exhaustion; Garp fell asleep to Cushie complaining.

'The first time you don't have any,' she was saying, 'and now you run out? It is lucky we're such old friends.'

It was still dark and far from dawn when Stewart Percy woke them. Fat Stew's voice violated the old infirmary like an unnamable disease. 'Open up!' they heard him hollering, and they crept to the window to see.

On the green, green lawn, in his bathrobe and slippers – and with Bonkers leashed beside him – Cushie's father bleated at the windows of the infirmary annex. It was not long before Jenny appeared in the light.

'Are you ill?' she asked Stewart.

'I want my daughter!' Stewart yelled.

'Are you drunk?' Jenny asked.

'You let me in!' Stewart screamed.

'The doctor is out,' said Jenny Fields, 'and I doubt there is anything I can treat you for.'

'Bitch!' Stewart bellowed. 'Your bastard son has seduced my daughter! I know they're in there, in that fucking infirmary!'

It *is* a fucking infirmary now, Garp thought, delighting in the touch and scent of Cushie trembling beside him. In the cool air, through the dark window, they shivered in silence.

'You should see my *dog!*' Stewart screeched to Jenny. 'Blood everywhere! The dog hiding under the hammock! Blood on the porch!' Stewart croaked. 'What the hell did that bastard do to Bonkers?'

Garp felt Cushie flinch beside him when his mother spoke. What Jenny said must have made Cushie Percy remember *her* remark, thirteen years earlier. What Jenny Fields said was, 'Garp bit Bonkie.' Then her light went out, and in the darkness cast over the infirmary and its annex only Fat Stew's breathing was audible with the runoff from the rain – washing over the Steering School, rinsing everything clean.

5

In the City Where Marcus Aurelius Died

When Jenny took Garp to Europe, Garp was better prepared for the solitary confinement of a writer's life than most eighteen-year-olds. He was already thriving in a world of his own imagination; after all, he had been brought up by a woman who thought that solitary confinement was a perfectly natural way to live. It would be years before Garp noticed that he didn't have any friends, and this oddity never struck Jenny Fields as odd. In his distant and polite fashion, Ernie Holm was the first friend Jenny Fields ever had.

Before Jenny and Garp found an apartment, they lived in more than a dozen pensions all over Vienna. It was Mr Tinch's idea that this would be the ideal way for them to choose the part of the city they liked best: they would live in all the districts and decide for themselves. But short-term life in a pension must have been more pleasant for Tinch in the summer of 1913; when Jenny and Garp came to Vienna, it was 1961; they quickly tired of lugging their typewriters from pension to pension. It was this experience, however, that gave Garp the material for his first major short story, 'The Pension Grillparzer.' Garp hadn't even known what a pension *was* before he came to Vienna, but he quickly discovered that a pension had somewhat less to offer than a hotel; it was always smaller, and never elegant; it sometimes offered breakfast, and sometimes not. A pension was sometimes a bargain and sometimes a mistake. Jenny and

Garp found pensions that were clean and comfortable and friendly, but they were often seedy.

Jenny and Garp wasted little time deciding that they wanted to live within or near the Ringstrasse, the great round street that circles the heart of the old city; it was the part of the city where almost everything was, and where Jenny could manage a little better without speaking any German – it was the more sophisticated, cosmopolitan part of Vienna, if there really is such a part of Vienna.

It was fun for Garp to be in charge of his mother; three years of Steering German made Garp their leader, and he clearly enjoyed being Jenny's boss.

'Have the schnitzel, Mom,' he would tell her.

'I thought this Kalbsnieren sounded interesting,' Jenny said.

'Veal kidney, Mom,' Garp said. 'Do you like kidney?'

'I don't know,' Jenny admitted. 'Probably not.'

When they finally moved into a place of their own, Garp took over the shopping. Jenny had spent eighteen years eating in the Steering dining halls; she had never learned how to cook, and now she couldn't read the directions. It was in Vienna that Garp learned how he loved to cook, but the first thing he claimed to like about Europe was the W.C. – the water closet. In his time spent in pensions, Garp discovered that a water closet was a tiny room with nothing but a toilet in it; it was the first thing about Europe that made sense to Garp. He wrote Helen that 'it is the wisest system – to urinate and move your bowels in one place, and to brush your teeth in another.' The W.C., of course, would also feature prominently in Garp's story, 'The Pension Grillparzer,' but Garp would not write that story, or anything else, for a while.

Although he was unusually self-disciplined for an eighteen-year-old, there were simply too many things to see; together with those things he was suddenly responsible for, Garp was very busy and for months the only satisfying writing he did was to Helen. He was too excited with his new territory to develop the necessary routine for writing, although he tried.

He tried to write a story about a family; all he knew when he began was that the family had an interesting life and the members were all close to each other. That was not enough to know.

Jenny and Garp moved into a cream-colored, high-ceilinged apartment on the second floor of an old building on the Schwindgasse, a little street in the fourth district. They were right around the corner from the Prinz-Eugen-Strasse, the Schwarzenbergplatz, and the Upper and Lower Belvedere. Garp eventually went to all the art museums in the city, but Jenny never went to any except the Upper Belvedere. Garp explained to her that the Upper Belvedere contained only the nineteenth- and twentieth-century paintings, but Jenny said that the nineteenth and twentieth centuries were enough for her. Garp explained that she could at least walk through the gardens to the Lower Belvedere and see the baroque collection, but Jenny shook her head; she had taken several art history courses at Steering – she'd had enough education, she said.

'And the Brueghels, Mom!' Garp said. 'You just take the Strassenbahn up the Ring and get off at Mariahilferstrasse. The big museum across from the streetcar stop is the Kunsthistorisches.'

'But I can *walk* to the Belvedere,' Jenny said. 'Why take a streetcar?'

She could also walk to the Karlskirche, and there were some interesting-looking embassy buildings a short distance up Argentinierstrasse. The Bulgarian Embassy was right across the street from their apartment on the Schwindgasse. Jenny said she liked staying in her own neighborhood. There was a coffeehouse a block away and she sometimes went there and read the newspapers in English. She never went out to eat anywhere unless Garp took her; and unless he cooked for her in their apartment, she didn't eat anything at home.

She was completely taken with the idea of writing something – more taken, at this phase, than Garp.

'I don't have time to be a tourist at this point in my life,' she told her son. 'But *you* go ahead, soak up the culture. That's what you *should* be doing.'

'Absorb, ab-ab-absorb,' Tinch had told them. That seemed to Jenny to be just what Garp should do; for herself, she found she'd already absorbed enough to have plenty to say. Jenny Fields was forty-one. She imagined that the interesting part of her life was behind her; all she wanted to do was write about it.

Garp gave her a piece of paper to carry with her. It had her address written on it, in case she got lost: Schwindgasse 15/2, Wien IV. Garp had to teach her how to pronounce her address – a tedious lesson. '*Schwindgassefünfzehnzwei!*' Jenny spat.

'Again,' Garp said. 'Do you want to *stay* lost when you get lost?'

Garp investigated the city by day and found places to take Jenny to at night, and in the late afternoons when she was through with her writing; they would have a beer, or a glass of wine, and Garp would describe his whole day to her. Jenny listened politely. Wine or beer made her sleepy. Usually they ate a nice dinner somewhere and Garp escorted Jenny home on the Strassenbahn; he took special pride in never using taxis, because he had learned the streetcar system so thoroughly. Sometimes he went to the open markets in the morning and came home early and cooked all afternoon. Jenny never complained; it didn't matter to her whether they ate in or out.

'This is a Gumpoldskirchner,' Garp would say, explaining the wine. 'It goes very well with the Schweinebraten.'

'What funny words,' Jenny remarked.

In a typical evaluation of Jenny's prose style, Garp later wrote: 'My mother had such a struggle with her English, it's no wonder she never bothered to learn German.'

* * *

Although Jenny Fields sat every day at her typewriter, she did not know how to write. Although she was – physically – writing, she did not enjoy reading over what she'd written. Before long, she tried to remember the good things she'd read and what made them different from her own first-draft attempt. She'd simply begun at the beginning. 'I was born,' and so forth. 'My parents wanted me to stay at Wellesley; however . . .' And, of course: 'I decided I wanted a child of my own and eventually got one in the following manner . . .' But Jenny had read enough good stories to know that hers didn't *sound* like the good stories in her memory. She wondered what could be wrong, and she frequently sent Garp on errands to the few bookstores that sold books in English. She wanted to look more closely at how books began; she had quickly produced over three hundred typed pages, yet she felt that her book never really *started*.

But Jenny suffered her writing problems silently; she was cheerful with Garp, even if she was rarely very attentive. Jenny Fields felt all her life that things began and came to an end. Like Garp's education – like her own. Like Sergeant Garp. She had not lost any affection for her son, but she felt that a phase of her mothering him was over; she felt she had brought Garp along this far, and now she should let him find something to do by himself. She could not go through their lives signing him up for wrestling, or for something else. Jenny liked living with her son; in fact, it didn't occur to her that they would ever live apart. But Jenny expected Garp to entertain himself every day in Vienna, and so Garp did.

He had gotten no further with his story about a close, interesting family except that he had found something interesting for them to do. The father of the family was some sort of inspector and his family went with him when he did his job. The job involved scrutinizing all the restaurants and hotels and pensions in Austria – evaluating them and giving them a rating according to A, B, C. It was a job Garp imagined that *he'd* like to have. In a country like Austria, so dependent on tourism, the classification and reclassification of the places the tourists ate in and slept in *should* have a kind of desperate importance, but Garp couldn't imagine what could be important about it – or for whom. So far all he had was this family: they had a funny job. They exposed flaws; they gave out the grades. So what? It was easier to write to Helen.

That late summer and early fall, Garp walked and rode the trolleys all over Vienna, meeting no one. He wrote Helen that 'a part of adolescence is feeling that there's no one else around who's enough like yourself to understand you'; Garp wrote that he believed Vienna enhanced that feeling in him 'because in Vienna there really *isn't* anyone like myself around.'

His perception was at least numerically correct. There were very few people in Vienna who were even the same age as Garp. Not many Viennese were born in 1943; for that matter, not many Viennese were born from the start of the Nazi occupation in 1938 through the end of the war in 1945. And although there were a surprising number of babies born out of rapes, not many Viennese *wanted* babies until after 1955 – the end of the Russian occupation. Vienna was a city occupied by foreigners for seventeen years. To most Viennese, it is understandable, those seventeen years did not seem like a good and wise time to have children. It was Garp's experience to live in a city that made him feel peculiar to be eighteen years old. This must have made him grow older faster, and this must have contributed to his increasing sense that Vienna was more of 'a museum housing a dead city' – as he wrote Helen – than it was a city that was still alive.

Garp's observation was not offered as criticism. Garp *liked* wandering around in a museum. 'A more real city might not have suited me so well,' he later wrote. 'But Vienna was in its death phase; it lay still and let me look at it, and think about it, and look again. In a *living* city, I could never have noticed so much. Living cities don't hold still.'

Thus T. S. Garp spent the warm months *noticing* Vienna, writing letters to Helen Holm, and managing the domestic life of his mother, who had added the isolation of writing to her chosen life of solitude. 'My mother, the writer,' Garp referred to her, facetiously, in countless letters to Helen. But he envied Jenny, that she was writing at all. He felt stuck with his story. He realized he could go on giving his made-up family one adventure after another, but where were they going? To one more B restaurant with such a weakness in their desserts that an A rating was a lifetime out of reach; to one more B hotel, sliding to C as surely as the mildew smell in the lobby would never go away. Perhaps someone in the inspector's family could be poisoned, in a class A restaurant, but what would it *mean*? And there could be crazy people, or even criminals, hiding out in one of the pensions, but what would they have to do with the scheme of things?

Garp knew that he did not have a scheme of things.

He saw a four-member circus unload from Hungary, or Yugoslavia, at a railroad station. He tried to imagine *them* in his story. There had been a bear who rode a motorcycle, around and around a parking lot. A small crowd gathered and a man who walked on his hands collected money for the bear's performance in a pot balanced on the soles of his feet; he fell, occasionally, but so did the bear.

Finally, the motorcycle wouldn't start anymore. It never became clear what the two other members of this circus did; just as they were trying to take over for the bear and the man who walked on his hands the police came and asked them to fill out a lot of forms. That had not been interesting to watch and the crowd – what there was of one – had gone away. Garp had stayed the longest, not because he was interested in further performances by this decrepit circus but because he was interested in getting them into his story. He couldn't imagine how. As Garp was leaving the railroad station, he could hear the bear throwing up.

For weeks Garp's only progress with his story was a title:

'The Austrian Tourist Bureau.' He didn't like it. He went back to being a tourist instead of a writer.

But when the weather grew colder, Garp tired of tourism; he took to carping at Helen for not writing him back enough – a sign he was writing to her too much. She was much busier than he was; she was in college, where she'd been accepted with sophomore standing, and she was carrying more than double the average load of courses. If Helen and Garp were similar, in these early years, it was that they both behaved as if they were going somewhere in a *hurry*. 'Leave poor Helen alone,' Jenny advised him. 'I thought you were going to write something beside letters.' But Garp did not like to think of competing in the same apartment with his mother. Her typewriter never paused for thought; Garp knew that its steady pounding would probably end his career as a writer before he could properly begin. 'My mother never knew about the silence of revision,' Garp once remarked.

By November Jenny had six hundred manuscript pages, but still she had the feeling that she had not really begun. Garp had no subject that could spill out of him in this fashion. Imagination, he realized, came harder than memory.

His 'breakthrough,' as he would call it when he wrote Helen, occurred one cold and snowy day in the Museum of the History of the City of Vienna. It was a museum within easy walking distance of the Schwindgasse; somehow he had skipped seeing it, knowing he could walk there any day. Jenny told him about it. It was one of the two or three places she had actually visited herself, only because it was right across the Karlsplatz and well within what she called her neighborhood.

She mentioned there was a writer's room in the museum; she forgot whose. She'd thought having a writer's room in a museum was an interesting idea.

'A writer's *room*, Mom?' Garp asked.

'Yes, it's a whole room,' Jenny said. 'They took all the

writer's furniture, and maybe the walls and floor, too. I don't
know how they did it.'

'I don't know *why* they did it,' Garp said. 'The whole room
is in the museum?'

'Yes, I think it was a bedroom,' Jenny said, 'but it was also
where the writer actually *wrote.*'

Garp rolled his eyes. It sounded obscene to him.
Would the writer's toothbrush be there? And the chamber
pot?

It was a perfectly ordinary room, but the bed looked too
small – like a child's bed. The writing table looked small,
too. Not the bed or the table of an expansive writer, Garp
thought. The wood was dark; everything looked easily
breakable; Garp thought his mother had a better room
to write in. The writer whose room was enshrined in the
Museum of the History of the City of Vienna was named
Franz Grillparzer; Garp had never heard of him.

Franz Grillparzer died in 1872; he was an Austrian poet
and dramatist, whom very few people outside Austria have
ever heard of. He is one of those nineteenth-century writers
who did not survive the nineteenth century with any enduring popularity, and Garp would later argue that Grillparzer
did not deserve to survive the nineteenth century. Garp was
not interested in plays and poems, but he went to the library
and read what is considered to be Grillparzer's outstanding
prose work: the long short story 'The Poor Fiddler.' Perhaps,
Garp thought, his three years of Steering German were not
enough to allow him to appreciate the story; in German, he
hated it. He then found an English translation of the story
in a secondhand bookstore on Habsburgergasse; he still
hated it.

Garp thought that Grillparzer's famous story was a
ludicrous melodrama; he also thought it was ineptly told
and baldly sentimental. It was only vaguely remindful to
him of nineteenth-century Russian stories, where often
the character is an indecisive procrastinator and a failure
in every aspect of practical life; but Dostoevsky, in Garp's

opinion, could compel you to be interested in such a wretch; Grillparzer bored you with tearful trivia.

In the same secondhand bookstore Garp bought an English translation of the *Meditations* of Marcus Aurelius; he had been made to read Marcus Aurelius in a Latin class at Steering, but he had never read him in English before. He bought the book because the bookstore owner told Garp that Marcus Aurelius had died in Vienna.

'In the life of a man,' Marcus Aurelius wrote, 'his time is but a moment, his being an incessant flux, his sense a dim rushlight, his body a prey of worms, his soul an unquiet eddy, his fortune dark, his fame doubtful. In short, all that is body is as coursing waters, all that is of the soul as dreams and vapors.' Garp somehow thought that Marcus Aurelius must have lived in Vienna when he wrote that.

The subject of Marcus Aurelius's dreary observations was certainly the *subject* of most serious writing, Garp thought; between Grillparzer and Dostoevsky the difference was not subject matter. The difference, Garp concluded, was intelligence and grace; the difference was art. Somehow this obvious discovery pleased him. Years later, Garp read in a critical introduction to Grillparzer's work that Grillparzer was 'sensitive, tortured, fitfully paranoid, often depressed, cranky, and choked with melancholy; in short, a complex and modern man.'

'Maybe so,' Garp wrote. 'But he was also an extremely bad writer.'

Garp's conviction that Franz Grillparzer was a 'bad' writer seemed to provide the young man with his first real confidence as an artist – even before he had written anything. Perhaps in every writer's life there needs to be that moment when some other writer is attacked as unworthy of the job. Garp's killer instinct in regard to poor Grillparzer was almost a wrestling secret; it was as if Garp had observed an opponent in a match with another wrestler; spotting the weaknesses, Garp *knew* he could do better. He even forced Jenny to read 'The Poor Fiddler.'

It was one of the few times he would seek her *literary* judgment.

'Trash,' Jenny pronounced it. 'Simplistic. Maudlin. Cream puff.'

They were *both* delighted.

'I didn't like his room, really,' Jenny told Garp. 'It was just not a writer's room.'

'Well, I don't think that matters, Mom,' Garp said.

'But it was a very cramped room,' Jenny complained. 'It was too dark, and it looked very *fussy.*'

Garp peered into his mother's room. Over her bed and dresser, and taped to her wall mirror – nearly obscuring his mother's own image – were the scattered pages of her incredibly long and messy manuscript. Garp didn't think his mother's room looked very much like a writer's room, either, but he didn't say so.

He wrote Helen a long, cocky letter, quoting Marcus Aurelius and slamming Franz Grillparzer. In Garp's opinion, 'Franz Grillparzer died forever in 1872 and like a cheap local wine does not travel very far from Vienna without spoiling.' The letter was a kind of muscle-flexing; perhaps Helen knew that. The letter was calisthenics; Garp made a carbon copy of it and decided he liked it so well that he kept the original and sent Helen the carbon. 'I feel a little like a library,' Helen wrote him. 'It's as if you intend to use me as your file drawer.'

Was Helen really complaining? Garp was not sensitive enough to Helen's own life to bother to ask her. He merely wrote back that he was 'getting ready to write.' He was confident she would like the results. Helen may have felt warned away from him, but she didn't indicate any anxiety; at college, she was gobbling courses at nearly triple the average rate. Approaching the end of her first semester, she was about to become a second-semester junior. The self-absorption and ego of a young writer did not frighten Helen Holm; she was moving at her own rapid pace, and she appreciated someone who was determined. Also, she liked

Garp's writing to her; she had an ego, too, and his letters, she kept telling him, were awfully well written.

In Vienna, Jenny and Garp went on a spree of Grillparzer jokes. They began to uncover little signs of the dead Grillparzer all over the city. There was a Grillparzergasse, there was a Kaffeehaus des Grillparzers; and one day in a pastry shop they were amazed to find a sort of layer cake named after him: Grillparzertorte! It was much too sweet. Thus, when Garp cooked for his mother, he asked her if she wanted her eggs soft-boiled or Grillparzered. And one day at the Schönbrunn Zoo they observed a particularly gangling antelope, its flanks spindly and beshitted; the antelope stood sadly in its narrow and foul winter quarters. Garp identified it: der Gnu des Grillparzers.

Of her own writing, Jenny one day remarked to Garp that she was guilty of 'doing a Grillparzer.' She explained that this meant she had introduced a scene or a character 'like an alarm going off.' The scene she had in mind was the scene in the movie house in Boston when the soldier had approached her. 'At the movie,' wrote Jenny Fields, 'a soldier consumed with lust approached me.'

'That's awful, Mom,' Garp admitted. The phrase 'consumed with lust' was what Jenny meant by 'doing a Grillparzer.'

'But that's what it *was*,' Jenny said. 'It was lust, all right.'

'It's better to say he was *thick* with lust,' Garp suggested.

'Yuck,' Jenny said. Another Grillparzer. It was the *lust* she didn't care for, in general. They discussed lust, as best they could. Garp confessed his lust for Cushie Percy and rendered a suitably tame version of the consummation scene. Jenny did not like it. 'And Helen?' Jenny asked. 'Do you feel that for Helen?'

Garp admitted he did.

'How terrible,' Jenny said. She did not understand the feeling and did not see how Garp could ever associate it with pleasure, much less with affection.

'"All that is body is as coursing waters,"' Garp said lamely, quoting Marcus Aurelius; his mother just shook her head.

They ate dinner in a very red restaurant in the vicinity of Blutgasse. 'Blood Street,' Garp translated for her, happily.

'Stop translating everything,' Jenny told him. 'I don't want to know everything.' She thought the decor of the restaurant was *too* red and the food was too expensive. The service was slow and they started for home too late. It was very cold and the gay lights of the Kärntnerstrasse did little to warm them.

'Let's get a taxi,' Jenny said. But Garp insisted that in another five blocks they could take a streetcar just as easily. 'You and your damn Strassenbahns,' Jenny said.

It was clear that the subject of 'lust' had spoiled their evening.

The first district glittered with Christmas gaudiness; between the towering spires of Saint Stephen's and the massive bulk of the opera house lay seven blocks of shops and bars and hotels; in those seven blocks, they could have been anywhere in the world at wintertime. 'Some night we've got to go to the opera, Mom,' Garp suggested. They had been in Vienna for six months without going to the opera, but Jenny did not like to stay up late at night.

'Go by yourself,' Jenny said. She saw, ahead of them, three women standing in long fur coats; one of them had a matching fur muff and she held the muff in front of her face and breathed into it to warm her hands. She was quite elegant to look at, although there was something of the tinsel of Christmas about the other two women with her. Jenny envied the woman her muff. 'That's what I want,' Jenny announced. 'Where can I get one of those?' She pointed to the women ahead of them, but Garp didn't know what she meant.

The women, he knew, were whores.

When the whores saw Jenny coming up the street with Garp, they were puzzled at the relationship. They saw a handsome boy with a plain but handsome woman who was old enough to be his mother; but Jenny hooked Garp's arm rather formally when she walked with him, and there was something like tension and confusion in the conversation Garp and Jenny were having – which made the whores think Jenny could *not* have been Garp's mother. Then Jenny pointed at them and they were angry; they thought Jenny was another whore who was working their territory and had snagged a boy who looked well-off and not sinister – a pretty boy who might have paid *them*.

In Vienna, prostitution is legal and complexly controlled. There is something like a union; there are medical certificates, periodical checkups, identification cards. Only the best-looking prostitutes are allowed to work the posh streets in the first district. In the outlying districts, the prostitutes are uglier or older, or both; they are also cheaper, of course. District by district, their prices are supposed to be fixed. When the whores saw Jenny, they stepped out on the sidewalk to block Jenny's and Garp's way. They had quickly decided that Jenny was not quite up to the standard of a first-district prostitute, and that she was probably working independently – which is illegal – or had stepped out of her assigned district to try to pull a little more money; that would get her in a lot of trouble with the other prostitutes.

In truth, Jenny would not have been mistaken for a prostitute by most people, but it is hard to say exactly what she looked like. She had dressed as a nurse for so many years that she did not really know how to dress in Vienna; she tended to overdress when she went out with Garp, perhaps in compensation for the old bathrobe in which she wrote. She had no experience in buying clothes for herself, and in a foreign city all the clothes looked slightly different to her. With no particular taste in mind, she simply bought the more expensive things; after all, she *did* have money and she did not have the patience or the interest for any comparative shopping. As a consequence, she looked new and shiny in her clothes, and beside Garp she did not look as if she came from the same family. Garp's constant dress, at Steering, had been a jacket and tie and comfortable pants – a kind of sloppy city standard uniform that made him anonymous almost anywhere.

'Would you ask that woman where she got that muff?' Jenny said to Garp. To her surprise, the women blocked the sidewalk to meet them.

'They're *whores*, Mom,' Garp whispered to her.

Jenny Fields froze. The woman with the muff spoke sharply to her. Jenny didn't understand a word, of course; she stared at Garp for a translation. The woman spoke a stream of things to Jenny, who never took her eyes off her son.

'My mother wanted to ask you where you got your pretty muff,' Garp said in his slow German.

'Oh, they're *foreigners*,' said one.

'God, it's his *mother*,' said another.

The woman with the muff stared at Jenny, who now stared at the woman's muff. One of the whores was a young girl with her hair piled very high and sprinkled with little gold and silver stars; she also had a green star tattoo on one cheek and a scar, which pulled her upper lip only slightly out of line – so that, for a moment, you didn't know *what* was wrong with her face, only that something was wrong. There was nothing at all wrong with her body, though; she was tall and lean and very hard to look at, though Jenny now found herself staring at her.

'Ask her how old she is,' Jenny said to Garp.

'*Ich bin* eighteen,' the girl said. 'I know good English.'

'That's how old my son is,' Jenny said, nudging Garp. She did not understand that they had mistaken *her* for one of them; when Garp told her, later, she was furious – but only at herself. 'It's my clothes!' she cried. 'I don't know how to dress!' And from that moment on, Jenny Fields would never dress as anything but a nurse; she put her uniform back on and wore it everywhere – as if she were forever on duty, though she would never be a nurse again.

'May I see your muff?' Jenny asked the woman who had one; Jenny had assumed that they all spoke English, but only the young girl knew the language. Garp translated and the woman reluctantly removed her muff – a scent of perfume emerging from the warm nest where her long hands, sparkling with rings, had been clutched together.

The third whore had a pockmark on her forehead, like an impression made with a peach pit. Aside from this flaw, and a small fat mouth like the mouth of an overweight child, she was standardly ripe – in her twenties, Garp guessed; she probably had an enormous bosom, but under her black fur coat it was hard to be sure.

The woman with the muff, Garp thought, was beautiful. She had a long, potentially sad face. Her body, Garp imagined, was serene. Her mouth was very calm. Only her eyes and her bare hands in the cold night let Garp see that she was his mother's age, at least. Maybe she was older. 'It was a gift,' she said to Garp, about the muff. 'It came with the coat.' They were a silver-blond fur, very sleek.

'It is the real thing,' said the young whore who spoke English; she obviously admired everything about the older prostitute.

'Of course, you can buy something, not quite so expensive, almost anywhere,' the pockmarked woman told Garp. 'Go to Stef's,' she said, in a queer slang that Garp barely understood, and she pointed up the Kärntnerstrasse. But Jenny didn't look and Garp only nodded and continued to gaze at the older woman's long bare fingers twinkling with rings.

'My hands are cold,' she said softly to Garp, and Garp took the muff from Jenny and gave it back to the whore. Jenny seemed in a daze.

'Let's *talk* to her,' Jenny told Garp. 'I want to ask her about it.'

'About *what*, Mom?' Garp said. 'Jesus Christ.'

'What we were talking about,' Jenny said. 'I want to ask her about *lust.*'

The two older whores looked at the one who knew English, but her English was not fast enough to catch any of this.

'It's cold, Mom,' Garp complained. 'And it's late. Let's just go home.'

'Tell her we want to go to some place warm, just to sit and talk,' Jenny said. 'She'll let us pay her for *that*, won't she?'

'I suppose so,' Garp groaned. 'Mom, *she* doesn't know anything about lust. They probably don't feel anything very much like that.'

'I want to know about *male* lust,' Jenny said. 'About *your* lust. She must know something about *that*.'

'For God's sake, Mom!' Garp said.

'*Was macht's?*' the lovely prostitute asked him. 'What's the matter?' she asked. 'What's going on here? Does she want to buy the muff?'

'No, no,' Garp said. 'She wants to buy *you*.'

The older whore looked stunned; the whore with the pockmark laughed.

'No, no,' Garp explained. 'Just to *talk*. My mother just wants to ask you some questions.'

'It's cold,' the whore told him, suspiciously.

'Some place inside?' Garp suggested. 'Anyplace you like.'

'Ask her what she charges,' Jenny said.

'*Wie viel kostet?*' mumbled Garp.

'It costs five hundred schillings,' the whore said, 'usually.' Garp had to explain to Jenny that this was about twenty dollars. Jenny Fields would live for more than a year in Austria and never learn the numbers, in German, or the money system.

'Twenty dollars, just to talk?' Jenny said.

'No, no, Mom,' Garp said, 'that's for the *usual*.' Jenny thought. Was twenty dollars a lot for the usual? She didn't know.

'Tell her we'll give her ten,' Jenny said, but the whore looked doubtful – as if talk, for her, might be more difficult than the 'usual.' Her indecision was influenced by more than price, however; she didn't trust Garp and Jenny. She asked the young whore who spoke English if they were British or

American. Americans, she was told; this seemed to relieve her, slightly.

'The British are often perverse,' she told Garp, simply. 'Americans are usually ordinary.'

'We just want to *talk* with you,' Garp insisted, but he could see that the prostitute firmly imagined some mother-and-son act of monstrous oddity.

'Two hundred and fifty schillings,' the lady with the mink muff finally agreed. 'And you buy my coffee.'

So they went to the place all the whores went to get warm, a tiny bar with miniature tables; the phone rang all the time but only a few men lurked sullenly by the coat rack, looking the women over. There was some rule that the women could not be approached when they were in this bar; the bar was a kind of home base, a time-out zone.

'Ask her how old she is,' Jenny said to Garp; but when he asked her, the woman softly shut her eyes and shook her head. 'Okay,' said Jenny, 'ask her why she thinks men like her.' Garp rolled his eyes. 'Well, you *do* like her?' Jenny asked him. Garp said he did. 'Well, what *is* it about her that you *want*?' Jenny asked him. 'I don't mean just her sex parts, I mean is there something else that's satisfying? Something to imagine, something to think about, some kind of *aura*?' Jenny asked.

'Why don't you pay *me* two hundred and fifty schillings and not ask her any questions, Mom,' Garp said tiredly.

'Don't be fresh,' Jenny said. 'I want to know if it degrades her to feel *wanted* in that way – and then to be *had* in that way, I suppose – or whether she thinks it only degrades the men?' Garp struggled to translate this. The woman appeared to think very seriously about it; or else she didn't understand the question, or Garp's German.

'I don't know,' she finally said.

'I have other questions,' Jenny said.

For an hour, it continued. Then the whore said she had to get back to work. Jenny seemed neither satisfied nor disappointed by the interview's lack of concrete results;

she just seemed insatiably curious. Garp had never wanted anyone as much as he wanted the woman.

'Do you want her?' Jenny asked him, so suddenly that he couldn't lie. 'I mean, after all this – and looking at her, and talking with her – do you really want to have sex with her, too?'

'Of course, Mom,' Garp said, miserably. Jenny looked no closer to understanding lust than she was before dinner. She looked puzzled and surprised at her son.

'All right,' she said. She handed him the 250 schillings that they owed the woman, and another 500 schillings. 'You do what you want to do,' she told him, 'or what you *have* to do, I guess. But please take me home first.'

The whore had watched the money change hands; she had an eye for recognizing the correct amount. 'Look,' she said to Garp, and touched his hand with her fingers, as cold as her rings. 'It's all right with me if your mother wants to buy me for you, but she can't come along with us. I will *not* have her watch us, absolutely not. I'm still a Catholic, believe it or not,' she said, 'and if you want anything funny like that, you'll have to ask Tina.'

Garp wondered who Tina was; he gave a shudder at the thought that nothing must be too 'funny' for her. 'I'm going to take my mother home,' Garp told the beautiful woman. 'And I won't be back to see you.' But she smiled at him and he thought his erection would burst through his pocket of loose schillings and worthless groschen. Just one of her perfect teeth – but it was a big front upper tooth – was all gold.

In the taxi (that Garp agreed to take home) Garp explained to his mother the Viennese system of prostitution. Jenny was not surprised to hear that prostitution was legal; she was surprised to learn that it was *illegal* in so many other places. 'Why shouldn't it be legal?' she asked. 'Why can't a woman use her body the way she wants to? If someone wants to pay for it, it's just one more crummy deal. Is twenty dollars a lot of money for it?'

'No, that's pretty good,' Garp said. 'At least, it's a very low price for the good-looking ones.'

Jenny slapped him. 'You know all about it!' she said. Then she said she was sorry – she had never struck him before, she just didn't understand this fucking lust, lust, lust! at all.

At the Schwindgasse apartment, Garp made a point of *not* going out; in fact, he was in his own bed and asleep before Jenny, who paced through her manuscript pages in her wild room. A sentence boiled in her, but she could not yet see it clearly.

Garp dreamed of other prostitutes; he had visited two or three of them in Vienna – but he had never paid the first-district prices. The next evening, after an early supper at the Schwindgasse, Garp went to see the woman with the mink muff streaked with light.

Her working name was Charlotte. She was not surprised to see him. Charlotte was old enough to know when she'd successfully hooked someone, although she never did tell Garp exactly how old she was. She had taken very fine care of herself, and only when she was completely undressed was her age apparent anywhere except in the veins on her long hands. There were stretch marks on her belly and her breasts, but she told Garp that the child had died a long time ago. She did not mind if Garp touched the Cesarean scar.

After he had seen Charlotte four times at the fixed first-district rate, he happened to run into her at the Naschmarkt on a Saturday morning. She was buying fruit. Her hair was probably a little dirty; she'd covered it with a scarf and wore it like a young girl's – with bangs and two short braids. The bangs were slightly greasy against her forehead, which seemed paler in the daylight. She had no makeup on and wore a pair of American jeans and tennis sneakers and a long coat-style sweater with a high roll collar. Garp would not have recognized her if he hadn't seen her hands clutching the fruit; she had all her rings on.

At first she wouldn't answer him when he spoke to her,

but he had already told her that he did all the shopping, and the cooking, for himself and his mother, and she found this amusing. After her irritation at meeting a customer in her off-duty hours, she seemed good-humored. It did not become clear to Garp, for a while, that he was the same age as Charlotte's child would have been. Charlotte took some vicarious interest in the way Garp was living with his mother.

'How's your mother's writing coming?' Charlotte would ask him.

'She's still pounding away,' Garp would say. 'I don't think she's solved the lust problem yet.'

But only to a point did Charlotte allow Garp to joke about his mother.

Garp was insecure enough about himself with Charlotte that he never told her *he* was trying to write, too; he knew she would think he was too young. Sometimes, he thought so, too. And his story wasn't ready to tell someone about. The most he had done was change the title. He now called it 'The Pension Grillparzer,' and that title was the first thing about it that solidly pleased him. It helped him to focus. Now he had a place in mind, just *one* place where almost everything that was important was going to happen. This helped him to think in a more focused way about his characters, too – about the family of classifiers, about the other residents of one small, sad pension somewhere (it would *have* to be small and sad, and in Vienna, to be named after Franz Grillparzer). Those 'other residents' would include a kind of circus; not a very good kind, either, he imagined, but a circus with no other place to stay. No other place would have them.

In the world of ratings, the whole thing would be a kind of C experience. This kind of imagining got Garp started, slowly, in what he thought was a real direction; he was right about that, but it was too new to write it down – or even to write about it. Anyway, the more he wrote to Helen the less he wrote in other, important ways; and he couldn't discuss this with his mother: imagination was not her greatest strength. Of course, he'd have felt foolish discussing *any* of this with Charlotte.

Garp often met Charlotte at the Naschmarkt on Saturdays. They shopped and sometimes they ate lunch together in a Serbian place not far from the Stadtpark. On these occasions Charlotte paid for herself. At one such lunch Garp confessed to her that the first-district rate was hard for him to pay regularly without admitting to his mother where this steady flow of money was going. Charlotte was angry at him for bringing up business when she wasn't working. She would have been angrier if he'd admitted that he was seeing less of her, professionally, because the sixth-district prices of someone whom he met at the corner of Karl Schweighofergasse and Mariahilfer were much easier to conceal from Jenny.

Charlotte had a low opinion of her colleagues who operated out of the first district. She'd once told Garp she was planning to retire at the first sign that her first-district appeal was slipping. She would never do business in the outer districts. She had a lot of money saved, she told him, and she was going to move to Munich (where nobody knew she was a whore) and marry a young doctor who could take care of her, in every way, until she died; it was unnecessary for her to explain to Garp that she had always appealed to younger men, but Garp thoroughly resented her assumption that doctors were – in the long run – desirable. It may be this early exposure to the desirability of doctors that caused Garp, in his literary career, often to people his novels and stories with such unlikable characters from the medical profession. If so, it didn't occur to him until later. There is no doctor in 'The Pension Grillparzer.' In the beginning there is very little about death, either, although that is the subject the story would come to. In the beginning Garp had only a *dream* of death, but it was a whale of a dream and he gave it to the oldest person alive in his story: a grandmother. Garp guessed this meant that she would be the first to die.

THE PENSION GRILLPARZER

My father worked for the Austrian Tourist Bureau. It was my mother's idea that our family travel with him when he went on the road as a Tourist Bureau spy. My mother and brother and I would accompany him on his secretive missions to uncover the discourtesy, the dust, the badly cooked food, the shortcuts taken by Austria's restaurants and hotels and pensions. We were instructed to create difficulties whenever we could, never to order exactly what was on the menu, to imitate a foreigner's odd requests – the hours we would like to have our baths, the need for aspirin and directions to the zoo. We were instructed to be civilized but troublesome; and when the visit was over, we reported to my father in the car.

My mother would say, 'The hairdresser is always closed in the morning. But they make suitable recommendations outside. I guess it's all right, provided they don't claim to have a hairdresser actually *in* the hotel.'

'Well, they *do* claim it,' my father would say. He'd note this in a giant pad.

I was always the driver. I said, 'The car is parked off the street, but someone put fourteen kilometers on the gauge between the time we handed it over to the doorman and picked it up at the hotel garage.'

'That is a matter to report directly to the management,' my father said, jotting it down.

'The toilet leaked,' I said.

'I couldn't open the door to the W.C.,' said my brother, Robo.

'Robo,' Mother said, 'you always have trouble with doors.'

'Was that supposed to be Class C?' I asked.

'I'm afraid not,' Father said. 'It is still listed as Class B.' We drove for a short while in silence; our most serious judgment concerned changing a hotel's or a pension's rating. We did not suggest reclassification frivolously.

'I think this calls for a letter to the management,' Mother suggested. 'Not too nice a letter, but not a really rough one. Just state the facts.'

'Yes, I rather liked him,' Father said. He always made a point of getting to meet the managers.

'Don't forget the business of them driving our car,' I said. 'That's really unforgivable.'

'And the eggs were bad,' said Robo; he was not yet ten and his judgments were not considered seriously.

We became a far harsher team of evaluators when my grandfather died and we inherited grandmother – my mother's mother, who thereafter accompanied us on our travels. A regal dame, Johanna was accustomed to Class A travel, and my father's duties more frequently called for investigations of Class B and Class C lodgings. They were the places, the B and C hotels (and the pensions), that most interested the tourists. At restaurants we did a little better. People who couldn't afford the classy places to sleep were still interested in the best places to eat.

'I shall not have dubious food tested on me,' Johanna told us. 'This strange employment may give you all glee about having free vacations, but I can see there is a terrible price paid: the anxiety of not knowing what sort of quarters you'll have for the night. Americans may find it charming that we still have rooms without private baths and toilets, but I am an old woman and I'm not charmed by walking down a public corridor in search of cleanliness and my relievement. Anxiety is only half of it. Actual diseases are possible – and not only from food. If the bed is questionable, I promise I shan't put my head down. And the children are young and impressionable; you should think of the clientele in some of these lodgings and seriously ask yourselves about the influences.' My mother and father nodded; they said nothing. 'Slow down!' Grandmother said sharply to me. 'You're just a young boy who likes to show off.' I slowed down. 'Vienna,' Grandmother sighed. 'In Vienna I always stayed at the Ambassador.'

'Johanna, the Ambassador is not under investigation,' Father said.

'I should think not,' Johanna said. 'I suppose we're not even headed toward a Class A place?'

'Well, it's a B trip,' my father admitted. 'For the most part.'

'I trust,' Grandmother said, 'that you mean there is one A place en route?'

'No,' Father admitted. 'There is one C place.'

'It's okay,' Robo said. 'There are fights in Class C.'

'I should imagine so,' Johanna said.

'It's a Class C pension, very small,' Father said, as if the size of the place forgave it.

'And they're applying for a B,' said Mother.

'But there have been some complaints,' I added.

'I'm sure there have,' Johanna said.

'And animals,' I added. My mother gave me a look.

'Animals?' said Johanna.

'Animals,' I admitted.

'A *suspicion* of animals,' my mother corrected me.

'Yes, be fair,' Father said.

'Oh, wonderful!' Grandmother said. 'A suspicion of animals. Their hair on the rugs? Their terrible waste in the corners! Did you know that my asthma reacts, severely, to any room in which there has recently been a cat?'

'The complaint was not about cats,' I said. My mother elbowed me sharply.

'Dogs?' Johanna said. 'Rabid dogs! Biting you on the way to the bathroom.'

'No,' I said. 'Not dogs.'

'Bears!' Robo cried.

But my mother said, 'We don't know for sure about the bear, Robo.'

'This isn't serious,' Johanna said.

'Of course it's not serious!' Father said. 'How could there be bears in a pension?'

'There was a letter saying so,' I said. 'Of course, the Tourist Bureau assumed it was a crank complaint. But then there was another sighting – and a second letter claiming there had been a bear.'

My father used the rearview mirror to scowl at me, but I thought that if we were all supposed to be in on the investigation, it would be wise to have Grandmother on her toes.

'It's probably not a real bear,' Robo said, with obvious disappointment.

'A man in a bear suit!' Johanna cried. 'What unheard-of perversion is *that*? A *beast* of a man sneaking about in disguise! Up to what? It's a man in a bear suit, I know it is,' she said. 'I want to go to that one *first*. If there's going to be a Class C experience on this trip, let's get it over with as soon as possible.'

'But we haven't got reservations for tonight,' Mother said.

'Yes, we might as well give them a chance to be at their best,' Father said. Although he never revealed to his victims that he worked for the Tourist Bureau, Father believed that reservations were simply a decent way of allowing the personnel to be as prepared as they could be.

'I'm sure we don't need to make a reservation in a place frequented by men who disguise themselves as animals,' Johanna said. 'I'm sure there is *always* a vacancy there. I'm sure the guests are regularly dying in their beds – of fright, or else of whatever unspeakable injury the madman in the foul bear suit does to them.'

'It's probably a *real* bear,' Robo said, hopefully – for in the turn the conversation was taking, Robo certainly saw that a real bear would be preferable to Grandmother's imagined ghoul. Robo had no fear, I think, of a real bear.

I drove us as inconspicuously as possible to the dark, dwarfed corner of Planken and Seilergasse. We were looking for the Class C pension that wanted to be a B.

'No place to park,' I said to Father, who was already making note of that in his pad.

I double-parked and we sat in the car and peered up at the Pension Grillparzer; it rose only four slender stories between a pastry shop and a Tabak Trafik.

'See?' Father said. 'No bears.'

'No *men*, I hope,' said Grandmother.

'They come at night,' Robo said, looking cautiously up and down the street.

We went inside to meet the manager, a Herr Theobald, who instantly put Johanna on her guard. 'Three generations traveling together!' he cried. 'Like the old days,' he added, especially to Grandmother, 'before all these divorces and the young people wanting apartments by themselves. This is a *family* pension! I just wish you had made a reservation – so I could put you more closely together.'

'We're not accustomed to sleeping in the same room,' Grand-mother told him.

'Of course not!' Theobald cried. 'I just meant that I wished your *rooms* could be closer together.' This worried Grand-mother, clearly.

'How far apart must we be put?' she asked.

'Well, I've only two rooms left,' he said. 'And only one of them is large enough for the two boys to share with their parents.'

'And my room is how far from theirs?' Johanna asked coolly.

'You're right across from the W.C.!' Theobald told her, as if this were a plus.

But as we were shown to our rooms, Grandmother staying with Father – contemptuously to the rear of our procession – I heard her mutter, 'This is not how I conceived of my retirement. Across the hall from a W.C., listening to all the visitors.'

'Not one of these rooms is the same,' Theobald told us. 'The furniture is all from my family.' We could believe it. The one large room Robo and I were to share with my parents was a hall-sized museum of knickknacks, every dresser with a different style of knob. On the other hand, the sink had brass faucets and the headboard of the bed was carved. I could see my father balan-cing things up for future notation in the giant pad.

'You may do that later,' Johanna informed him. 'Where do *I* stay?'

As a family, we dutifully followed Theobald and my grand-mother down the long, twining hall, my father counting the paces to the W.C. The hall rug was thin, the color of a shadow. Along the walls were old photographs of speed-skating teams – on their feet the strange blades curled up at the tips like court jesters' shoes or the runners of ancient sleds.

Robo, running far ahead, announced his discovery of the W.C.

Grandmother's room was full of china, polished wood, and the hint of mold. The drapes were damp. The bed had an unsettling ridge at its center, like fur risen on a dog's spine – it was almost as if a very slender body lay stretched beneath the bedspread.

Grandmother said nothing, and when Theobald reeled out of the room like a wounded man who's been told he'll live, Grandmother asked my father, 'On what basis can the Pension Grillparzer hope to get a B?'

'Quite decidedly C,' Father said.

'Born C and will die C,' I said.

'I would say, myself,' Grandmother told us, 'that it was E or F.'

In the dim tearoom a man without a tie sang a Hungarian song. 'It does not mean he's Hungarian,' Father reassured Johanna, but she was skeptical.

'I'd say the odds are not in his favor,' she suggested. She would not have tea or coffee. Robo ate a little cake, which he claimed to like. My mother and I smoked a cigarette; she was trying to quit and I was trying to start. Therefore, we shared a cigarette between us – in fact, we'd promised never to smoke a whole one alone.

'He's a great guest,' Herr Theobald whispered to my father; he indicated the singer. 'He knows songs from all over.'

'From Hungary, at least,' Grandmother said, but she smiled.

A small man, clean-shaven but with that permanent gun-blue shadow of a beard on his lean face, spoke to my grandmother. He wore a clean white shirt (but yellow from age and laundering), suit pants, and an unmatching jacket.

'Pardon me?' said Grandmother.

'I said that I tell dreams,' the man informed her.

'You *tell* dreams,' Grandmother said. 'Meaning, you *have* them?'

'Have them and tell them,' he said mysteriously. The singer stopped singing.

'Any dream you want to know,' said the singer. 'He can tell it.'

'I'm quite sure I don't want to know any,' Grandmother said. She viewed with displeasure the ascot of dark hair bursting out at the open throat of the singer's shirt. She would not regard the man who 'told' dreams at all.

'I can see you are a lady,' the dream man told Grandmother. 'You don't respond to just every dream that comes along.'

'Certainly not,' said Grandmother. She shot my father one of her how-could-you-have-let-this-happen-to-me? looks.

'But I know one,' said the dream man; he shut his eyes. The singer slipped a chair forward and we suddenly realized he was sitting very close to us. Robo, though he was much too old for it, sat in Father's lap. 'In a great castle,' the dream man began, 'a woman lay beside her husband. She was wide awake, suddenly, in the middle of the night. She woke up without the slightest idea of what had awakened her, and she felt as alert as if she'd been up for hours. It was also clear to her, without a look, a word, or a touch, that her husband was wide awake too – and just as suddenly.'

'I hope this is suitable for the child to hear, ha ha,' Herr Theobald said, but no one even looked at him. My grandmother folded her hands in her lap and stared at them – her knees together, her heels tucked under her straight-backed chair. My mother held my father's hand.

I sat next to the dream man, whose jacket smelled like a zoo. He said, 'The woman and her husband lay awake listening for sounds in the castle, which they were only renting and did not know intimately. They listened for sounds in the courtyard, which they never bothered to lock. The village people always took walks by the castle; the village children were allowed to swing on the great courtyard door. What had woken them?'

'Bears?' said Robo, but Father touched his fingertips to Robo's mouth.

'They heard horses,' said the dream man. Old Johanna, her eyes shut, her head inclined toward her lap, seemed to shudder in her stiff chair. 'They heard the breathing and stamping of horses who were trying to keep still,' the dream man said. 'The husband reached out and touched his wife. "Horses?" he said. The woman got out of bed and went to the courtyard window. She would swear to this day that the courtyard was full of soldiers on horseback – but *what* soldiers they were! They wore *armor*! The visors on their helmets were closed and their murmuring voices were as tinny and difficult to hear as voices on a fading radio station. Their armor clanked as their horses shifted restlessly under them.

'There was an old dry bowl of a former fountain, there in the castle's courtyard, but the woman saw that the fountain was flowing; the water lapped over the worn curb and the horses were drinking it. The knights were wary, they would not dismount; they looked up at the castle's dark windows, as if they knew they were uninvited at this watering trough – this rest station on their way, somewhere.

'In the moonlight the woman saw their big shields glint. She crept back to bed and lay rigidly against her husband.

'"What is it?" he asked her.

'"Horses," she told him.

'"I thought so," he said. "They'll eat the flowers."

'"Who built this castle?" she asked him. It was a very old castle, they both knew that.

'"Charlemagne," he told her; he was going back to sleep.

'But the woman lay awake, listening to the water which now seemed to be running all through the castle, gurgling in every drain, as if the old fountain were drawing water from every available source. And there were the distorted voices of the whispering knights – *Charlemagne's* soldiers speaking their dead language! To this woman, the soldiers' voices were as morbid as the eighth century and the people called Franks. The horses kept drinking.

'The woman lay awake a long time, waiting for the soldiers to leave; she had no fear of actual attack from them – she was sure they were on a journey and had only stopped to rest at a place they once knew. But for as long as the water ran she felt that she mustn't disturb the castle's stillness or its darkness. When she fell asleep, she thought Charlemagne's men were still there.

'In the morning her husband asked her, "Did you hear water

running, too?" Yes, she had, of course. But the fountain was dry, of course, and out the window they could see that the flowers weren't eaten – and everyone knows horses eat flowers.

'"Look," said her husband; he went into the courtyard with her. "There are *no* hoofprints, there are no droppings. We must have *dreamed* we heard horses." She did not tell him that there were soldiers, too; or that, in her opinion, it was unlikely that two people would dream the same dream. She did not remind him that he was a heavy smoker who never smelled the soup simmering; the aroma of horses in the fresh air was too subtle for him.

'She saw the soldiers, or dreamed them, twice more while they stayed there, but her husband never again woke up with her. It was always sudden. Once she woke with the taste of metal on her tongue as if she'd touched some old, sour iron to her mouth – a sword, a chest plate, chain mail, a thigh guard. They were out there again, in colder weather. From the water in the fountain a dense fog shrouded them; the horses were snowy with frost. And there were not so many of them the next time – as if the winter or their skirmishes were reducing their numbers. The last time the horses looked gaunt to her, and the men looked more like unoccupied suits of armor balanced delicately in the saddles. The horses wore long masks of ice on their muzzles. Their breathing (or the men's breathing) was congested.

'Her husband,' said the dream man, 'would die of a respiratory infection. But the woman did not know it when she dreamed this dream.'

My grandmother looked up from her lap and slapped the dream man's beard-gray face. Robo stiffened in my father's lap; my mother caught her mother's hand. The singer shoved back his chair and jumped to his feet, frightened, or ready to fight someone, but the dream man simply bowed to Grandmother and left the gloomy tearoom. It was as if he'd made a contract with Johanna that was final but gave neither of them any joy. My father wrote something in the giant pad.

'Well, wasn't *that* some story?' said Herr Theobald. 'Ha ha.' He rumpled Robo's hair – something Robo always hated.

'Herr Theobald,' my mother said, still holding Johanna's hand, '*my father died of a respiratory infection.*'

'Oh, dear shit,' said Herr Theobald. 'I'm sorry, *meine Frau,*' he told Grandmother, but old Johanna would not speak to him.

We took Grandmother out to eat in a Class A restaurant, but she hardly touched her food. 'That person was a gypsy,' she told us. 'A satanic being, and a Hungarian.'

'Please, Mother,' my mother said. 'He couldn't have known about Father.'

'He knew more than *you* know,' Grandmother snapped.

'The schnitzel is excellent,' Father said, writing in the pad. 'The Gumpoldskirchner is just right with it.'

'The Kalbsnieren are fine,' I said.

'The eggs are okay,' said Robo.

Grandmother said nothing until we returned to the Pension Grillparzer, where we noticed that the door to the W.C. was hung a foot or more off the floor, so that it resembled the bottom half of an American toilet-stall door or a saloon door in the Western movies. 'I'm certainly glad I used the W.C. at the restaurant,' Grandmother said. 'How revolting! I shall try to pass the night without exposing myself where every passerby can peer at my ankles!'

In our family room Father said, 'Didn't Johanna live in a castle? Once upon a time, I thought she and Grandpa rented some castle.'

'Yes, it was before I was born,' Mother said. 'They rented Schloss Katzelsdorf. I saw the photographs.'

'Well, *that's* why the Hungarian's dream upset her,' Father said.

'Someone is riding a bike in the hall,' Robo said. 'I saw a wheel go by – under our door.'

'Robo, go to sleep,' Mother said.

'It went "squeak squeak,"' Robo said.

'Good night, boys,' said Father.

'If you can talk, we can talk,' I said.

'Then talk to each other,' Father said. 'I'm talking to your mother.'

'I want to go to sleep,' Mother said. 'I wish no one would talk.'

We tried. Perhaps we slept. Then Robo whispered to me that he had to use the W.C.

'You know where it is,' I said.

Robo went out the door, leaving it slightly open; I heard him walk down the corridor, brushing his hand along the wall. He was back very quickly.

'There's someone *in* the W.C.,' he said.

'Wait for them to finish,' I said.

'The light wasn't on,' Robo said, 'but I could still see under the door. Someone is in there, in the dark.'

'I prefer the dark myself,' I said.

But Robo insisted on telling me exactly what he'd seen. He said that under the door was a pair of *hands*.

'Hands?' I said.

'Yes, where the feet should have been,' Robo said; he claimed that there was a hand on either side of the toilet – instead of a foot.

'Get out of here, Robo!' I said.

'Please come see,' he begged. I went down the hall with him but there was no one in the W.C. 'They've gone,' he said.

'Walked off on their hands, no doubt,' I said. 'Go pee. I'll wait for you.'

He went into the W.C. and peed sadly in the dark. When we were almost back to our room together, a small dark man with the same kind of skin and clothes as the dream man who had angered Grandmother passed us in the hall. He winked at us, and smiled. I had to notice that he was walking on his hands.

'You see?' Robo whispered to me. We went into our room and shut the door.

'What is it?' Mother asked.

'A man walking on his hands,' I said.

'A man *peeing* on his hands,' Robo said.

'Class C,' Father murmured in his sleep; Father often dreamed that he was making notes in the giant pad.

'We'll talk about it in the morning,' Mother said.

'He was probably just an acrobat who was showing off for you, because you're a kid,' I told Robo.

'How did he know I was a kid when he was in the W.C.?' Robo asked me.

'Go to *sleep*,' Mother whispered.

Then we heard Grandmother scream down the hall.

Mother put on her pretty green dressing gown; Father put on his bathrobe and his glasses; I pulled on a pair of pants, over my pajamas. Robo was in the hall first. We saw the light coming from under the W.C. door. Grandmother was screaming rhythmically in there.

'Here we are!' I called to her.

'Mother, what is it?' my mother asked.

We gathered in the broad slot of light. We could see Grandmother's mauve slippers and her porcelain-white ankles under the door. She stopped screaming. 'I heard whispers when I was in my bed,' she said.

'It was Robo and me,' I told her.

'Then, when everyone seemed to have gone, I came into the W.C.,' Johanna said. 'I left the light *off*. I was *very* quiet,' she told us. 'Then I saw and heard the wheel.'

'The *wheel?*' Father asked.

'A wheel went by the door a few times,' Grandmother said. 'It rolled by and came back and rolled by again.'

Father made his fingers roll like wheels alongside his head; he made a face at Mother. 'Somebody needs a new set of wheels,' he whispered, but Mother looked crossly at him.

'I turned *on* the light,' Grandmother said, 'and the wheel went away.'

'I told you there was a bike in the hall,' said Robo.

'Shut up, Robo,' Father said.

'No, it was not a bicycle,' Grandmother said. 'There was only *one* wheel.'

Father was making his hands go crazy beside his head. 'She's got a wheel or two *missing*,' he hissed at my mother, but she cuffed him and knocked his glasses askew on his face.

'Then someone came and looked *under* the door,' Grandmother said, 'and *that* is when I screamed.'

'Someone?' said Father.

'I saw his hands, a man's hands – there was hair on his knuckles,' Grandmother said. 'His hands were on the rug right outside the door. He must have been looking *up* at me.'

'No, Grandmother,' I said. 'I think he was just standing out here on his hands.'

'Don't be fresh,' my mother said.

'But we saw a man walking on his hands,' Robo said.

'You did *not*,' Father said.

'We *did*,' I said.

'We're going to wake everyone up,' Mother cautioned us.

The toilet flushed and Grandmother shuffled out the door with only a little of her former dignity intact. She was wearing a gown over a gown over a gown; her neck was very long and her face was creamed white. Grandmother looked like a troubled goose. 'He was evil and vile,' she said to us. 'He knew terrible magic.'

'The man who looked at you?' Mother asked.

'That man who told my *dream*,' Grandmother said. Now a tear made its way through her furrows of face cream. 'That was *my* dream,' she said, 'and he told everyone. It is unspeakable that he even *knew* it,' she hissed to us. 'My dream – of Charlemagne's horses and soldiers – *I* am the only one who should know it. I had that dream before you were born,' she told Mother. 'And that vile evil magic man told my dream as if it were *news*.

'I never even told your father all there was to that dream. I was never sure that it *was* a dream. And now there are men on their hands, and their knuckles are hairy, and there are magic wheels. I want the boys to sleep with *me*.'

So that was how Robo and I came to share the large family room, far away from the W.C., with Grandmother, who lay on my mother's and father's pillows with her creamed face shining like the face of a wet ghost. Robo lay awake watching her. I do not think Johanna slept very well; I imagine she was dreaming her dream of death again – reliving the last winter of Charlemagne's cold soldiers with their strange metal clothes covered with frost and their armor frozen shut.

When it was obvious that I had to go to the W.C., Robo's round, bright eyes followed me to the door.

There was someone in the W.C. There was no light shining from under the door, but there was a unicycle parked against the wall outside. Its rider sat in the dark W.C.; the toilet was flushing over and over again – like a child, the unicyclist was not giving the tank time to refill.

I went closer to the gap under the W.C. door, but the occupant was not standing on his or her hands. I saw what were clearly feet, in almost the expected position, but the feet did not touch the floor; their soles tilted up to me – dark, bruise-colored pads. They were *huge* feet attached to short, furry shins. They were a *bear's* feet, only there were no claws. A bear's claws are not retractable, like a cat's; if a bear had claws, you would see them. Here, then, was an imposter in a bear suit, or a declawed bear. A domestic bear, perhaps. At least – by its presence in the W.C. – a *housebroken* bear. For by its smell I could tell it was no man in a bear suit; it was all bear. It was real bear.

I backed into the door of Grandmother's former room, behind which my father lurked, waiting for further disturbances. He snapped open the door and I fell inside, frightening us both. Mother sat up in bed and pulled the feather quilt over her head. 'Got him!' Father cried, dropping down on me. The floor trembled; the bear's unicycle slipped against the wall and fell into the door of the W.C., out of which the bear suddenly shambled, stumbling over its unicycle and lunging for its balance. Worriedly, it stared across the hall, through the open door, at Father sitting on my chest. It picked up the unicycle in its front paws. '*Grauf?*' said the bear. Father slammed the door.

Down the hall we heard a woman call, 'Where are you, Duna?'

'*Harf!*' the bear said.

Father and I heard the woman come closer. She said, 'Oh, Duna, practicing again? Always practicing! But it's better in the daytime.' The bear said nothing. Father opened the door.

'Don't let anyone else in,' Mother said, still under the featherbed.

In the hall a pretty, aging woman stood beside the bear, who now balanced in place on its unicycle, one huge paw on the woman's shoulder. She wore a vivid red turban and a long wraparound dress that resembled a curtain. Perched on her high bosom was a necklace strung with bear claws; her earrings touched the shoulder of her curtain-dress and her other, bare shoulder where my father and I stared at her fetching mole. 'Good evening,' she said to Father. 'I'm sorry if we've disturbed you. Duna is forbidden to practice at night – but he loves his work.'

The bear muttered, pedaling away from the woman. The bear had very good balance but he was careless; he brushed against the walls of the hall and touched the photographs of the speed-skating teams with his paws. The woman, bowing away from Father, went after the bear calling, 'Duna, Duna,' and straightening the photographs as she followed him down the hall.

'*Duna* is the Hungarian word for the Danube,' Father told me. 'That bear is named after our beloved *Donau*.' Sometimes it seemed to surprise my family that the Hungarians could love a river, too.

'Is the bear a *real* bear?' Mother asked – still under the featherbed – but I left Father to explain it all to her. I knew that in the morning Herr Theobald would have much to explain, and I would hear everything reviewed at that time.

I went across the hall to the W.C. My task there was hurried by the bear's lingering odor, and by my suspicion of bear hair on everything; it was only my suspicion, though, for the bear had left everything quite tidy – or at least neat for a bear.

'I saw the bear,' I whispered to Robo, back in our room, but Robo had crept into Grandmother's bed and had fallen asleep beside her. Old Johanna was awake, however.

'I saw fewer and fewer soldiers,' she said. 'The last time they came there were only nine of them. Everyone looked so hungry; they must have eaten the extra horses. It was so cold. Of course

I wanted to help them! But we weren't alive at the same time; how could I help them if I wasn't even born? Of course I knew they would die! But it took such a long time.

'The last time they came, the fountain was frozen. They used their swords and their long pikes to break the ice into chunks. They built a fire and melted the ice in a pot. They took bones from their saddlebags – bones of all kinds – and threw them in the soup. It must have been a very thin broth because the bones had long ago been gnawed clean. I don't know what bones they were. Rabbits, I suppose, and maybe a deer or a wild boar. Maybe the extra horses. I do not choose to think,' said Grandmother, 'that they were the bones of the missing soldiers.'

'Go to sleep, Grandmother,' I said.

'Don't worry about the bear,' she said.

And *then* what? Garp wondered. What can happen next? He wasn't altogether sure what *had* happened, or why. Garp was a natural storyteller; he could make things up, one right after the other, and they seemed to fit. But what did they mean? That dream and those desperate entertainers, and what would happen to them all – everything had to connect. What sort of explanation would be natural? What sort of ending might make them all part of the same world? Garp knew he did not know enough; not yet. He trusted his instincts; they had brought him this far with 'The Pension Grillparzer'; now he had to trust the instinct that told him not to go any further until he knew much more.

What made Garp older and wiser than his nineteen years had nothing to do with his experience or with what he had learned. He had some instincts, some determination, better than average patience; he loved to work hard. Altogether, with the grammar Tinch had taught him, that was all. Only two facts impressed Garp: that his mother actually believed she could write a book and that the most meaningful relationship in his present life was with a whore. These facts contributed greatly to the young man's developing sense of humor.

He put 'The Pension Grillparzer' – as they say – aside. It will come, Garp thought. He knew he had to know more; all he could do was look at Vienna and learn. It was holding still for him. Life seemed to be holding still for him. He made a great many observations of Charlotte, too, and he noticed everything his mother did, but he was simply too young. What I need is *vision*, he knew. An overall scheme of things, a vision all his own. It will come, he repeated to himself, as if he were training for another wrestling season – jumping rope, running laps on a small track, lifting weights, something almost that mindless but that necessary.

Even Charlotte has a vision, he thought; he certainly knew that his mother had one. Garp had no parallel wisdom for the absolute clarity of the world according to Jenny Fields. But he knew it would take only time to imagine a world of his own – with a little help from the real world. The real world would soon cooperate.

6

The Pension Grillparzer

When spring came to Vienna, Garp had still not finished 'The Pension Grillparzer'; he had not, of course, even written to Helen about his life with Charlotte and her colleagues. Jenny had kicked her writing habit into yet a higher gear; she had found the sentence that had been boiling in her since that night she discussed lust with Garp and Charlotte: it was an old sentence, actually, from her life long ago, and it was the sentence with which she truly *began* the book that would make her famous.

'In this dirty-minded world,' Jenny wrote, 'you are either somebody's wife or somebody's whore – or fast on your way to becoming one or the other.' The sentence set a tone for the book, which the book had been lacking; Jenny was discovering that when she began with that sentence, an aura was cast over her autobiography that bound the disharmonious parts of her life's story together – the way fog shrouds an uneven landscape, the way heat reaches through a rambling house into every room. That sentence inspired others like it, and Jenny wove them as she might have woven a bright and binding thread of brilliant color through a sprawling tapestry of no apparent design.

'I wanted a job and I wanted to live alone,' she wrote. 'That made me a sexual suspect.' And that gave her a title, too. *A Sexual Suspect*, the autobiography of Jenny Fields. It would go through eight hardcover printings and be translated into six languages even before the paperback sale that could keep Jenny, and a regiment of nurses, in new uniforms for a century.

'Then I wanted a baby, but I didn't want to have to share my body or my life to have one,' Jenny wrote. 'That made me a sexual suspect, too.' Thus Jenny had found the string with which to sew her messy book together.

But when spring came to Vienna, Garp felt like a trip; maybe Italy; possibly, they could rent a car.

'Do you know how to drive?' Jenny asked him. She knew perfectly well that he hadn't ever learned; there had never been a need. 'Well, I don't know how, either,' she told him. 'And besides, I'm working; I can't stop now. If you want to take a trip, take a trip by yourself.'

It was in the American Express office, where Garp and Jenny got their mail, that Garp met his first traveling young Americans. Two girls who had formerly gone to Dibbs, and a boy named Boo who had gone to Bath. 'Hey, how about us?' one of the girls said to Garp, when they had all met. 'We're all prep school stuff.'

Her name was Flossie and it appeared to Garp that she had a relationship with Boo. The other girl was called Vivian, and under the tiny café table on the Schwarzenbergplatz, Vivian squeezed Garp's knee between her own and drooled while sipping her wine. 'I just went to a *dent*-hisht,' she explained to him. 'Got so much Novocain in my goddamn mouth I don't know whether it's open or shut.'

'Sort of half and half,' Garp said to her. But he thought: Oh, what the hell. He missed Cushie Percy, and his relationships with prostitutes were beginning to make *him* feel like a sexual suspect. Charlotte, it was now clear, was interested in mothering him; though he tried to imagine her on another level, he knew, sadly, that this level would never carry beyond the professional.

Flossie and Vivian and Boo were all going to Greece but they let Garp show them Vienna for three days. In that time Garp slept twice with Vivian, whose Novocain finally wore off; he also slept once with Flossie, while Boo was out cashing travelers' checks and changing the oil in the car. There was no love lost between Steering and Bath boys, Garp knew; but Boo had the last laugh.

It is impossible to know whether Garp got gonorrhea from Vivian or from Flossie, but Garp was convinced that the *source* of the dose was Boo. It was, in Garp's opinion, 'Bath clap.' By the time of the first symptoms, of course, the threesome had left for Greece and Garp faced the dripping and the burning alone. There could be no worse a case of clap to catch in all of Europe, he thought. 'I caught a dose of Boo's goo,' he wrote, but much later; it was not funny when it happened, and he didn't dare seek his mother's professional advice. He knew she would refuse to believe that he hadn't caught it from a whore. He got up the nerve to ask Charlotte to recommend a doctor who was familiar with the matter; he thought she would know. He thought later that Jenny would possibly have been *less* angry with him.

'You'd think Americans would know a little simple hygiene!' Charlotte said furiously. 'You should think of your mother! I'd expect you to have better taste. People who give it away for free to someone they hardly know – well, they should make you suspicious, shouldn't they?' Once again, Garp had been caught without a condom.

Thus Garp winced his way to Charlotte's personal physician, a hearty man named Thalhammer who was missing his left thumb. 'And I was once left-handed,' Herr Doktor Thalhammer told Garp. 'But everything is surmountable if we have energy. We can learn anything we can set our minds to!' he said, with firm good cheer; he demonstrated for Garp how he could write the prescription, with an enviable penmanship, with his right hand. It was a simple and painless cure. In Jenny's day, at good old Boston Mercy, they would have given Garp the Valentine treatment and he'd have learned, more emphatically, how not all rich kids are clean kids.

He didn't write Helen about this, either.

His spirits slumped; spring wore on, the city opened in

many small ways – like buds. But Garp felt he had walked
Vienna out. He could barely get his mother to stop writing
long enough to eat dinner with him. When he sought out
Charlotte, her colleagues told him she was sick; she hadn't
worked for weeks. For three Saturdays, Garp did not see
her at the Naschmarkt. When he stopped her colleagues
one May evening on the Kärntnerstrasse, he saw they were
reluctant to discuss Charlotte. The whore whose forehead
appeared to have been pockmarked by a peach pit merely
told Garp that Charlotte was sicker than she first thought.
The young girl, Garp's age, with the misshapen lip and the
half-knowledge of English, tried to explain to him. 'Her *sex*
is sick,' she said.

That was a curious way to put it, Garp thought. Garp was
not surprised to hear that *anyone's* sex was sick, but when he
smiled at the remark, the young whore who spoke English
frowned at him and walked away.

'You don't understand,' said the overlush prostitute with
the pockmark. 'Forget Charlotte.'

It was mid-June, and Charlotte had still not come back,
when Garp called Herr Doktor Thalhammer and asked
where he could find her. 'I doubt that she wants to see anybody,' Thalhammer told him, 'but human beings can adjust
to almost anything.'

Very near Grinzing and the Vienna Woods, out in the
nineteenth district where the whores don't go, Vienna looks
like a village imitation of itself; in these suburbs, many of
the streets are still cobblestoned and trees grow along the
sidewalks. Unfamiliar with this part of the city, Garp rode
the No. 38 Strassenbahn too far out the Grinzinger Allee;
he had to walk back to the corner of Billrothstrasse and
Rudolfinergasse to the hospital.

The Rudolfinerhaus is a private hospital in a city of
socialized medicine; its old stone walls are the same Maria
Theresa yellow as the palace at Schönbrunn, or the Upper
and Lower Belvedere. Its own gardens are enclosed in its

own courtyard, and it costs as much as almost any hospital in the United States. The Rudolfinerhaus does not normally provide pajamas for its patients, for example, because its patients usually prefer their own nightclothes. The well-to-do Viennese treat themselves to the luxury of being sick there – and most foreigners who are afraid of socialized medicine end up there, where they are shocked at the prices.

In June, when Garp went there, the hospital struck him as full of pretty young mothers who'd just delivered babies. But it was also full of well-off people who'd come there to get seriously well again, and it was partially full of well-off people, like Charlotte, who'd come there to die.

Charlotte had a private room because, she said, there was no reason to save her money now. Garp knew she was dying as soon as he saw her. She had lost almost thirty pounds. Garp saw that she wore what was left of her rings on her index and middle fingers; her other fingers were so shrunken that her rings would slide off. Charlotte was the color of the dull ice on the brackish Steering River. She did not appear very surprised to see Garp, but she was so heavily anesthetized that Garp imagined Charlotte was fairly unsurprised in general. Garp had brought a basket of fruit; since they had shopped together, he knew what Charlotte liked to eat, but she had a tube down her throat for several hours each day and it left her throat too sore to swallow anything but liquid. Garp ate a few cherries while Charlotte enumerated the parts of her body that had been removed. Her sex parts, she thought, and much of her digestive tract, and something that had to do with the process of elimination. 'Oh, and my breasts, I think,' she said, the whites of her eyes very gray and her hands held above her chest where she flattered herself to imagine her breasts used to be. To Garp it appeared that they had not touched her breasts; under the sheet, there was still something there. But he later thought that Charlotte had been such a lovely woman that she could hold her body in such a way as to inspire the *illusion* of breasts.

'Thank God I've got money,' Charlotte said. 'Isn't this a Class A place?'

Garp nodded. The next day he brought a bottle of wine; the hospital was very relaxed about liquor and visitors; perhaps this was one of the luxuries one paid for. 'Even if I got out,' Charlotte said, 'what could I do? They cut my purse out.' She tried to drink some wine, then fell asleep. Garp asked a nurse's aide to explain what Charlotte meant by her 'purse,' though he thought he knew. The nurse's aide was Garp's age, nineteen or maybe younger, and she blushed and looked away from him when she translated the slang.

A purse was a prostitute's word for her vagina.

'Thank you,' Garp said.

Once or twice when he visited Charlotte he encountered her two colleagues, who were shy and girlish with Garp in the daylight of Charlotte's sunny room. The young one who spoke English was named Wanga; she had cut her lip that way as a child when she tripped while running home from the store with a jar of mayonnaise. 'We were on a picnic going,' she explained, 'but my whole family had me instead to the hospital to bring.'

The riper, sulkish woman with the peach pit pockmark on her forehead, and the breasts like two full pails, did not offer to explain *her* scar; she was the notorious 'Tina,' for whom nothing was too 'funny.'

Occasionally Garp ran into Herr Doktor Thalhammer there, and once he walked with Thalhammer to Thalhammer's car; they happened to be leaving the hospital together. 'Do you want a lift?' Thalhammer offered him, pleasantly. In the car was a pretty young schoolgirl whom Thalhammer introduced to Garp as his daughter. They all talked easily about *Die Vereinigten Staaten* and Thalhammer assured Garp it was no trouble to drive Garp all the way to his doorstep at the Schwindgasse. Thalhammer's daughter reminded Garp of Helen, but he could not even imagine asking to see the girl again; that her father had recently treated him for clap seemed to Garp to be an insurmountable awkwardness – despite Thalhammer's optimism that people can adjust to *anything*. Garp doubted that Thalhammer could have adjusted to that.

All around Garp, now, the city looked ripe with dying. The teeming parks and gardens reeked of decay to him, and the subject of the great painters in the great museums was always death. There were always cripples and old people riding the No. 38 Strassenbahn out to Grinzinger Allee, and the heady flowers planted along the pruned paths of the courtyard in the Rudolfinerhaus reminded Garp only of funeral parlors. He recalled the pensions he and Jenny had stayed in when they first arrived, over a year ago: the faded and unmatched wallpaper, the dusty bric-a-brac, the chipped china, the hinges crying for oil. 'In the life of a man,' wrote Marcus Aurelius, 'his time is but a moment . . . his body a prey of worms . . .'

The young nurse's aide whom Garp had embarrassed by asking about Charlotte's 'purse' was increasingly snotty to him. One day when he arrived early, before visitors were permitted, she asked him a little too aggressively what he was to Charlotte, anyway. A member of the family? She had seen Charlotte's other visitors – her gaudy colleagues – and she assumed Garp was just an old hooker's customer. 'She's my mother,' Garp said; he didn't know why, but he appreciated the shock of the young nurse's aide, and her subsequent respect.

'What did you tell them?' Charlotte whispered to him, a few days later. 'They think you're my *son*.' He confessed his lie; Charlotte confessed she had done nothing to correct it. 'Thank you,' she whispered. 'It's nice to trick the swine. They think they're so superior.' And mustering her former and fading lewdness, she said, 'I'd let you have it once for free, if I still had the equipment. Maybe twice for half price,' she said.

He was touched and cried in front of her.

'Don't be a baby,' she said. 'What *am* I to you, really?'

When she was asleep, he read on her hospital chart that she was fifty-one.

She died a week later. When Garp went to her room, it was whisked clean, the bed stripped back, the windows wide open. When he asked for her, there was a nurse in charge of the floor whom he didn't recognize – an iron-gray maiden who kept shaking her head. 'Fräulein Charlotte,' Garp said. 'She was Herr Doktor Thalhammer's patient.'

'He has lots of patients,' said the iron-gray maiden. She was consulting a list, but Garp did not know Charlotte's real name. Finally, he could think of no other way to identify her.

'The whore,' he said. 'She was a whore.' The gray woman regarded him coolly; if Garp could detect no satisfaction in her expression, he could detect no sympathy either.

'The prostitute is dead,' the old nurse said. Perhaps Garp only imagined that he heard a little triumph in her voice.

'One day, *meine Frau*,' he said to her, 'you will be dead, too.'

And that, he thought – leaving the Rudolfinerhaus – was a properly Viennese thing to say. Take that, you old gray city, you dead bitch, he thought.

He went to his first opera that night; to his surprise, it was in Italian, and since he understood none of it, he took the whole performance to be a kind of religious service. He walked in the night to the lit spires of Saint Stephen's; the south tower of the cathedral, he read on some plaque, was started in the middle of the fourteenth century and completed in 1439. Vienna, Garp thought, was a cadaver; all Europe, maybe, was a dressed-up corpse in an open coffin. 'In the life of a man,' wrote Marcus Aurelius, 'his time is but a moment . . . his fortune dark . . .'

In this mood Garp walked home on the Kärntnerstrasse, where he met the notorious Tina. Her deep pockmark, harboring the neon of the city lights, was a greenish blue.

'*Guten Abend*, Herr Garp,' she said. 'Guess what?'

Tina explained that Charlotte had bought Garp a favor.

The favor was that Garp could have Tina and Wanga for free; he could have them one at a time or both together, Tina explained. Together, Tina thought, was more interesting – and quicker. But perhaps Garp did not like both of them. Garp admitted that Wanga did not appeal to him; she was too close to his own age, and though he would never say this if she were here and her feelings could be hurt, he did not care for the way the mayonnaise jar had pulled her lip askew.

'Then you can have me twice,' Tina said, cheerfully. 'Once now, and once,' she added, 'after you've had a long time to catch your breath. Forget Charlotte,' Tina said. Death happened to everyone, Tina explained. Even so, Garp politely declined the offer.

'Well, it's here,' Tina said. 'When you want it.' She reached out and frankly cupped him in her warm palm; her big hand was an ample codpiece for him, but Garp only smiled and bowed to her – as the Viennese do – and walked home to his mother.

He enjoyed his slight pain. He took pleasure in this silly self-denial – and more pleasure in his *imagination* of Tina, he suspected, than he ever could have derived from her vaguely gross flesh. The silvery gouge on her forehead was nearly as big as her mouth; her pockmark looked to Garp like a small, open grave.

What Garp was savoring was the beginning of a writer's long-sought trance, wherein the world falls under one embracing tone of voice. 'All that is body is as coursing waters,' Garp remembered, 'all that is of the soul as dreams and vapors.' It was July when Garp went back to work on 'The Pension Grillparzer.' His mother was finishing up the manuscript that would soon change both their lives.

It was August when Jenny finished her book and announced that *she* was ready to travel, to at last see something of Europe – maybe Greece? she suggested. 'Let's take the train somewhere,' she said. 'I always wanted to take the Orient Express. Where's it go?'

'From Paris to Istanbul, I think,' Garp said. 'But *you* take it, Mom. I've got too much work to do.'

Tit for tat, Jenny had to admit. She was so sick of *A Sexual Suspect* that she couldn't even proofread it one more time. She didn't even know what to do with it, now; did one just go to New York and hand over one's life story to a stranger? She wanted Garp to read it, but she saw that Garp was at last engrossed in a task of his own; she felt she shouldn't bother him. Besides, she was unsure; a large part of her life story was *his* life story, too – she thought the story might upset him.

Garp worked through August on the conclusion of his short story, 'The Pension Grillparzer.' Helen, exasperated, wrote to Jenny. 'Is Garp dead?' she asked. 'Kindly send details.' That Helen Holm is a bright girl, Jenny thought. Helen got more of an answer than she counted on. Jenny sent her a copy of the manuscript of *A Sexual Suspect* with a note explaining that this was what she'd been doing all year, and now Garp was writing something, too. Jenny said she would appreciate Helen's candid opinion of the manuscript. Perhaps, said Jenny, some of Helen's college teachers would know what one *did* with a finished book?

Garp relaxed, when he wasn't writing, by going to the zoo; it was a part of the great grounds and gardens surrounding the Schönbrunn Palace. It appeared to Garp that many of the buildings in the zoo were war ruins, three-quarters destroyed; they had been partially restored to house the animals. This gave Garp the eerie impression that the zoo still existed in Vienna's war period; it also interested him in the period. To fall asleep at night he took to reading some very specific, historical accounts of Vienna during the Nazi and the Russian occupations. This was not unrelated to the death themes that haunted his writing of 'The Pension Grillparzer.' Garp discovered that when you are writing something, everything seems related to everything else. Vienna was dying, the zoo was not as well restored from the war damage as the homes the *people* lived in; the history of a city was like the history of a family – there is closeness, and even affection, but death eventually separates everyone from each other. It is only the vividness of memory that keeps the dead alive forever; a writer's job is to imagine everything so personally that the fiction is as vivid as our personal memories. He felt the holes from the machine-gun fire in the stone walls of the lobby of the apartment on the Schwindgasse.

Now he knew what the grandmother's dream meant.

He wrote Helen that a young writer needs desperately to live with someone and he had decided that he wanted to live with her; even *marry* her, he offered, because sex was simply necessary but it took too much of one's time if one had to be constantly *planning* how one was going to get it. Therefore, Garp reasoned, it is better to live with it!

Helen revised several letters before she finally sent him one that said he could, so to speak, go stick it in his ear. Did he think she was going through college so rigorously so that she could provide him with sex that was not even necessary to *plan?*

He did not revise, at all, his letter back to her; he said he was too busy writing to take the time to explain it to her; she would have to read what he was working on and judge for herself how serious he was.

'I don't doubt that you're quite serious,' she told him. 'And right now I have more to read than I need to know.'

She did not tell him that she was referring to Jenny's book, *A Sexual Suspect*; it was 1,158 manuscript pages long. Though Helen would later agree with Garp that it was no literary jewel, she had to admit that it was a very compelling story.

While Garp put the finishing touches on his much shorter story, Jenny Fields plotted her next move. In her restlessness she had bought an American news magazine at a large Vienna newsstand; in it she had read that a courageous New York editor at a well-known publishing house had just rejected the manuscript submitted by an infamous former member

of the government who had been convicted of stealing
government money. The book was a thinly disguised 'fiction'
of the criminal's own sordid, petty, political dealings. 'It was
a lousy novel,' the editor was quoted as saying. 'The man
can't write. Why should he make any money off his crummy
life?' The book, of course, would be published elsewhere,
and it would eventually make its despicable author and
its publisher lots of money. 'Sometimes I feel it is my
responsibility to say no,' the editor was quoted as saying,
'even if I know people *do* want to read this slop.' The slop,
eventually, would be treated to several serious reviews, just
as if it were a serious book, but Jenny was greatly impressed
with the editor who had said no and she clipped the article
out of the news magazine. She drew a circle around the
editor's name – a plain name, almost like an actor's name,
or the name of an animal in a children's book: John Wolf.
There was a picture of John Wolf in the magazine; he looked
like a man who took care of himself, and he was very well
dressed; he looked like any number of people who work
and live in New York – where good business and good
sense suggest that you'd *better* take care of yourself and dress
as well as you can – but to Jenny Fields he looked like an
angel. He was going to be *her* publisher, she was sure. She
was convinced that *her* life was *not* 'crummy,' and that John
Wolf would believe she deserved to make money off it.

Garp had other ambitions for 'The Pension Grillparzer.'
It would never make him much money; it would first
appear in a 'serious' magazine where almost no one would
read it. Years later, when he was better known, it would be
published in a more attentive way, and several appreciative
things would be written about it, but in his lifetime 'The
Pension Grillparzer' wouldn't make Garp enough money to
buy a good car. Garp, however, expected more than money
or transportation from 'The Pension Grillparzer.' Very
simply, he expected to get Helen Holm to live with him –
even marry him.

When he finished 'The Pension Grillparzer,' he announced

to his mother that he wanted to go home and see Helen; he would send her a copy of the story and she could have read it by the time he arrived back in the United States. Poor Helen, Jenny thought; Jenny knew that Helen had a lot to read. Jenny also worried how Garp referred to Steering as 'home'; but she had reasons of her own for wanting to see Helen, and Ernie Holm would not mind their company for a few days. There was always the parental mansion at Dog's Head Harbor – if Garp and Jenny needed a place to recover, or to make their plans.

Garp and Jenny were such singularly obsessed people that they did not pause to wonder why they had seen so little of Europe, and now they were leaving. Jenny packed her nursing uniforms. There remained, in Garp's mind, only the favors that Charlotte had left up to Tina's devising.

Garp's imagination of these favors had sustained him during the writing of 'The Pension Grillparzer,' but as he would learn all his life, the demands of writing and of real life are not always similar. His imagination sustained him when he was writing; now that he *wasn't* writing, he wanted Tina. He went to look for her on the Kärntnerstrasse, but the mayonnaise-jar whore, who spoke English, told him that Tina had moved from the first district.

'So goes it,' Wanga said. 'Forget Tina.'

Garp found that he *could* forget her; lust, as his mother called it, was tricky that way. And time, he discovered, had softened his dislike of Wanga's mayonnaise-jar lip; suddenly, he liked it. And so he had *her*, twice, and as he would learn all his life, nearly everything seems a letdown after a writer has finished writing something.

Garp and Jenny had spent fifteen months in Vienna. It was September. Garp and Helen were only nineteen, and Helen would be going back to college very soon. The plane flew from Vienna to Frankfurt. The slight tingling (that was Wanga) quietly left Garp's flesh. When Garp thought of Charlotte, he imagined that Charlotte had been happy. After all, she had never had to leave the first district.

The plane flew from Frankfurt to London; Garp reread 'The Pension Grillparzer' and hoped that Helen would not turn him down. From London to New York, Jenny read her son's story. In terms of what *she'd* spent more than a year doing, Garp's story struck Jenny as rather unreal. But her taste for literature was never keen and she marveled at her son's imagination. Later she would say that 'The Pension Grillparzer' was just the sort of story she'd expect a boy without a proper family to make up.

Maybe so. Helen would later say that it is in the conclusion of 'The Pension Grillparzer' that we can glimpse what the world according to Garp would be like.

THE PENSION GRILLPARZER [*Conclusion*]

In the breakfast room of the Pension Grillparzer we confronted Herr Theobald with the menagerie of his other guests who had disrupted our evening. I knew that (as never before) my father was planning to reveal himself as a Tourist Bureau spy.

'Men walking about on their hands,' said Father.

'Men looking under the door of the W.C.,' said Grandmother.

'*That* man,' I said, and pointed to the small, sulking fellow at the corner table, seated for breakfast with his cohorts – the dream man and the Hungarian singer.

'He does it for his living,' Herr Theobald told us, and as if to demonstrate that this was so, the man who stood on his hands began to stand on his hands.

'Make him stop that,' Father said. 'We know he can do it.'

'But did you know that he can't do it any other way?' the dream man asked suddenly. 'Did you know his legs were useless? He has no shinbones. It is *wonderful* that he can walk on his hands! Otherwise, he wouldn't walk at all.' The man, although it was clearly hard to do while standing on his hands, nodded his head.

'Please sit down,' Mother said.

'It is perfectly all right to be crippled,' Grandmother said, boldly. 'But *you* are evil,' she told the dream man. 'You know things you have no right to know. He knew my *dream*,' she told Herr Theobald, as if she were reporting a theft from her room.

'He is a *little* evil, I know,' Theobald admitted. 'But not usually! And he behaves better and better. He can't help what he knows.'

'I was just trying to straighten you out,' the dream man told Grandmother. 'I thought it would do you good. Your husband has been dead quite a while, after all, and it's about time you stopped making so much of that dream. You're not the only person who's had such a dream.'

'Stop it,' Grandmother said.

'Well, you ought to know,' said the dream man.

'No, be quiet, please,' Herr Theobald told him.

'I am from the Tourist Bureau,' Father announced, probably because he couldn't think of anything else to say.

'Oh my God shit!' Herr Theobald said.

'It's not Theobald's fault,' said the singer. 'It's *our* fault. He's nice to put up with us, though it costs him his reputation.'

'They married my sister,' Theobald told us. 'They are *family*, you see. What can I do?'

'"They" married your sister?' Mother said.

'Well, she married *me* first,' said the dream man.

'And then she heard *me* sing!' the singer said.

'She's never been married to the *other* one,' Theobald said, and everyone looked apologetically toward the man who could only walk on his hands.

Theobald said, 'They were once a circus act, but politics got them in trouble.'

'We were the best in Hungary,' said the singer. 'You ever hear of the Circus Szolnok?'

'No, I'm afraid not,' Father said, seriously.

'We played in Miskolc, in Szeged, in Debrecen,' said the dream man.

'*Twice* in Szeged,' the singer said.

'We would have made it to Budapest if it hadn't been for the Russians,' said the man who walked on his hands.

'Yes, it was the Russians who removed his shinbones!' said the dream man.

'Tell the truth,' the singer said. 'He was *born* without shinbones. But it's true that we couldn't get along with the Russians.'

'They tried to jail the bear,' said the dream man.

'Tell the truth,' Theobald said.

'We rescued his sister from them,' said the man who walked on his hands.

'So of course I must put them up,' said Herr Theobald, 'and they work as hard as they can. But who's interested in their act in this country? It's a Hungarian thing. There's no *tradition* of bears on unicycles here,' Theobald told us. 'And the damn dreams mean nothing to us Viennese.'

'Tell the truth,' said the dream man. 'It is because I have told the wrong dreams. We worked a nightclub on the Kärntnerstrasse, but then we got banned.'

'You should never have told *that* dream,' the singer said gravely.

'Well, it was your wife's responsibility, too!' the dream man said.

'She was *your* wife, then,' the singer said.

'Please stop it,' Theobald begged.

'We get to do the balls for children's diseases,' the dream man said. 'And some of the state hospitals – especially at Christmas.'

'If you would only do more with the bear,' Herr Theobald advised them.

'Speak to your sister about that,' said the singer. 'It's *her* bear – she's trained him, she's let him get lazy and sloppy and full of bad habits.'

'He is the only one of you who never makes fun of me,' said the man who could only walk on his hands.

'I would like to leave all this,' Grandmother said. 'This is, for me, an awful experience.'

'Please, dear lady,' Herr Theobald said, 'we only wanted to show you that we meant no offense. These are hard times. I need the B rating to attract more tourists, and I can't – in my heart – throw out the Circus Szolnok.'

'*In his heart,* my ass!' said the dream man. 'He's afraid of his sister. He wouldn't dream of throwing us out.'

'If he dreamed it, you would know it!' cried the man on his hands.

'I am afraid of the *bear*,' Herr Theobald said. 'It does everything she tells it to do.'

'Say "he," not "it,"' said the man on his hands. 'He is a fine bear, and he never hurt anybody. He has no claws, you know perfectly well – and very few teeth, either.'

'The poor thing has a terribly hard time eating,' Herr Theobald admitted. 'He is quite old, and he's messy.'

Over my father's shoulder, I saw him write in the giant pad: 'A depressed bear and an unemployed circus. This family is centered on the sister.'

At that moment, out on the sidewalk, we could see her tending to the bear. It was early morning and the street was not especially busy. By law, of course, she had the bear on a leash, but it was a token control. In her startling red turban the woman walked up and down the sidewalk, following the lazy movements of the bear on his unicycle. The animal pedaled easily from parking meter to parking meter, sometimes leaning a paw on the meter as he turned. He was very talented on the unicycle, you could tell, but you could also tell that the unicycle was a dead end for him. You could see that the bear felt he could go no further with unicycling.

'She should bring him off the street now,' Herr Theobald fretted. 'The people in the pastry shop next door complain to me,' he told us. 'They say the bear drives their customers away.'

'That bear makes the customers *come!*' said the man on his hands.

'It makes some people come, it turns some away,' said the dream man. He was suddenly somber, as if his profundity had depressed him.

But we had been so taken up with the antics of the Circus Szolnok that we had neglected old Johanna. When my mother saw that Grandmother was quietly crying, she told me to bring the car around.

'It's been too much for her,' my father whispered to Theobald. The Circus Szolnok looked ashamed of themselves.

Outside on the sidewalk the bear pedaled up to me and handed me the keys; the car was parked at the curb. 'Not everyone likes to be given the keys in that fashion,' Herr Theobald told his sister.

'Oh, I thought he'd rather like it,' she said, rumpling my hair. She was as appealing as a barmaid, which is to say that she was more appealing at night; in the daylight I could see that she was older than her brother, and older than her husbands too – and in time, I imagined, she would cease being lover and sister to them, respectively, and become a mother to them all. She was already a mother to the bear.

'Come over here,' she said to him. He pedaled listlessly in place on his unicycle, holding on to a parking meter for support. He licked the little glass face of the meter. She tugged his leash. He stared at her. She tugged again. Insolently, the bear began to pedal – first one way, then the next. It was as if he took interest, seeing that he had an audience. He began to show off.

'Don't try anything,' the sister said to him, but the bear pedaled faster and faster, going forward, going backward, angling sharply and veering among the parking meters; the sister had to let go of the leash. 'Duna, stop it!' she cried, but the bear was out of control. He let the wheel roll too close to the curb and the unicycle pitched him hard into the fender of a parked car. He sat on the sidewalk with the unicycle beside him; you could tell that he hadn't injured himself, but he looked very embarrassed and nobody laughed. 'Oh, Duna,' the sister said, scoldingly, but she went over and crouched beside him at the curb. 'Duna, Duna,' she reproved him, gently. He shook his big head; he would not look at her. There was some saliva strung on the fur near his mouth and she wiped this away with her hand. He pushed her hand away with his paw.

'Come back again!' cried Herr Theobald, miserably, as we got into our car.

Mother sat in the car with her eyes closed and her fingers massaging her temples; this way she seemed to hear nothing we said. She claimed it was her only defense against traveling with such a contentious family.

I did not want to report on the usual business concerning the care of the car, but I saw that Father was trying to maintain order and calm; he had the giant pad spread on his lap as if we'd just completed a routine investigation. 'What does the gauge tell us?' he asked.

'Someone put thirty-five kilometers on it,' I said.

'That terrible bear has been in here,' Grandmother said. 'There are hairs from the beast on the backseat, and I can *smell* him.'

'I don't smell anything,' Father said.

'And the perfume of that gypsy in the turban,' Grandmother said. 'It is hovering near the ceiling of the car.' Father and I sniffed. Mother continued to massage her temples.

On the floor by the brake and clutch pedals I saw several of the mint-green toothpicks that the Hungarian singer was in the habit of wearing like a scar at the corner of his mouth. I didn't mention them. It was enough to imagine them all – out on the town, in our car. The singing driver, the man on his hands beside him – waving out the window with his feet. And in back, separating the dream man from his former wife – his great head brushing the upholstered roof, his mauling paws relaxed in his large lap – the old bear slouched like a benign drunk.

'Those poor people,' Mother said, her eyes still closed.

'Liars and criminals,' Grandmother said. 'Mystics and refugees and broken-down animals.'

'They were trying hard,' Father said, 'but they weren't coming up with the prizes.'

'Better off in a zoo,' said Grandmother.

'I had a good time,' Robo said.

'It's hard to break out of Class C,' I said.

'They have fallen past Z,' said old Johanna. 'They have disappeared from the human alphabet.'

'I think this calls for a letter,' Mother said.

But Father raised his hand – as if he were going to bless us – and we were quiet. He was writing in the giant pad and wished to be undisturbed. His face was stern. I knew that Grandmother felt confident of his verdict. Mother knew it was useless to argue. Robo was already bored. I steered us off through the tiny streets; I took Spiegelgasse to Lobkowitzplatz. Spiegelgasse is so narrow that you can see the reflection of your own car in the windows of the shops you pass, and I felt our movement through Vienna was superimposed (like that) – like a trick with a movie camera, as if we made a fairy-tale journey through a toy city.

When Grandmother was asleep in the car, Mother said, 'I don't suppose that in this case a change in the classification will matter very much, one way or another.'

'No,' Father said, 'not much at all.' He was right about that, though it would be years until I saw the Pension Grillparzer again.

When Grandmother died, rather suddenly and in her sleep, Mother announced that she was tired of traveling. The real reason, however, was that she began to find herself plagued by Grandmother's dream. 'The horses are so thin,' she told me, once. 'I mean, I always knew they would be thin, but not *this* thin. And the soldiers – I knew they were miserable,' she said, 'but not *that* miserable.'

Father resigned from the Tourist Bureau and found a job with a local detective agency specializing in hotels and department stores. It was a satisfactory job for him, though he refused to work during the Christmas season – when, he said, some people ought to be allowed to steal a little.

My parents seemed to me to relax as they got older, and I really felt they were fairly happy near the end. I know that the strength of Grandmother's dream was dimmed by the *real* world, and specifically by what happened to Robo. He went to a private school and was well liked there, but he was killed by a home-made bomb in his first year at the university. He was not even 'political.' In his last letter to my parents he wrote: 'The self-seriousness of the radical factions among the students is much overrated. And the food is execrable.' Then Robo went to his history class, and his classroom was blown apart.

It was after my parents died that I gave up smoking and took up traveling again. I took my second wife back to the Pension Grillparzer. With my first wife, I never got as far as Vienna.

The Grillparzer had not kept Father's B rating very long, and it had fallen from the ratings altogether by the time I returned to it. Herr Theobald's sister was in charge of the place. Gone was her tart appeal and in its place was the sexless cynicism of some maiden aunts. She was shapeless and her hair was dyed a sort of bronze, so that her head resembled one of those copper scouring pads that you use on a pot. She did not remember me and was suspicious of my questions. Because I appeared to know so much about her past associates, she probably knew I was with the police.

The Hungarian singer had gone away – another woman thrilled by his voice. The dream man had been *taken* away – to an institution. His own dreams had turned to nightmares and he'd awakened the pension each night with his horrifying howls. His removal from the seedy premises, said Herr Theobald's sister, was almost simultaneous with the loss of the Grillparzer's B rating.

Herr Theobald was dead. He had dropped down clutching his heart in the hall, where he ventured one night to investigate what he thought was a prowler. It was only Duna, the malcontent bear, who was dressed in the dream man's pin-striped suit. Why Theobald's sister had dressed the bear in this fashion was not explained to me, but the shock of the sullen animal unicycling in the lunatic's left-behind clothes had been enough to scare Herr Theobald to death.

The man who could only walk on his hands had also fallen into the gravest trouble. His wristwatch snagged on a tine of an escalator and he was suddenly unable to hop off; his necktie, which he rarely wore because it dragged on the ground when he walked on his hands, was drawn under the step-off grate at the end of the escalator – where he was strangled. Behind him a line of people formed – marching in place by taking one step back and allowing the escalator to carry them forward, then taking

another step back. It was quite a while before anyone got up the
nerve to step over him. The world has many unintentionally
cruel mechanisms that are not designed for people who walk on
their hands.

After that, Theobald's sister told me, the Pension Grillparzer
went from Class C to much worse. As the burden of management
fell more heavily on her, she had less time for Duna and the
bear grew senile and indecent in his habits. Once he bullied
a mailman down a marble staircase at such a ferocious pace
that the man fell and broke his hip; the attack was reported
and an old city ordinance forbidding unrestrained animals in
places open to the public was enforced. Duna was outlawed at
the Pension Grillparzer.

For a while, Theobald's sister kept the bear in a cage in
the courtyard of the building, but he was taunted by dogs and
children, and food (and worse) was dropped into his cage from
the apartments that faced the courtyard. He grew unbearlike
and devious – only pretending to sleep – and he ate most of
someone's cat. Then he was poisoned twice and became afraid
to eat anything in this perilous environment. There was no
alternative but to donate him to the Schönbrunn Zoo, but there
was even some doubt as to his acceptability. He was toothless
and ill, perhaps contagious, and his long history of having been
treated as a human being did not prepare him for the gentler
routine of zoo life.

His outdoor sleeping quarters in the courtyard of the
Grillparzer had inflamed his rheumatism, and even his one
talent, unicycling, was irretrievable. When he first tried it in
the zoo, he fell. Someone laughed. Once anyone laughed at
something Duna did, Theobald's sister explained, Duna would
never do that thing again. He became, at last, a kind of charity
case at Schönbrunn, where he died a short two months after he'd
taken up his new lodgings. In the opinion of Theobald's sister,
Duna died of mortification – the result of a rash that spread over
his great chest, which then had to be shaved. A shaved bear,
one zoo official said, is embarrassed to death.

In the cold courtyard of the building I looked in the bear's empty cage. The birds hadn't left a fruit seed, but in a corner of his cage was a looming mound of the bear's ossified droppings – as void of life, and even odor, as the corpses captured by the holocaust at Pompeii. I couldn't help thinking of Robo; of the bear, there were more remains.

In the car I was further depressed to notice that not one kilometer had been added to the gauge, not one kilometer had been driven in secret. There was no one around to take liberties anymore.

'When we're a safe distance away from your precious Pension Grillparzer,' my second wife said to me, 'I'd like you to tell me why you brought me to such a shabby place.'

'It's a long story,' I admitted.

I was thinking I had noticed a curious lack of either enthusiasm or bitterness in the account of the world by Theobald's sister. There was in her story the flatness one associates with a storyteller who is accepting of unhappy endings, as if her life and her companions had never been exotic to *her* – as if they had always been staging a ludicrous and doomed effort at reclassification.

7

More Lust

And so she married him; she did what he asked. Helen thought it was a pretty good story for a start. Old Tinch liked it, too. 'It is rich with lu-lu-lunacy and sorrow,' Tinch told Garp. Tinch recommended that Garp send 'The Pension Grillparzer' to Tinch's favorite magazine. Garp waited three months for this reply:

> The story is only mildly interesting, and it does nothing new with language or with form. Thanks for showing it to us, though.

Garp was puzzled and he showed the rejection to Tinch. Tinch was also puzzled.

'I guess they're interested in n-n-*newer* fiction,' Tinch said.

'What's that?' Garp asked.

Tinch admitted he didn't really know. 'The new fiction is interested in language and in f-f-form, I guess,' Tinch said. 'But I don't understand what it's really about. Sometimes it's about it-it-itself, I think,' Tinch said.

'About itself?' Garp said.

'It's sort of fiction about fi-fi-*fiction*,' Tinch told him.

Garp still didn't understand, but what mattered to Garp was that Helen liked the story.

Almost fifteen years later, when Garp published his third novel, that same editor at Tinch's favorite magazine would write Garp a letter. The letter would be very flattering to Garp, and to his work, and it would ask Garp to submit anything *new* he might have written to Tinch's favorite magazine. But T. S. Garp had a tenacious memory and the indignation of a badger. He found the old rejection note that had called his Grillparzer story 'only mildly interesting'; the note was crusty with coffee stains and had been folded so many times that it was torn at the creases, but Garp enclosed it with a letter to the editor at Tinch's favorite magazine. Garp's letter said:

> I am only mildly interested in your magazine, and I am still doing nothing new with language or with form. Thanks for asking me, though.

Garp had a foolish ego that went out of its way to remember insults to and rejections of his work. It is fortunate for Helen that she had a ferocious ego of her own, for if she hadn't highly esteemed herself, she would have ended up hating him. As it was, they were lucky. Many couples live together and discover they're not in love; some couples never discover it. Others marry, and the news comes to them at awkward moments in their lives. In the case of Garp and Helen, they hardly knew each other but they had their hunches – and in their stubborn, deliberate ways they fell in love with each other sometime after they had married.

Perhaps because they were so busy pursuing their singular careers they did not overscrutinize their relationship. Helen would graduate from college two years after she began; she would have a Ph.D. in English literature when she was only twenty-three, and her first job – an assistant professor at a women's college – when she was twenty-four. It would take Garp five years to finish his first novel, but it would be a good novel and it would earn him a respectable reputation for a young writer – even if it wouldn't make him any money. By then, Helen would be making money for them. All the time that Helen went to school, and Garp was writing, Jenny took care of the money.

Jenny's book was more of a shock to Helen, when she first read it, than it was to Garp – who, after all, had lived with his mother and was unsurprised by her eccentricity; it had become commonplace to him. Garp, however, *was* shocked by the book's success. He had not counted on becoming a public figure – a leading character in someone else's book before he'd even written a book of his own.

The editor, John Wolf, would never forget the first morning at his office where he met Jenny Fields.

'There's a nurse to see you,' his secretary said, rolling her eyes – as if this might be a paternity suit that her boss had on his hands. John Wolf and his secretary could not have known that a manuscript of 1,158 typed pages was what made Jenny's suitcase so heavy.

'It's about me,' she told John Wolf, opening her suitcase and hefting the monster manuscript to the top of his desk. 'When can you read it?' It looked to John Wolf as if the woman intended to stay in his office *while* he read it. He glanced at the first sentence ('In this dirty-minded world . . .'), and he thought: Oh boy, how do I get rid of *this* one?

Later, of course, he was panic-stricken when he could not find a phone number for her; when he wanted to tell her that yes! – they would certainly publish *this!* – he could not have known that Jenny Fields was the proper guest of Ernie Holm at Steering, where Jenny and Ernie talked into the night, every night (the usual parental concern when parents discover that their nineteen-year-old children plan to get married).

'Where can they go every night?' Jenny asked. 'They don't come back here until two or three, and last night it rained. It rained all night, and they don't even have a car.'

They went to the wrestling room. Helen, of course, had a key. And a wrestling mat was as comfortable and familiar to them as any bed. And much bigger.

'They say they want children,' Ernie complained. 'Helen should finish her education.'

'Garp will never finish a book, with children,' Jenny said.

After all, she was thinking that she'd had to wait eighteen years to *begin* her book.

'They're both hard workers,' Ernie said, to reassure himself and Jenny.

'They'll *have* to be,' Jenny said.

'I don't know why they can't just *live* together,' Ernie said. 'And if it works out, *then* let them get married; then let them have a baby.'

'I don't know why *any*one wants to live with anyone else,' said Jenny Fields. Ernie looked a little hurt.

'Well, you like Garp living with you,' he reminded her, 'and I like Helen living with me. I really miss her when she's away at school.'

'It's *lust*,' Jenny said, ominously. 'The world is sick with lust.'

Ernie felt worried about her; he didn't know she was about to become rich and famous forever. 'Do you want a beer?' he asked Jenny.

'No, thank you,' Jenny said.

'They're good kids,' Ernie reminded her.

'But lust gets them all, in the end,' said Jenny Fields, morosely, and Ernie Holm walked delicately to his kitchen and opened another beer for himself.

It was the 'lust' chapter of *A Sexual Suspect* that especially embarrassed Garp. It was one thing to be a famous child born out of wedlock, quite another to be a famous case history of adolescent need – his private randiness become a popular story. Helen thought it was very funny, though she confessed to not understanding his attraction to whores.

'Lust makes the best of men behave out of character,' wrote Jenny Fields – a line that particularly infuriated Garp.

'What the hell does *she* know about it?' he screamed. 'She never felt it, not once. Some authority *she* is! It's like listening to a plant describe the motives of a mammal!'

But other reviewers were kinder to Jenny; though the more serious journals occasionally chided her for her actual writing, the media, in general, felt warmly toward the book. 'The first truly feminist autobiography that is as full of celebrating one kind of life as it is full of putting down another,' somebody wrote. 'This brave book makes the important assertion that a woman can have a whole life without a sexual attachment of *any* kind,' wrote somebody else.

'These days,' John Wolf had forewarned Jenny, 'you're either going to be taken as the right voice at the right time, or you're going to be put down as all wrong.' She was taken as the right voice at the right time, but Jenny Fields, sitting whitely in her nurse's uniform – in the restaurant where John Wolf took only his favorite writers – felt discomfort at the word *feminism*. She was not sure what it meant, but the *word* reminded her of feminine hygiene and the Valentine treatment. After all, her formal training had been nursing. She said shyly that she'd only thought she made the right choice about how to live her life, and since it had not been a popular choice, she'd felt goaded into saying something to defend it. Ironically, a rash of young women at Florida State University in Tallahassee found Jenny's choice *very* popular; they generated a small controversy by plotting their own pregnancies. For a while, in New York, this syndrome among singular-minded women was called 'doing a Jenny Fields.' But Garp always called it 'doing a Grillparzer.' As for Jenny, she felt only that women – just like men – should at least be able to make conscious decisions about the course of their lives; if that made her a feminist, she said, then she guessed she *was* one.

John Wolf liked Jenny Fields very much, and he did what he could to warn her that she might not understand either the attacks or the praise her book would receive. But Jenny never wholly understood how 'political' a book it was – or how it would be used as such a book.

'I was trained to be a nurse,' she said later, in one of her disarming interviews. 'Nursing was the first thing I took to, and the first thing I ever wanted to do. It simply seemed very practical, to me, for someone who was healthy – and I have always been healthy – to help people who weren't healthy or who couldn't help themselves. I think it was simply in that spirit that I wanted to write a book, too.'

In Garp's opinion, his mother never stopped being a nurse. She had nursed him through the Steering School; she had been a plodding midwife to her own strange life story; finally, she became a kind of nurse to women with problems. She became a figure of famous strength; women sought her advice. With the sudden success of *A Sexual Suspect*, Jenny Fields uncovered a nation of women who faced making choices about how to live; these women felt encouraged by Jenny's own example of making unpopular decisions.

She could have started an advice column for any newspaper, but Jenny Fields felt through with writing, now – just as she'd decided, once before, that she was through with education; just as she'd decided she was through with Europe. In a way, she was *never* through with nursing. Her father, the shocked shoe king, died of a heart attack shortly after the publication of *A Sexual Suspect*; although Jenny's mother never blamed Jenny's book for the tragedy – and Jenny never blamed herself – Jenny knew that her mother could not live alone. Unlike Jenny Fields, Jenny's mother had developed a habit of living with someone else; she was old now, and Jenny thought of her as rattling about in the great rooms at Dog's Head Harbor, purposeless and wholly without her few remaining wits in the absence of her mate.

Jenny went to care for her, and it was at the Dog's Head Harbor mansion that Jenny first began her role as counselor to the women who sought some comfort from her no-nonsense ability to make decisions.

'Even *weird* decisions!' Garp wailed, but he was happy, and taken care of. He and Helen had their first child, almost immediately. It was a boy named Duncan. Garp often joked that the reason his first novel was written with so many short chapters was because of Duncan. Garp wrote between feedings and naps and changes of diapers. 'It was a novel of short takes,' he claimed, later, 'and the credit is wholly

Duncan's.' Helen was at school every day; she had agreed
to have a child only if Garp would agree to take care of it.
Garp loved the idea of never having to go out. He wrote and
took care of Duncan; he cooked and wrote and took care
of Duncan some more. When Helen came home, she came
home to a reasonably happy homemaker; as long as Garp's
novel progressed, no routine, however mindless, could upset
him. In fact, the more mindless, the better. He left Duncan
for two hours every day with the woman in the downstairs
apartment; he went to the gym. He later became an oddity
at the women's college where Helen taught – running
endless laps around the field hockey field, or jumping rope
for half an hour in a corner of the gymnasium reserved for
gymnastics. He missed wrestling and complained to Helen
that she should have gotten a job somewhere where there
was a wrestling team; Helen complained that the English
Department was too small, and she disliked having no male
students in her classes, but it was a good job and she would
keep it until something better came along.

Everything in New England is at least near everything else.
They got to visit Jenny at the shore and Ernie at Steering.
Garp would take Duncan to the Steering wrestling room
and roll him around like a ball. 'This is where your daddy
wrestled,' he told him.

'It's where your daddy did *everything*,' Helen told Duncan,
referring – of course – to Duncan's own conception, and
to her first rainy night with Garp in the locked and empty
Seabrook Gymnasium, on the warm crimson mats stretch-
ing wall to wall.

'Well, you finally got me,' Helen had whispered to him,
tearfully, but Garp had sprawled there, on his back on the
wrestling mat, wondering who had gotten *whom*.

When Jenny's mother died, Jenny visited Helen and Garp
more frequently, though Garp objected to what he called his
mother's 'entourage.' Jenny Fields traveled with a small core
of adorers, or with occasional other figures who felt they

were part of what would be called the women's movement; they often wanted Jenny's support or her endorsement. There was often a case or a cause that needed Jenny's pure white uniform on the speaker's platform, although Jenny rarely spoke very much or for very long.

After the other speeches, they would introduce the author of *A Sexual Suspect*. In her nurse's uniform, she was instantly recognizable. Into her fifties, Jenny Fields would remain an athletically attractive woman, crisp and plain. She would rise and say, 'This is right.' Or, sometimes, 'This is wrong' – depending on the occasion. She was the decision maker who'd made the hard choices in her own life and therefore she could be counted on to be on the right side of a woman's problem.

The logic behind all this made Garp fume and stew for days, and once an interviewer from a women's magazine asked if she could come interview him about what it was like to be the son of a famous feminist. When the interviewer discovered Garp's chosen life, his 'housewife's role,' as she gleefully called it, Garp blew up at her.

'I'm doing what I want to do,' he said. 'Don't call it by any other name. I'm just doing what I want to do – and that's all my mother ever did, too. Just what *she* wanted to do.'

The interviewer pressed him; she said he sounded bitter. Of course, it must be hard, she suggested, being an unknown writer with a mother whose book was known around the world. Garp said it was mainly painful to be misunderstood, and that he did not resent his mother's success; he only occasionally disliked her new associates. 'Those stooges who are living off her,' he said.

The article in the women's magazine pointed out that *Garp* was also 'living off' his mother, very comfortably, and that he had no right to be hostile toward the women's movement. That was the first time Garp heard of it: 'the women's movement.'

It was not many days after this that Jenny came to visit him. One of her goons, as Garp called them, was with her:

a large, silent, sullen woman who lurked in the doorway of Garp's apartment and declined to take her coat off. She looked warily at little Duncan, as if she awaited, with extreme displeasure, the moment when the child might touch her.

'Helen's at the library,' Garp told Jenny. 'I was going to take Duncan for a walk. You want to come?' Jenny looked questioningly at the big woman with her; the woman shrugged. Garp thought that his mother's greatest weakness, since her success, was to be, in his words, 'used by all the crippled and infirm women who wished they'd written *A Sexual Suspect*, or something equally successful.'

Garp resented standing cowed in his own apartment by his mother's speechless companion, a woman large enough to be his mother's bodyguard. Perhaps that's what she is, he thought. And an unpleasant image of his mother with a tough dyke escort crossed his mind – a vicious killer who would keep the men's hands off Jenny's white uniform.

'Is there something the matter with that woman's *tongue*, Mom?' Garp whispered to Jenny. The superiority of the big woman's silence outraged him; Duncan was trying to talk with her, but the woman merely fixed the child with a quieting eye. Jenny quietly informed Garp that the woman wasn't talking because the woman was without a tongue. Literally.

'It was cut off,' Jenny said.

'Jesus,' Garp whispered. 'How'd it happen?'

Jenny rolled her eyes; it was a habit she'd picked up from her son. 'You really read nothing, don't you?' Jenny asked him. 'You just never have bothered to keep up with what's going on.' What was 'going on,' in Garp's opinion, was never as important as what he was making up – what he was working on. One of the things that upset him about his mother (since she'd been adopted by women's politics) was that she was always discussing the *news*.

'This is *news*, you mean?' Garp said. 'It's such a famous tongue accident that I should have heard about it?'

'Oh, God,' Jenny said wearily. 'Not a famous accident. Very deliberate.'

'Mother, did someone cut her tongue off?'

'Precisely,' Jenny said.

'Jesus,' Garp said.

'You haven't heard of Ellen James?' Jenny asked.

'No,' Garp admitted.

'Well, there's a whole *society* of women now,' Jenny informed him, 'because of what happened to Ellen James.'

'What happened to her?' Garp asked.

'Two men raped her when she was eleven years old,' Jenny said. 'Then they cut her tongue off so she couldn't tell anyone who they were or what they looked like. They were so stupid that they didn't know an eleven-year-old could *write*. Ellen James wrote a very careful description of the men, and they were caught, and they were tried and convicted. In jail, someone murdered them.'

'Wow,' Garp said. 'So *that's* Ellen James?' he whispered, indicating the big quiet woman with new respect.

Jenny rolled her eyes again. 'No,' she said. 'That is someone from the Ellen James *Society*. Ellen James is still a child; she's a wispy-looking little blond girl.'

'You mean this Ellen James Society goes around not talking,' Garp said, 'as if *they* didn't have any tongues?'

'No, I mean they *don't* have any tongues,' Jenny said. 'People in the Ellen James Society have their tongues cut *off*. To protest what happened to Ellen James.'

'Oh boy,' Garp said, looking at the large woman with renewed dislike.

'They call themselves Ellen Jamesians,' Jenny said.

'I don't want to hear any more of this shit, Mom,' Garp said.

'Well, that woman there is an Ellen Jamesian,' Jenny said. 'You wanted to know.'

'How old is Ellen James now?' Garp asked.

'She's twelve,' Jenny said. 'It happened only a year ago.'

'And these Ellen Jamesians,' Garp asked, 'do they have meetings, and elect presidents and treasurers and stuff like that?'

'Why don't you ask her?' Jenny said, indicating the lunk by the door. 'I thought you didn't want to hear any more about it.'

'How can I ask her if she doesn't have a tongue to answer me?' Garp hissed.

'She *writes*,' Jenny said. 'All Ellen Jamesians carry little notepads around with them and they *write* you what they want to say. You know what writing is, don't you?'

Fortunately, Helen came home.

Garp would see more of the Ellen Jamesians. Although he felt deeply disturbed by what had happened to Ellen James, he felt only disgust at her grown-up, sour imitators whose habit was to present you with a card. The card said something like:

Hello, I'm Martha. I'm an Ellen Jamesian. Do you know what an Ellen Jamesian is?

And if you didn't know, you were handed another card.

The Ellen Jamesians represented, for Garp, the kind of women who lionized his mother and sought to use her to help further their crude causes.

'I'll tell you something about those women, Mom,' he said to Jenny once. 'They were probably all lousy at talking, anyway; they probably never had a worthwhile thing to say in their lives – so their tongues were no great sacrifice; in fact, it probably saves them considerable embarrassment. If you see what I mean.'

'You're a little short on sympathy,' Jenny told him.

'I have *lots* of sympathy – for Ellen James,' Garp said.

'These women must have suffered, in other ways, themselves,' Jenny said. 'That's what makes them want to get closer to each other.'

'And inflict more suffering on themselves, Mom?'

'Rape is every woman's problem,' Jenny said. Garp hated his mother's 'everyone' language most of all. A case, he thought, of carrying democracy to an idiotic extreme.

'It's every man's problem, too, Mom. The next time there's a rape, suppose I cut my *prick* off and wear it around my neck. Would you respect *that*, too?'

'We're talking about *sincere* gestures,' Jenny said.

'We're talking about *stupid* gestures,' Garp said.

But he would always remember his first Ellen Jamesian – the big woman who came to his apartment with his mother; when she left, she wrote Garp out a note and slipped it into his hand as if it were a tip.

'Mom's got a new bodyguard,' Garp whispered to Helen as they waved good-bye. Then he read the bodyguard's note.

Your mother is worth 2 of you,

the note said.

But he couldn't really complain about his mother; for the first five years Garp and Helen were married, Jenny paid their bills.

Garp joked that he called his first novel *Procrastination* because it had taken him so long to write it, but he had worked on it steadily and carefully; Garp was rarely a procrastinator.

The novel was called 'historical.' It is set in the Vienna of the war years, 1938–45, and through the period of the Russian occupation. The main character is a young anarchist who has to lie low, after the Anschluss, waiting for just the right blow he can strike against the Nazis. He waits too long. The point being, he should better have struck before the Nazi takeover; but there is nothing he can be sure of, then, and he is too young to recognize what is happening. Also, his mother – a widow – cherishes her private life; unconcerned with politics, she hoards her dead husband's money.

Through the war years, the young anarchist works as a zookeeper at Schönbrunn. When the population of Vienna begins seriously starving, and midnight raids on the zoo are a common source of stolen food, the anarchist decides to liberate the remaining animals – who are, of course, innocent of his country's own procrastination and its acquiescence to Nazi Germany. But by then the animals themselves are starving; when the anarchist frees them, they eat him. 'That was only natural,' Garp wrote. The animals, in turn, are slaughtered easily by a starving mob now roaming Vienna for food – just ahead of the Russian forces. That, too, was 'only natural.'

The anarchist's mother survives the war and lives in the Russian zone of occupation (Garp gave her the same apartment he and his mother shared on the Schwindgasse); the miserly widow's tolerance is finally wearied by the repeated atrocities she now sees committed by the Soviets – rape, chief among them. She watches the city restored to moderation and complacency, and she remembers her own inertia during the Nazi rise to power with great regret. Finally, the Russians leave; it is 1956, and Vienna retreats into itself again. But the woman mourns her son and her damaged country; she strolls the partially rebuilt and once again healthy zoo at Schönbrunn every weekend, recalling her secretive visits to her son there, during the war. It is the Hungarian Revolution that prompts the old lady's final action. Hundreds of thousands of new refugees come into Vienna.

In an effort to awaken the complacent city – that it must not sit back and watch things develop again – the mother tries to do what her son did: she releases the animals in the Schönbrunn Zoo. But the animals are well fed and content now; only a few of them can even be goaded into leaving their cages, and those who do wander out are easily confined in the Schönbrunn paths and gardens; eventually they're returned to their cages, unharmed. One elderly bear suffers a bout of violent diarrhea. The old woman's gesture of liberation is well intended but it is completely meaningless and totally unrealized. The old woman is arrested and an examining police doctor discovers that she has cancer; she is a terminal case.

Finally, and ironically, her hoarded money is of some use to her. She dies in luxury – in Vienna's only private hospital, the Rudolfinerhaus. In her death dream she imagines that some animals escape from the zoo: a couple of young Asiatic Black Bears. She imagines them surviving and multiplying so successfully that they become famous as a new animal species in the valley of the Danube.

But this is only her imagination. The novel ends – after the old woman's death – with the death of the diarrhetic bear in the Schönbrunn Zoo. 'So much for revolution in modern times,' wrote one reviewer, who called *Procrastination* 'an anti-Marxist novel.'

The novel was praised for the accuracy of its historical research – a point of no particular interest to Garp. It was also cited for originality and for having unusual scope for a first novel by such a young author. John Wolf had been Garp's publisher, and although he had agreed with Garp *not* to mention on the jacket flap that this was the first novel by the son of the feminist heroine Jenny Fields, there were few reviewers who failed to sound that chime.

'It is amazing that the now-famous son of Jenny Fields,' wrote one, 'has actually grown up to be what he said he wanted to be when he grew up.' This, and other irrelevant cuteness concerning Garp's relationship to Jenny, made Garp very angry that his book couldn't be read and discussed for its own faults and/or merits, but John Wolf explained to him the hard fact that most readers were probably more interested in who he was than in what he'd actually written.

'Young Mr Garp is still writing about bears,' chided one wit, who'd been energetic enough to uncover the Grillparzer story from its obscure publication. 'Perhaps, when he grows up, he'll write something about people.'

But altogether, it was a literary debut more astonishing than most – and more noticed. It was, of course, never a popular book, and it hardly made T. S. Garp into a brand name; it would not make him 'the household product' – as he called her – that his mother had become. But it was not that kind of book; he was not that kind of writer, and never would be, John Wolf told him.

'What do you expect?' John Wolf wrote him. 'If you want to be rich and famous, get in another line. If you're serious about it, don't bitch. You wrote a serious book, it was published seriously. If you want to make a *living* off it, you're talking about another world. And remember: you're twenty-four years old. I think you'll write a lot more books.'

John Wolf was an honorable and intelligent man, but Garp wasn't sure – and he wasn't content. He had made a little money, and now Helen had a salary; now that he didn't *need* Jenny's money, Garp felt all right about accepting some when she simply gave it out. And he felt he'd at least earned another reward to himself: he asked Helen to have another baby. Duncan was four; he was old enough to appreciate a brother or a sister. Helen agreed, knowing how easy Garp had made it for her to have Duncan. If he wanted to change diapers between the chapters of his next book, that was up to him.

But it was actually more than merely wanting a second child that prompted Garp to reproduce again. He knew he was an overwatchful, worrisome father and he felt he might relieve Duncan of some of the pressure of fatherly fears if there was *another* child to absorb some of Garp's excess anxiety.

'I'm very happy,' Helen told him. 'If you want another baby, we'll make one. I just wish you'd *relax,* I wish you'd be happier. You wrote a good book, now you'll write another one. Isn't it just what you always wanted?'

But he bitched about the reviews of *Procrastination,* and he moaned about the sales. He carped at his mother, and roared about her 'sycophantic friends.' Finally Helen said to him, 'You want too much. Too much unqualified praise, or love – or *something* that's unqualified, anyway. You want the world to say, "I love your writing, I love you," and that's too much to want. That's really sick, in fact.'

'That's what *you* said,' he reminded her. '"I love your writing, I love you." That's exactly what you said.'

'But there can only be one of me,' Helen reminded him.

Indeed, there would only be one of her, and he loved her very much. He would always call her 'the wisest of my life's decisions.' He made some unwise decisions, he would admit; but in the first five years of his marriage to Helen, he was unfaithful to her only once – and it was brief.

It was a babysitter from the college where Helen taught, a freshman girl from Helen's Freshman English class; she was nice with Duncan, though Helen said that the girl was not a very special student. Her name was Cindy; she had read Garp's *Procrastination*, and she'd been properly awed. When he drove her home, she would ask him one question after another about his writing: How did you think of THAT? and what made you do it THIS way? She was a tiny thing, all flutters and twitches and coos – as trusting, as constant, and as stupid as a Steering pigeon. 'Little Squab Bones,' Helen called her, but Garp was attracted; he called her nothing. The Percy family had given him a permanent dislike of nicknames. And he liked Cindy's questions.

Cindy was dropping out of school because she felt a women's college was not right for her; she needed to live with grown-ups, and with men, she said, and although the college allowed her to move off-campus – into her own apartment, in the second semester of her freshman year – still she felt the college was too 'restricted' and she wanted to live in a 'more real environment.' She imagined that Garp's Vienna had been a 'more real environment,' though Garp struggled to assure her that it had not been. Little Squab Bones, Garp thought, was puppy-brained, and as soft and as easily influenced as a banana. But he wanted her, he realized, and he saw her as simply available – like the whores on the Kärntnerstrasse, she would be there when he asked her. And she would cost him only lies.

Helen read him a review from a famous news magazine; the review called *Procrastination* 'a complex and moving novel with sharp historic resonances . . . the drama encompasses the longings and agonies of youth.'

'Oh *fuck* "the longings and agonies of youth,"' Garp said. One of those youthful longings was embarrassing him now.

As for the 'drama': in the first five years of his marriage to Helen, T. S. Garp experienced only one real-life drama, and it did not have that much to do with him.

Garp had been running in the city park when he found the girl, a naked ten-year-old running ahead of him on the bridle path. When she realized he was gaining on her, she fell down and covered her face, then covered her crotch, then tried to hide her insubstantial breasts. It was a cold day, late fall, and Garp saw the blood on the child's thighs and her frightened, swollen eyes. She screamed and screamed at him.

'What happened to you?' he asked, though he knew very well. He looked all around them, but there was no one there. She hugged her raw knees to her chest and screamed. 'I won't hurt you,' Garp said. 'I want to help you.' But the child wailed even louder. My God, of course! Garp thought: the terrible molester had probably said those very words to her, not long ago. 'Where did he go?' Garp asked her. Then he changed his tone, trying to convince her he was on her side. 'I'll kill him for you,' he told her. She stared quietly at him, her head shaking and shaking, her fingers pinching and pinching the tight skin on her arms. 'Please,' Garp said, 'can you tell me where your clothes are?' He had nothing to give her to wear except his sweaty T-shirt. He was dressed in his running shorts, his running shoes. He pulled his T-shirt off over his head and felt instantly cold; the girl cried out, awfully loud, and hid her face. 'No, don't be frightened, it's for you to put on,' Garp told her. He let the T-shirt drop on her but she writhed out from under it and kicked at it; then she opened her mouth very wide and bit her own fist.

'She was not old enough to be Boy or Girl yet,' Garp

wrote. 'Only in the pudginess around her nipples was there anything faintly girlish. There was certainly no visible sex about her hairless pudenda, and she had a child's sexless hands. Perhaps there was something sensual about her mouth – her lips were puffy – but she had not done that to herself.'

Garp began to cry. The sky was gray, dead leaves were all around them, and when Garp began to wail aloud, the girl picked up his T-shirt and covered herself with it. They were in this queer position to each other – the child crouched under Garp's T-shirt, cringing at Garp's feet with Garp crying over her – when the mounted park police, a twosome, rode up the bridle path and spotted the apparent child molester with his victim. Garp wrote that one of the policemen split the girl and Garp apart by steering his horse between them, 'nearly trampling the girl.' The other policeman brought his billy down on Garp's collarbone; one side of his body, he wrote, felt paralyzed – 'but not the other.' With 'the other,' Garp unseated the policeman and tipped him from the saddle. 'It's not *me*, you son of a bitch!' Garp howled. 'I just found her, just here – just a minute ago.'

The policeman, sprawled in the leaves, held his drawn gun very still. The other policeman, mounted and prancing, shouted to the girl. 'Is it *him*?' he yelled. The child seemed terrified of the horses. She stared back and forth from the horses to Garp. She probably isn't sure what *happened*, Garp thought – much less who. But the girl, violently, shook her head. 'Where'd he go?' said the policeman on his horse. But the girl still looked at Garp. She tugged her chin and rubbed her cheeks – she tried to talk to him with her hands. Apparently, her words were gone; or her *tongue*, Garp thought, recalling Ellen James.

'It's the *beard*,' said the cop in the leaves; he had gotten to his feet but he had not holstered his gun. 'She's telling us there was a beard.' Garp had a beard then.

'It was *someone* with a beard,' said Garp. 'Like *mine*?' he asked the girl, stroking his dark, round beard, glossy with sweat. But she shook her head and ran her fingers over her sore upper lip.

'A mustache!' cried Garp, and the girl nodded.

She pointed back the way Garp had come, but Garp remembered seeing no one near the entrance to the park. The policeman hunched on his horse and through the thrown leaves he rode away from them. The other policeman was calming his horse, but he had not remounted. 'Cover her, or find her clothes,' Garp said to him; he started to run down the bridle path after the first policeman; he knew there were things you could see from ground level that you couldn't see on a horse. Also, Garp was such a fool about his running that he imagined he could outlast, if not outrun, any horse.

'Hey, you better wait here!' the policeman called after him, but Garp was in stride and clearly not stopping.

He followed the great rents in the ground that the horse had made. He had not gone even half a mile back along the path before he saw the bent figure of a man, maybe twenty-five yards off the path and almost hidden by the trees. Garp yelled at the figure, an elderly gentleman with a white mustache, who looked over his shoulder at Garp with an expression so surprised and ashamed that Garp was sure he'd found the child molester. He thundered through the vines and small, whiplike trees to the man, who had been peeing and was hastening to fold himself back into his trousers. He looked very much like a man caught doing something he shouldn't have done.

'I was just . . .' the man began, but Garp was upon him and thrust his stiff, cropped beard into the man's face. Garp sniffed him over like a hound.

'If it's you, you bastard, I can *smell* it on you!' Garp said. The man flinched away from this half-naked brute, but Garp seized both the man's wrists and snapped the man's hands up under his nose. He sniffed again, and the man cried out as if he feared Garp was going to bite him. 'Hold still!' Garp said. 'Did you do it? Where are the child's clothes?'

'Please!' the man piped. 'I was just going to the bathroom.'

He had not had time to close his fly and Garp eyed his crotch suspiciously.

'There is no smell like sex,' Garp wrote. 'You cannot disguise it. It is as rich and clear as spilled beer.'

So Garp dropped to his knees in the woods and unbuckled the man's belt and tore open the man's pants and yanked the man's undershorts straight down to the man's ankles; he stared at the man's frightened equipment.

'Help!' the old gentleman screamed. Garp took a deep sniff and the man collapsed in the young trees; staggering like a puppet strung under the arms, he thrashed in a thicket of slender trunks and branches too dense to allow him to fall. 'Help, *God!*' he cried, but Garp was already running back out to the bridle path, his legs digging through the leaves, his arms pummeling the air, his struck collarbone throbbing.

At the entrance to the park the mounted policeman clattered about the parking lot, peering in parked cars, circling the squat brick hut where the restrooms were. A few people watched him, sensing his eagerness. 'No mustaches,' the policeman called to Garp.

'If he got back here before you did, he could have driven away,' Garp said.

'Go look in the men's room,' the policeman said, riding toward a woman with a baby carriage piled high with blankets.

Every men's room made Garp remember every W.C.; at the door to this sour place, Garp passed a young man who was just leaving. He was clean-shaven, his upper lip so smooth that it almost shone; he looked like a college kid. Garp entered the men's room like a dog with his hair standing up on the back of his neck and his hackles curling. He checked for feet under the crapper-stall doors; he would not have been surprised to see a pair of hands – or a bear. He looked for backs turned toward him at the long urinal – or for anyone at the dirty brown sinks, peering into the pitted mirrors. But there was no one in the men's room.

Garp sniffed. He had worn a full but trimmed beard for a long time and the smell of shaving cream was not instantly recognizable to him. He just knew he smelled something foreign to this dank place. Then he looked in the nearest sink: he saw the gobs of lather, he saw the whiskers rimming the bowl.

The young, clean-shaven man who looked like a college kid was crossing the parking lot, quickly but calmly, when Garp came out the men's room door. 'It's *him!*' Garp hollered. The mounted cop looked at the young molester, puzzled.

'*He* doesn't have a mustache,' the policeman said.

'He just shaved it off!' Garp cried; he ran across the lot, straight at the kid, who began to run toward the maze of paths lacing the park. A litter of things flew out from under his jacket as he ran: Garp saw the scissors, a razor, a shaving cream can, and then came the little batches of clothes – the girl's, of course. Her jeans with a ladybug sewn at the hip, a jersey with the beaming face of a frog on the breast. Of course there was no bra; there was no need. It was her panties that got to Garp. They were simply cotton, and a simple blue; stitched at the waistband was a blue flower, sniffed at by a blue bunny.

The mounted policeman simply rode over the kid who was running away. The chest of the horse pounded the kid face forward into the cinder entry path and one rear hoof took a U-shaped bite of flesh out of the kid's calf; he curled, fetal, on the ground, holding his leg. Garp came up then, the girl's blue-bunny panties in his hand; he gave them to the mounted cop. Other people – the woman with the blanketed carriage, two boys on bikes, a thin man carrying a newspaper – approached them. They brought the cop the other things the kid had dropped. The razor, the rest of the girl's clothes. Nobody spoke. Garp wrote later that at that moment he saw the short history of the young child molester spread out at the horse's hooves: the scissors, the shaving cream can. Of course! The kid would grow a mustache, attack a child, shave the mustache (which would be all most children would remember).

'Have you done this before?' Garp asked the kid.

'You're not supposed to ask him anything,' the policeman said.

But the kid grinned stupidly at Garp. 'I've never been *caught* before,' he told him, cockily. When he smiled, Garp saw that the young man had no upper front teeth; the horse had kicked them out. There was just a bleeding flap of gum. Garp realized that something had probably happened to this kid so that he didn't *feel* very much – not much pain, not much of anything else.

Out of the woods at the end of the bridle path the second policeman came walking his horse – the child in the saddle, covered by the policeman's coat. She clutched Garp's T-shirt in her hands. She did not seem to recognize anybody. The policeman led her right up to where the molester lay on the ground, but she didn't really look at him. The first policeman dismounted; he went to the molester and tilted his bleeding face up toward the child. 'Him?' he asked her. She stared at the young man, blankly. The molester gave a short laugh, spat out a mouthful of blood; the child made no response. Then Garp gently touched his finger to the molester's mouth; with the blood on his finger, Garp lightly smeared a mustache on the young man's upper lip. The child began to scream and scream. The horses needed quieting. The child kept screaming until the second policeman took the molester away. Then she stopped screaming and gave Garp back his T-shirt. She kept patting the thick ridge of black hair on the back of the horse's neck as if she had never been on a horse before.

Garp thought it must have hurt her to sit on horseback, but suddenly she asked, 'Can I have another ride?' Garp was at least glad to hear that she had a tongue.

It was then that Garp saw the nattily dressed, elderly gentleman whose mustache had been innocent; he was making his meek way out of the park, coming cautiously into the parking lot, looking anxiously about for the madman who'd so savagely snatched his pants down and sniffed him like some dangerous omnivore. When the man saw Garp standing beside the policeman, he seemed relieved – he assumed Garp had been apprehended – and he more boldly walked toward them. Garp contemplated running – to avoid the confusion, the explanation – but just then the policeman said, 'I have to get your name. And what it is that you do. Besides run in the park.' He laughed.

'I'm a writer,' Garp told him. The policeman was apologetic that he hadn't heard of Garp, but at the time Garp hadn't published anything except 'The Pension Grillparzer'; there was very little the policeman *could* have read. This seemed to puzzle the policeman.

'An unpublished writer?' he asked. Garp was rather glum about it. 'Then what do you do for a living?' the policeman said.

'My wife and my mother support me,' Garp admitted.

'Well, I have to ask you what *they* do,' the policeman said. 'For the record, we like to know how everyone makes a living.'

The offended gentleman with the white mustache, who had overheard only the last bits of this interrogation, said, 'Just as I would have thought! A vagrant, a despicable bum!'

The policeman stared at him. In his early, unpublished years Garp felt angry whenever he was forced to admit how he had enough to live on; he felt more like inviting confusion at this moment than he felt moved to clear things up.

'I'm glad to see you've caught him, anyway,' the old gentleman said. 'This used to be a nice park, but the people who get in here these days – you ought to patrol it more closely,' he told the policeman, who guessed that the old man was referring to the child molester. The cop didn't want the business discussed in front of the child, so he rolled his eyes up toward her – she sat rigid in the saddle – and tried to indicate to the old gentleman why he shouldn't continue.

'Oh no, he didn't do it to that *child!*' the man cried, as if he'd just noticed her, mounted beside him, or just noticed she was not dressed under the policeman's coat – her small clothes hugged in her arms. 'How vile!' he cried, glaring at Garp. 'How disgusting! You'll want my name, of course?' he asked the policeman.

'What for?' the policeman said. Garp had to smile.

'Look at him smirking there!' the old man cried. 'Why, as a *witness*, of course – I'd tell my story to any court in the country, if it could condemn such a man as that!'

'But what were you a witness to?' the policeman said.

'Why, he did that . . . thing . . . to *me*, too!' the man said.

The policeman looked at Garp; Garp rolled his eyes. The policeman still clung to the sanity that the old gentleman was referring to the child molester, but he didn't understand why Garp was being treated with such abuse. 'Well, sure,' the policeman said, to humor the old fool. He took his name and address.

Months later Garp was buying a package of three prophylactics when this same old gentleman walked into the drugstore.

'What?! It's *you!*' the old man shouted. 'They let you out already, did they? I thought they'd put you away for *years!*'

It took Garp a moment to recognize the person. The druggist assumed that the old codger was a lunatic. The gentleman in his trimmed, white mustache advanced cautiously on Garp.

'What's the law coming to?' he asked. 'I suppose you're out on good behavior? No old men or young girls to *sniff* in prison, I suppose! Or some lawyer got you off on some slick technicality? That poor child traumatized for all her years and you're free to roam the parks!'

'You've made a mistake,' Garp told him.

'Yes, this is Mr Garp,' the druggist said. He didn't add, 'the writer.' If he'd considered adding anything, Garp knew, it would have been 'the hero,' because the druggist had seen the ludicrous newspaper headlines about the crime and capture in the park.

UNSUCCESSFUL WRITER NO FAILURE AS HERO!
CITIZEN CATCHES PARK PERVERT;
SON OF FAMOUS FEMINIST HAS KNACK FOR HELPING
GIRLS . . .

Garp was unable to write for months because of it, but the article impressed all the locals who knew Garp only from the supermarket, the gymnasium, the drugstore. In the meantime, *Procrastination* had been published – but almost no one seemed to know. For weeks, clerks and salespeople would introduce him to other customers: 'Here's Mr Garp, the one who nabbed that molester in the park.'

'What molester?'

'That one in city park. The Mustache Kid. He went after little girls.'

'Children?'

'Well, Mr Garp here is the one who got him.'

'Well, actually,' Garp would say, 'it was the policeman on his horse.'

'Knocked all his teeth down his throat, too!' they would crow with delight – the druggist and the clerk and the salespeople here and there.

'Well, that was actually the horse,' Garp admitted, modestly.

And sometimes someone would ask, 'And what is it you *do*, Mister Garp?'

The following silence would pain Garp, as he stood thinking that it was probably best to say that he *ran* – for a living. He cruised the parks, a molester-nabber by profession. He hung around phone booths, like that man in the cape – waiting for disasters. Any of this would make more sense to them than what he really did.

'I write,' Garp would finally admit. Disappointment – even suspicion – all over their once-admiring faces.

In the drugstore – to make matters worse – Garp *dropped* the package of three prophylactics.

'A-*ha!*' the old man cried. 'Look there! What's he up to with those?'

Garp wondered what options there were for what he *could* be up to with those.

'A pervert on the loose,' the old man assured the druggist. 'Looking for innocence to violate and defile!'

The old geezer's self-righteousness was irritating to the point that Garp had no desire to settle the misunderstanding; in fact, he rather enjoyed the memory of unpantsing the old bird in the park and he was not in the least sorry for the accident.

It was some time later when Garp realized that the old gentleman had no monopoly on self-righteousness. Garp took Duncan to a high school basketball game and was appalled that the ticket-taker was none other than the Mustache Kid – the real molester, the attacker of that helpless child in the city park.

'You're *out*,' Garp said, amazed. The pervert smiled openly at Duncan.

'One adult, one kiddy,' he said, tearing off tickets.

'How'd you ever get free?' Garp asked; he felt himself tremble with violence.

'Nobody proved nothing,' the kid said, haughtily. 'That dumb girl wouldn't even *talk.*' Garp thought again of Ellen James with her tongue cut off at eleven.

He felt a sudden sympathy for the madness of the old man he had so unpleasantly unpantsed. He felt such a terrible sense of injustice that he could even imagine some very unhappy woman despairing enough to cut off her own tongue. He knew that he wanted to hurt the Mustache Kid, on the spot – in front of Duncan. He wished he could arrange a maiming as a kind of moral lesson.

But there was a crowd wanting basketball tickets; Garp was holding things up.

'Move along, hair pie,' the kid said to Garp. In the kid's

expression, Garp thought he recognized the leer of the world. On the kid's upper lip was the insipid evidence that he was growing *another* mustache.

It was *years* later when he saw the child, a girl grown up; it was only because she recognized him that he recognized her. He was coming out of a movie theater in another town; she was in the line waiting to come in. Some of her friends were with her.

'Hello, how are you?' Garp asked. He was glad to see she had friends. That meant, to Garp, that she was normal.

'Is it a good movie?' the girl asked.

'You've certainly grown!' Garp said; the girl blushed and Garp realized what a stupid thing he'd said. 'Well, I mean it's been a long time – and it was a time well worth forgetting!' he added, heartily. Her friends were moving inside the movie theater and the girl gave a quick look after them to make sure she was really alone with Garp.

'Yes, I'm graduating this month,' she said.

'High school?' Garp wondered aloud. Could it have been *that* long ago?

'Oh no, *junior* high,' the girl said, laughing nervously.

'Wonderful!' Garp said. And without knowing why, he said, 'I'll try to come.'

But the girl looked suddenly stricken. 'No, please,' she said. '*Please* don't come.'

'Okay, I won't,' Garp agreed quickly.

He saw her several times after this meeting, but she never recognized him again because he shaved off his beard. 'Why don't you grow another beard?' Helen occasionally asked him. 'Or at least a mustache.' But whenever Garp encountered the molested girl, and escaped unrecognized, he was convinced he should remain clean-shaven.

'I feel uneasy,' Garp wrote, 'that my life has come in contact with so much rape.' Apparently, he was referring to the ten-year-old in the city park, to the eleven-year-old Ellen James and her terrible society – his mother's wounded women with their symbolic, self-inflicted speechlessness. And later he would write a novel, which would make Garp more of 'a household product,' which would have much to do with rape. Perhaps rape's offensiveness to Garp was that it was an act that disgusted him with himself – with his own very male instincts, which were otherwise so unassailable. He never felt like raping anyone; but rape, Garp thought, made men feel guilt by association.

In Garp's own case, he likened his guilt for the seduction of Little Squab Bones to a rapelike situation. But it was hardly a rape. It was deliberate, though. He even bought the condoms weeks in advance, knowing what he would use them for. Are not the worst crimes premeditated? It would not be a sudden passion for the babysitter that Garp would succumb to; he would plan, and be ready when Cindy succumbed to *her* passion for him. It must have given him a twinge, then, to *know* what those rubbers were for when he dropped them in front of the gentleman from the city park and heard the old man accuse him: 'Looking for innocence to violate and defile!' How true.

Still, he arranged obstacles in the path of his desire for the girl; he twice hid the prophylactics, but he also remembered where he'd hidden them. And the day of the last evening that Cindy would babysit for them, Garp made desperate love to Helen in the late afternoon. When they should have been dressing for dinner, or fixing Duncan's supper, Garp locked the bedroom and wrestled Helen out of her closet.

'Are you crazy?' she asked him. 'We're going out.'

'Terrible lust,' he pleaded. 'Don't deny it.'

She teased him. '*Please,* sir, I make a point of never doing it before the hors d'oeuvres.'

'*You're* the hors d'oeuvres,' Garp said.

'Oh, *thanks,*' said Helen.

'Hey, the door's locked,' Duncan said, knocking.

'Duncan,' Garp called, 'go tell us what the weather is doing.'

'The weather?' Duncan said, trying to force the bedroom door.

'I think it's snowing in the backyard!' Garp called. 'Go see.'

Helen stifled her laughter, and her other sounds, against his hard shoulder; he came so quickly he surprised her. Duncan trotted back to the bedroom door, reporting that it was springtime in the backyard, and everywhere else. Garp let him in the bedroom now that he was finished.

But he wasn't finished. He knew it – driving home with Helen from the party, he knew exactly where the rubbers were: under his typewriter, quiet these dull months since the publication of *Procrastination*.

'You look tired,' Helen said. 'Want me to take Cindy home?'

'No, that's okay,' he mumbled. 'I'll do it.'

Helen smiled at him and nuzzled her cheek against his mouth. 'My wild afternoon lover,' she whispered. 'You can *always* take me out to dinner that way, if you like.'

He sat a long time with Little Squab Bones in the car outside her dark apartment. He had chosen the time well – the college was letting out; Cindy was leaving town. She was already upset at having to say good-bye to her favorite writer; he was, at least, the only writer she'd actually met.

'I'm sure you'll have a good year, next year, Cindy,' he said. 'And if you come back to see anyone, please stop and see us. Duncan will miss you.' The girl stared into the cold lights of the dashboard, then looked over at Garp, miserably – tears and the whole flushed story on her face.

'I'll miss *you*,' she whined.

'No, no,' Garp said. '*Don't* miss me.'

'I *love* you,' she whispered, and let her slim head bump awkwardly against his shoulder.

'No, don't say that,' he said, not touching her. Not yet.

The three-pack of condoms nestled patiently in his pocket, coiled like snakes.

In her musty apartment, he used only one of them. To his

surprise, all her furniture had been moved out; they jammed her lumpy suitcases together and made an uncomfortable bed. He was careful not to stay a second more than necessary, lest Helen think he'd spent too long a time for even a *literary* good-bye.

A thick swollen stream ran through the women's college grounds and Garp discarded the remaining two prophylactics there, throwing them furtively out the window of his moving car – imagining that an alert campus cop might have seen him and would already be scrambling down the bank to retrieve the evidence: the rubbers plucked out of the current! The discovered weapon that leads back to the crime for which it was used.

But no one saw him, no one found him out. Even Helen, already asleep, would not have found the smell of sex peculiar; after all, only hours before, he had legitimately acquired the odor. Even so, Garp showered, and slipped cleanly into his own safe bed; he curled against Helen, who murmured some affection; instinctively, she thrust one long thigh over his hip. When he failed to respond, she forced her buttocks back against him. Garp's throat ached at her trust, and at his love for her. He felt fondly the slight swell of Helen's pregnancy.

Duncan was a healthy, bright child. Garp's first novel had at least made him what he said he wanted to be. Lust still troubled Garp's young life, but he was fortunate that his wife still lusted for him, and he for her. Now a second child would join their careful, orderly adventure. He felt Helen's belly anxiously – for a kick, a sign of life. Although he'd agreed with Helen that it would be nice to have a girl, Garp *hoped* for another boy.

Why? he thought. He recalled the girl in the park, his image of the tongueless Ellen James, his own mother's difficult decisions. He felt fortunate to be with Helen; she had her own ambitions and he could not manipulate her. But he remembered the Kärntnerstrasse whores, and Cushie Percy (who would die making a baby). And now – her scent still on him, or at least on his mind, although he had washed – the plundered Little Squab Bones. Cindy had cried under him, her back bent against a suitcase. A blue vein had pulsed at her temple, which was the translucent temple of a fair-skinned child. And though Cindy still had her tongue, she'd been *unable* to speak to him when he left her.

Garp didn't want a daughter because of *men*. Because of *bad* men, certainly; but even, he thought, because of men like *me*.

8

Second Children, Second Novels,
Second Love

It was a boy; their second son. Duncan's brother was called
Walt – it was never Walter, and never the German *Valt*; he
was simply a *t* at the end of a wall. Walt: like a beaver's tail
smacking water, like a well-hit squash ball. He dropped into
their lives and they had two boys.

Garp tried to write a second novel. Helen took her second
job; she became an associate professor of English at the state
university, in the town next-door to the women's college.
Garp and his boys had a boys' gym to play in, and Helen
had an occasional bright graduate student to relieve her of
the monotony of younger people; she also had more, and
more interesting, colleagues.

One of them was Harrison Fletcher; his field was the
Victorian Novel, but Helen liked him for other reasons –
among them: he was also married to a writer. Her name
was Alice; she was also working on her second novel,
although she'd never finished her first. When the Garps
met her, they thought she could easily be mistaken for an
Ellen Jamesian – she simply didn't talk. Harrison, whom
Garp called Harry, had never been called Harry before
– but he liked Garp and he appeared to enjoy his new
name as if it were a present Garp had given him. Helen
would continue to call him Harrison, but to Garp he was
Harry Fletcher. He was Garp's first friend, though Garp

and Harrison both sensed that Harrison preferred Helen's company.

Neither Helen nor Garp knew what to make of Quiet Alice, as they called her. 'She must be writing one hell of a book,' Garp often said. 'It's taken all her words away.'

The Fletchers had one child, a daughter whose age put her awkwardly between Duncan and Walt; it was implied that they wanted another. But the book, Alice's second novel, came first; when it was over, they would have a second child, they said.

The couples had dinner together occasionally, but the Fletchers were strictly cookout people – which is to say, neither of them cooked – and Garp was in a period where he baked his own bread, he had a stockpot always simmering on the stove. Mostly, Helen and Harrison discussed books, teaching, and their colleagues; they ate lunch together at the university union, they conversed – at length – in the evening, on the phone. And Garp and Harry went to the football games, the basketball games, and the wrestling meets; three times a week they played squash, which was Harry's game – his only sport – but Garp could play even with him simply because Garp was a better athlete, in better shape from all his running. For the pleasure of these games, Garp suppressed his dislike of balls.

In the second year of this friendship, Harry told Garp that Alice liked to go to movies. 'I *don't*,' Harry admitted, 'but if you do – and Helen said that you did – why not take Alice?'

Alice Fletcher giggled at movies, especially serious movies; she shook her head in disbelief at almost everything she saw. It took months for Garp to realize that Alice had something of an impediment or a nervous defect in her speech; perhaps it was psychological. At first Garp thought it was the popcorn.

'You have a speech problem, I think, Alice,' he said, driving her home one night.

'Yeth,' she said, nodding her head. Often it was a simple

lisp; sometimes it was completely different. Occasionally, it wasn't there. Excitement seemed to aggravate it.

'How's the book coming?' he asked her.

'Good,' she said. At one movie she had blurted out that she'd liked *Procrastination*.

'Do you want me to read any of your work?' Garp asked her.

'Yeth,' she said, her small head bobbing. She sat with her short, strong fingers crushing her skirt in her lap, the way Garp had seen her daughter crinkle her clothes – the child would sometimes roll her skirt, like a window shade, right up above her panties (though Alice stopped short of this).

'Was it an accident?' Garp asked her. 'Your speech problem. Or were you born with it?'

'Born with,' Alice said. The car stopped at the Fletchers' house and Alice tugged Garp's arm. She opened her mouth and pointed inside, as if this would explain everything. Garp saw the rows of small, perfect teeth and a tongue that was fat and fresh-looking like the tongue of a child. He could see nothing peculiar, but it was dark in the car, and he wouldn't have known what was peculiar if he'd seen it. When Alice closed her mouth, he saw she was crying – and also smiling, as if this act of self-exposure had required enormous trust. Garp nodded his head as if he understood everything.

'I see,' he mumbled. She wiped her tears with the back of one hand, squeezed his hand with her other.

'Harrithon is having an affair,' she said.

Garp knew that Harry wasn't having an affair with Helen, but he didn't know what poor Alice thought.

'Not with Helen,' Garp said.

'Na, na,' Alice said, shaking her head. 'Thumone *elth*.'

'Who?' Garp asked.

'A thtudent!' Alice wailed. 'A thtupid little twat!'

It had been a couple of years since Garp had molested Little Squab Bones, but in that time he had indulged himself in one other babysitter; to his shame, he had even forgotten her name. He felt, honestly, that babysitters were an appetite he was forever through with. Yet he sympathized with Harry – Harry was his friend, and he was an important friend to Helen. He also sympathized with Alice. Alice was alertly lovable; a kind of terminal vulnerability was clearly a part of her, and she wore it as visibly as a too-tight sweater on her compact body.

'I'm sorry,' Garp said. 'Can I do anything?'

'Tell him to *thtop*,' Alice said.

It had never been hard for Garp to stop, but he had never been a teacher – with 'thtudents' on his mind, or on his hands. Perhaps what Harry was involved with was something else. The only thing Garp could think of – that would perhaps make Alice feel better – was to confess his own mistakes.

'It happens, Alice,' he said.

'Not to you,' Alice said.

'Twice to me,' Garp said. She looked at him, shocked.

'Tell the *truth*,' she insisted.

'The truth,' he said, 'is that it happened twice. A babysitter, both times.'

'Jesuth Chritht,' said Alice.

'But they weren't important,' Garp said. 'I love Helen.'

'*Thith* is important,' Alice said. 'He hurth me. And I can't *white*.'

Garp knew about writers who couldn't *white*; this made Garp love Alice, on the spot.

'Fucking Harry is having an affair,' Garp told Helen.

'I know,' Helen said. 'I've told him to stop, but he keeps going back for more. She's not even a very good student.'

'What can we do?' Garp asked her.

'Fucking *lust*,' Helen said. 'Your mother was right. It *is* a man's problem. *You* talk to him.'

'Alice told me about your babysitters,' Harry told Garp. 'It's not the same. This is a special girl.'

'A *student*, Harry,' Garp said. 'Jesus Christ.'

'A *special* student,' Harry said. 'I'm not like you. I've

been honest, I've told Alice from the first. She's just got to accommodate it. I've told her she's free to do this, too.'

'She doesn't know any students,' Garp said.

'She knows *you*,' Harry told him. 'And she's in love with you.'

'What can we do?' Garp asked Helen. 'He's trying to set me up with Alice so he'll feel better about what he's doing.'

'At least he's been honest with her,' Helen told Garp. There was one of those silences wherein a family can identify its separate, breathing parts in the night. Open doors off an upstairs hall: Duncan breathing lazily, an almost-eight-year-old with lots of time to live; Walt breathing those tentative two-year-old breaths, short and excited; Helen, even and cool. Garp held his breath. He knew she knew about the babysitters.

'Harry told you?' he asked.

'You might have told me before you told Alice,' Helen said. 'Who was the second one?'

'I forget her name,' Garp admitted.

'I think it's shabby,' Helen said. 'It's really beneath me; it's beneath *you*. I hope you've outgrown it.'

'Yes, I have,' Garp said. He meant he had outgrown babysitters. But lust itself? Ah, well. Jenny Fields had fingered a problem at the heart of her son's heart.

'We've got to help the Fletchers,' Helen said. 'We're too fond of them to do nothing about this.' Helen, Garp marveled, moved through their life together as if it were an essay she was structuring – with an introduction, a presentation of basic priorities, then the thesis.

'Harry thinks the student is *special*,' Garp pointed out.

'Fucking *men*,' Helen said. 'You look after Alice. *I'll* show Harrison what's special.'

So one night, after Garp had cooked an elegant Paprika Chicken and spätzle, Helen said to Garp, 'Harrison and I will do the dishes. You take Alice home.'

'Take her home?' Garp said. 'Now?'

'Show him your novel,' Helen said to Alice. 'Show him

everything you want. I'm going to show your husband what an asshole he is.'

'Hey, come on,' Harry said. 'We're all friends, we all want to *stay* friends, right?'

'You simple son of a bitch,' Helen told him. 'You fuck a student and call her special – you insult your wife, you insult me. *I'll* show you what's special.'

'Go easy, Helen,' Garp said.

'Go with Alice,' Helen said. 'And let Alice drive her own babysitter home.'

'Hey, come on!' Harrison Fletcher said.

'Shuth up, Harrithon!' Alice said. She grabbed Garp's hand and stood up from the table.

'Fucking *men*,' said Helen. Garp, as speechless as an Ellen Jamesian, took Alice home.

'I can take the babysitter home, Alice,' he said.

'Jutht get back *fatht*,' Alice said.

'Very fast, Alice,' Garp said.

She made him read the first chapter of her novel aloud to her. 'I want to *hear* it,' she told him, 'and I can't *thay* it mythelf.' So Garp said it to her; it read, he was relieved to hear, beautifully. Alice wrote with such fluency and care that Garp could have *sung* her sentences, unselfconsciously, and they would have sounded fine.

'You have a lovely voice, Alice,' he told her, and she cried. And they made love, of course, and despite what everyone knows about such things, it *was* special.

'Wasn't it?' asked Alice.

'Yes, it *was*,' Garp admitted.

Now, he thought, *here* is trouble.

'What can we do?' Helen asked Garp. She had made Harrison Fletcher forget his 'special' student; Harrison now thought that *Helen* was the most special thing in his life.

'You started it,' Garp said to her. 'If it's going to stop, you've got to stop it, I think.'

'That's easy to say,' Helen said. 'I *like* Harrison; he's my best friend, and I don't want to lose that. I'm just not very interested in sleeping with him.'

'*He's* interested,' Garp said.

'God, I know,' Helen said.

'He thinks you're the best he's had,' Garp told her.

'Oh, great,' Helen said. 'That must be lovely for Alice.'

'Alice isn't thinking about it,' Garp said. Alice was thinking about *Garp*, Garp knew; and Garp was afraid the whole thing would stop. There were times when Garp thought that Alice was the best he'd ever had.

'And what about you?' Helen asked him. ('Nothing is equal,' Garp would write, one day.)

'I'm fine,' Garp said. 'I like Alice, I like you, I like Harry.'

'And Alice?' Helen asked.

'Alice likes me,' Garp said.

'Oh boy,' Helen said. 'So we all like each other, except that I don't care that much for *sleeping* with Harrison.'

'So it's over,' Garp said, trying to hide the gloom in his voice. Alice had cried to him that it could *never* be over. ('Could it? Could it?' she had cried. 'I can't juht *thtop!*')

'Well, isn't it still better than it *was?*' Helen asked Garp.

'You made your point,' Garp said. 'You got Harry off his damn student. Now you've just got to let him down easy.'

'And what about you and Alice?' Helen asked.

'If it's over for one of us, it's over for all of us,' Garp said. 'That's only fair.'

'I know what's *fair*,' Helen said. 'I also know what's *human*.'

The good-byes that Garp imagined conducting with Alice were violent scenarios, fraught with Alice's incoherent speech and always ending in desperate lovemaking – another failed resolution, wet with sweat and sweet with the lush stickum of sex, oh yeth.

'I think Alice is a little *loony*,' Helen said.

'Alice is a pretty good writer,' Garp said. 'She's the real thing.'

'Fucking *writers*,' Helen mumbled.

'Harry doesn't appreciate how talented Alice is,' Garp heard himself say.

'Oh boy,' Helen murmured. 'This is the last time I try to save anyone's marriage except my own.'

It took six months for Helen to let Harry down easy, and in that time Garp saw as much of Alice as he could, while still trying to forewarn her that their foursome was going to be short-lived. He also tried to forewarn himself, because he dreaded the knowledge that he would have to give Alice up.

'It's not the same, for all four of us,' he told Alice. 'It will have to stop, and pretty soon.'

'Tho what?' Alice said. 'It hasn't thtopped yet, has it?'

'Not yet,' Garp admitted. He read all her written words aloud to her, and they made love so much he stung in the shower and couldn't stand to wear a jock when he ran.

'We've got to do and *do* it,' Alice said, fervently. 'Do it while we can.'

'You know, this *can't* last,' Garp tried to warn Harry, while they were playing squash.

'I know, I know,' Harry said, 'but it's great *while* it lasts, isn't it?'

'Isn't it?' Alice demanded. Did Garp love Alice? Oh yeth.

'Yes, yes,' Garp said, shaking his head. He thought he did.

But Helen, enjoying it the least of them, suffered it the most; when she finally called an end to it, she couldn't help but show her euphoria. The other three couldn't help but show their resentment: that she should appear so uplifted while they were cast into such gloom. Without formal imposition there existed a six-month moratorium on the couples' seeing each other, except by chance. Naturally, Helen and Harry ran into each other at the English Department. Garp encountered Alice in the supermarket. Once she deliberately crashed her shopping cart into his; little Walt was jarred among the produce and the juice cans, and Alice's daughter looked equally alarmed at the collision.

'I felt the need of thum *contact,*' Alice said. And she called the Garps one night, very late, after Garp and Helen had gone to bed. Helen answered the phone.

'Is Harrithon there?' she asked Helen.

'No, Alice,' Helen said. 'Is something wrong?'

'He's not *here,*' Alice said. 'I haven't theen Harrithon all night!'

'Let me come over and sit with you,' Helen suggested. 'Garp can go look for Harrison.'

'Can't *Garp* come over and thit with me?' Alice asked. '*You* look for Harrithon.'

'No, *I'll* come over and sit with you,' Helen said. 'I think that's better. Garp can go look for Harrison.'

'I want Garp,' Alice said.

'I'm sorry that you can't have him,' Helen said.

'I'm thorry, Helen,' Alice said. She cried into the phone and said a stream of things that Helen couldn't understand. Helen gave the phone to Garp.

Garp talked to Alice, and listened to her, for about an hour. Nobody looked for 'Harrithon.' Helen felt she had done a good job of holding herself together for the six months she'd allowed it all to continue; she expected them all to at least control themselves adequately, now that it was over.

'If Harrison is out screwing students, I'm *really* going to cross him off,' Helen said. 'That *asshole!* And if Alice calls herself a writer, why isn't she writing? If she's got so much to *thay,* why waste saying it on the phone?'

Time, Garp knew, would ease everything. Time would also prove him wrong about Alice's writing. She may have had a pretty voice but she couldn't complete anything; she never finished her second novel, not in all the years that the Garps would know the Fletchers – or in all the years after. She could say everything beautifully, but – as Garp remarked to Helen, when he was finally exasperated with Alice – she couldn't get to the end of anything. She couldn't *thtop.*

Harry, too, would not play his cards wisely or well. The university would deny him tenure – a bitter loss for Helen, because she truly loved having Harrison for a friend. But the student Harry had thrown over for Helen had not been let down so easy; she bitched about her seduction to the English Department – although, of course, it was her jilting that really made her bitch. This raised eyebrows among Harry's colleagues. And, of course, *Helen's* support of Harrison Fletcher's case for tenure was quietly not taken seriously – *her* relationship with Harry having also been made clear by the jilted student.

Even Garp's mother, Jenny Fields – with all she stood up for, for women – agreed with Garp that Helen's own tenure at the university, so easily granted her when she was younger than poor Harry, had been a token gesture on the part of the English Department. Someone had probably told them that they needed a woman on the department at the associate professor level, and Helen had come along. Although Helen did not doubt her own qualifications, she knew it hadn't been her quality that had gotten her tenure.

But Helen had not slept with any students; not yet. Harrison Fletcher had, unforgivably, allowed his sex life to be more special to him than his job. He got another job, anyway. And perhaps what remained of the friendship between the Garps and the Fletchers was actually saved by the Fletchers' having to move away. This way, the couples saw each other about twice a year; distance diffused what might have been hard feelings. Alice could speak her flawless prose to Garp – in letters. The temptation to touch each other, even to bash their shopping carts together, was removed from them, and they all settled into being the kind of friends many old friends become: that is, they were friends when they heard from each other – or when, occasionally, they got together. And when they were not in touch, they did not think of one another.

Garp threw away his second novel and began a *second* second novel. Unlike Alice, Garp was a real writer – not because he wrote more beautifully than she wrote but because he knew what every artist should know: as Garp put it,

'You only grow by coming to the end of something and by beginning something else.' Even if these so-called endings and beginnings are illusions. Garp did not write faster than anyone else, or *more*; he simply always worked with the *idea* of completion in mind.

His second book was swollen, he knew, with the energy he had left over from Alice.

It was a book full of wounding dialogue and sex that left the partners smarting; sex in the book also left the partners guilty, and usually wanting more sex. This paradox was cited by several reviewers who called the phenomenon, alternately, 'brilliant' and 'dumb.' One reviewer called the novel 'bitterly truthful,' but he hastened to point out that the bitterness doomed the novel to the status of 'only a minor classic.' If more of the bitterness had been 'refined away,' the reviewer theorized, 'a purer truth would have emerged.'

More nonsense was compiled concerning the novel's 'thesis.' One reviewer struggled with the idea that the novel seemed to be saying that *only* sexual relationships could profoundly reveal people to themselves; yet it was during sexual relationships that people appeared to lose what profundity they had. Garp said he never had a thesis and he grumpily told an interviewer that he had written 'a serious comedy about marriage, but a sexual farce.' Later he wrote that 'human sexuality makes farcical our most serious intentions.'

But no matter what Garp said – or the reviewers, either – the book was not a success. Titled *Second Wind of the Cuckold*, the novel confused nearly everyone; even its reviews were confusing. It undersold *Procrastination* by a few thousand copies, and even though John Wolf assured Garp that this was what often happened to second novels, Garp – for the first time in his life – felt he had failed.

John Wolf, who was a good editor, protected Garp from one particular review until he feared Garp would see the review by accident; then Wolf reluctantly sent the clipping, from a West Coast newspaper, with the attached note that he'd heard the reviewer suffered a hormone imbalance. The review remarked, curtly, that it was sordid and pathetic that T. S. Garp, 'the talentless son of the famous feminist, Jenny Fields, has written a sexist novel that wallows in sex – and not even instructively.' And so forth.

Growing up with Jenny Fields had not made Garp the sort of person who was easily influenced by other people's opinions of him, but even Helen did not like *Second Wind of the Cuckold*. And even Alice Fletcher, in all her loving letters, never once mentioned the book's existence.

Second Wind of the Cuckold was about two married couples who have an affair.

'Oh boy,' Helen said, when she first learned what the book was about.

'It's not about *us*,' Garp said. 'It's *not* about any of that. It just *uses* that.'

'And you're always telling me,' Helen said, 'that auto-biographical fiction is the *worst* kind.'

'This *isn't* autobiographical,' Garp said. 'You'll see.'

She didn't. Though the novel was not about Helen and Garp and Harry and Alice, it *was* about four people whose finally unequal and sexually striving relationship is a bust.

Each person in the foursome is physically handicapped. One of the men is blind. The other man has a stutter of such monstrous proportions that his dialogue is infuriatingly difficult to read. Jenny blasted Garp for taking a cheap shot at poor departed Mr Tinch, but writers, Garp sadly knew, were just observers – good and ruthless imitators of human behavior. Garp had meant no offense to Tinch; he was just using one of Tinch's habits.

'I don't know how you could have done such a thing to Alice,' Helen despaired.

Helen meant the handicaps, especially the women's handicaps. One has muscle spasms in her right arm – her hand is always lashing out, striking wineglasses, flowerpots, children's faces, once nearly emasculating her husband (accidentally) with a pruning hook. Only her lover, the other woman's husband, is able to soothe this terrible, uncontrollable spasm – so that the woman is, for the first time in her life, the possessor of a flawless body, entirely intentional in its movement, truly ruled and contained by herself alone.

The other woman suffers unpredictable, unstoppable flatulence. The farter is married to the stutterer, the blind man is married to the dangerous right arm.

Nobody in the foursome, to Garp's credit, is a writer. ('We should be grateful for small favors?' Helen asked.) One of the couples is childless, and wants to be. The other couple is trying to have a child; this woman conceives, but her elation is tempered by everyone's anxiety concerning the identity of the natural father. Which one was it? The couples watch for telltale habits in the newborn child. Will it stutter, fart, lash out, or be blind? (Garp saw this as his ultimate comment – on his mother's behalf – on the subject of *genes*.)

It is to some degree an optimistic novel, if only because the friendship between the couples finally convinces them to break off their liaison. The childless couple later separates, disillusioned with each other – but not necessarily as a result of the experiment. The couple with the child succeeds as a couple; the child develops without a detectable flaw. The last scene in the novel is the chance meeting of the two women; they pass on an escalator in a department store at Christmastime, the farter going up, the woman with the dangerous right arm going down. Both are laden with packages. At the moment they pass each other, the woman stricken with uncontrollable flatulence releases a keen, treble fart – the spastic stiff-arms an old man on the escalator in front of her, bowling him down the moving staircase, toppling a sea of people. But it's Christmas. The escalators are jam-packed and noisy; no one is hurt and everything, in season, is forgivable. The two women, moving apart on their mechanical conveyors, seem to serenely acknowledge each other's burdens; they grimly smile at each other.

'It's a comedy!' Garp cried out, over and over again. 'No one got it. It's supposed to be very *funny*. What a film it would make!'

But no one even bought the paperback rights.

As could be seen by the fate of the man who could only walk on his hands, Garp had a thing about escalators.

Helen said that no one in the English Department ever spoke to her about *Second Wind of the Cuckold*; in the case of *Procrastination*, many of her well-meaning colleagues had at least attempted a discussion. Helen said that the book was an invasion of her privacy and she hoped the whole thing had been a kick that Garp would soon be off.

'Jesus, do they think it's *you*?' Garp asked her. 'What the hell's the matter with your dumb colleagues, anyway? Do *you* fart in the halls over there? Does your shoulder drop out of socket in department meetings? Was poor Harry a stutterer in the classroom?' Garp yelled. 'Am I blind?'

'*Yes*, you're blind,' Helen said. 'You have your own terms for what's fiction, and what's fact, but do you think other people know your system? It's all your *experience* – somehow, however much you make up, even if it's only an *imagined* experience. People *think* it's me, they *think* it's you. And sometimes I think so, too.'

The blind man in the novel is a geologist. 'Do they see me playing with rocks?' Garp hollered.

The flatulent woman does volunteer work in a hospital; she is a nurse's aide. 'Do you see my mother complaining?' Garp asked. 'Does she write me and point out that she never once farted in a hospital – only at home, and always under control?'

But Jenny Fields *did* complain to her son about *Second Wind of the Cuckold*. She told him he had chosen a disappointingly narrow subject of little universal importance. 'She means sex,' Garp said. 'This is classic. A lecture on what's universal by a woman who's never once felt sexual desire. And the Pope, who takes vows of chastity, decides

the issue of contraception for millions. The world *is* crazy!'
Garp cried.

Jenny's newest colleague was a six-foot-four transsexual
named Roberta Muldoon. Formerly Robert Muldoon, a
standout tight end for the Philadelphia Eagles, Roberta's
weight had dropped from 235 to 180 since her successful
sex-change operation. The doses of estrogen had cut into
her once-massive strength and some of her endurance; Garp
guessed also that Robert Muldoon's former and famous
'quick hands' weren't so quick anymore, but Roberta Muldoon was a formidable companion to Jenny Fields. Roberta
worshiped Garp's mother. It had been Jenny's book, *A Sexual
Suspect,* that had given Robert Muldoon the courage to have
the sex-change operation – one winter as he lay recovering
from knee surgery in a Philadelphia hospital.

Jenny Fields was now supporting Roberta's case with the
television networks, who, Roberta claimed, had secretly
agreed not to hire her as a sports announcer for the football
season. Roberta's *knowledge* of football had not decreased
one drop since all the estrogen, Jenny was arguing; waves of
support from the college campuses around the country had
made the six-foot-four Roberta Muldoon a figure of striking
controversy. Roberta was intelligent and articulate, and of
course she knew her football; she'd have been an improvement on the usual morons who commented on the game.

Garp liked her. They talked about football together and
they played squash. Roberta always took the first few games
from Garp – she was more powerful than he was, and a
better athlete – but her stamina was not quite up to his, and
being the much bigger person in the court, she wore down.
Roberta would also tire of her case against the television
networks, but she would develop great endurance for other,
more important things.

'You're certainly an improvement on the Ellen James
Society, Roberta,' Garp would tell her. He enjoyed his
mother's visits better when Jenny came with Roberta. And

Roberta tossed a football for hours with Duncan. Roberta promised to take Duncan to an Eagles game, but Garp was anxious about that. Roberta was a target figure; she had made some people very angry. Garp imagined various assaults and bomb threats on Roberta – and Duncan disappearing in the vast and roaring football stadium in Philadelphia, where he would be defiled by a child molester.

It was the fanaticism of some of Roberta Muldoon's hate mail that gave Garp such an imagination, but when Jenny showed him some hate mail of her own, Garp was anxious about that, too. It was an aspect of the publicity of his mother's life that he had not considered: some people truly hated her. They wrote Jenny that they wished she had cancer. They wrote Roberta Muldoon that they hoped his or her parents were no longer living. One couple wrote Jenny Fields that they would like to artificially inseminate her, with elephant sperm – and blow her up from the inside. That note was signed: 'A Legitimate Couple.'

One man wrote Roberta Muldoon that he had been an Eagles' fan all his life, and even his grandparents had been born in Philadelphia, but now he was going to be a Giants or a Redskins fan, and drive to New York or Washington – 'or even Baltimore, if necessary' – because Roberta had perverted the entire Eagles offensive line with his pansy ways.

One woman wrote Roberta Muldoon that she hoped Roberta would get gang-banged by the Oakland Raiders. The woman thought that the Raiders were the most disgusting team in football; maybe they would show Roberta how much fun it was to be a woman.

A high school tight end from Wyoming wrote Roberta Muldoon that she had made him ashamed to be a tight end anymore and he was changing his position – to linebacker. So far, there were no transsexual linebackers.

A college offensive guard from Michigan wrote Roberta that if she were ever in Ypsilanti, he would like to fuck her with her shoulder pads on.

'This is nothing,' Roberta told Garp. 'Your mother gets much worse. Lots more people hate *her.*'

'Mom,' Garp said. 'Why don't you drop out for a while? Take a vacation. Write another book.' He never thought he'd ever hear himself suggesting such a thing to her, but he suddenly saw Jenny as a potential victim, exposing herself, through other victims, to all the hatred and cruelty and violence in the world.

When asked by the press, always, Jenny would say that she *was* writing another book; only Garp and Helen and John Wolf knew this was a lie. Jenny Fields wasn't writing a word.

'I've done all I want to do about *me*, already,' Jenny told her son. 'Now I'm interested in other people. You just worry about *you*,' she said, gravely, as if in her opinion her son's introversion – his imaginative life – was the more dangerous way to live.

Helen actually feared this, too – especially when Garp wasn't writing; and for more than a year after *Second Wind of the Cuckold*, Garp didn't write. Then he wrote for a year and threw it all away. He wrote letters to his editor; they were the most difficult letters John Wolf ever had to read, much less answer. Some of them were ten and twelve pages long; most of them accused John Wolf of not 'pushing' *Second Wind of the Cuckold* as hard as he could have.

'Everyone *hated* it,' John Wolf reminded Garp. 'How could we have pushed it?'

'You never supported the book,' Garp wrote.

Helen wrote John Wolf that he must be patient with Garp, but John Wolf knew writers pretty well and he was as patient and as kind as he could be.

Eventually, Garp wrote letters to other people. He answered some of his mother's hate mail – those rare cases with return addresses. He wrote long letters trying to talk these people out of their hatred. 'You're becoming a social worker,' Helen told him. But Garp even offered to answer some of Roberta Muldoon's hate mail; Roberta had a new lover, however, and her hate mail was rolling off her like water.

'Jesus,' Garp complained to her, 'first a sex reassignment and now you're in love. For a tight end with tits, you're really boring, Roberta.' They were very good friends and they played squash fervently whenever Roberta and Jenny came to town, but this was not frequently enough to occupy all of Garp's restless time. He spent hours playing games with Duncan – and waiting for Walt to get old enough to play games, too. He cooked up a storm.

'The third novel's the big one,' John Wolf told Helen, because he sensed she was wearying of Garp's restlessness and she was in need of a pep talk. 'Give him time, it will come.'

'How *he* know the third novel's the big one?' Garp fumed. 'My third novel doesn't even exist. And the way it was published, my second novel might as well not exist. These editors are full of myths and self-fulfilling prophecies! If he knows so much about third novels, why doesn't he write his *own* third novel? Why doesn't he write his *first?*'

But Helen smiled and kissed him and took up going to the movies with him, although she hated movies. She was happy with her job; the kids were happy. Garp was a good father and a good cook and he made love to her more elaborately when he wasn't writing than he did when he was hard at work. Let it come, Helen thought.

Her father, good old Ernie Holm, had shown signs of early heart trouble, but her father was happy at Steering. He and Garp took a trip together, every winter, to see one of those big wrestling matches out in Iowa. Helen was sure that Garp's writing block was a small thing to endure.

'It will come,' Alice Fletcher told Garp, on the phone. 'You can't *forth* it.'

'I'm not trying to *force* anything,' he assured her. 'There's just nothing there.' But he thought that desirable Alice, who could never finish anything – not even her love for him – was a poor one to understand what he meant.

Then Garp got some hate mail of his own. He was

addressed in a lively letter by someone who took offense at *Second Wind of the Cuckold*. It was not a blind, stuttering, spastic farter – as you might imagine – either. It was just what Garp needed to lift himself out of his slump.

Dear Shithead,

[wrote the offended party]

I have read your novel. You seem to find other people's problems very funny. I have seen your picture. With your fat head of hair I suppose you can laugh at bald persons. And in your cruel book you laugh at people who can't have orgasms, and people who aren't blessed with happy marriages, and people whose wives and husbands are unfaithful to each other. You ought to know that persons who have these problems do not think everything is so *funny*. Look at the world, shithead – it is a bed of pain, people suffering and nobody believing in God or bringing their children up right. You shithead, you don't have any problems so you can make fun of poor people who do!

Yours sincerely,

(Mrs.) I. B. Poole

Findlay, Ohio

That letter stung Garp like a slap; rarely had he felt so importantly misunderstood. Why did people insist that if you were 'comic' you couldn't also be 'serious'? Garp felt most people confused being profound with being sober, being earnest with being deep. Apparently, if you *sounded* serious, you were. Presumably, other animals could not laugh at themselves, and Garp believed that laughter was related to sympathy, which we were always needing more of. He had been, after all, a humorless child – and never religious – so perhaps he now took comedy more seriously than others.

But for Garp to see his vision interpreted as making *fun* of people was painful to him; and to realize that his art had made him appear cruel gave Garp a keen sense of failure. Very carefully, as if he were speaking to a potential suicide high up in a foreign and unfamiliar hotel, Garp wrote to his reader in Findlay, Ohio.

Dear Mrs Poole:

The world *is* a bed of pain, people suffer terribly, few of us believe in God or bring up our children very well; you're right about that. It is also true that people who have problems do not, as a rule, think their problems are 'funny.'

Horace Walpole once said that the world is comic to those who think and tragic to those who feel. I hope you'll agree with me that Horace Walpole somewhat simplifies the world by saying this. Surely both of us think *and* feel; in regard to what's comic and what's tragic, Mrs Poole, the world is all mixed up. For this reason I have never understood why 'serious' and 'funny' are thought to be opposites. It is simply a truthful contradiction to me that people's problems are often funny and that the people are often and nonetheless sad.

I am ashamed, however, that you think I am laughing at people, or making fun of them. I take people very seriously. People are all I take seriously, in fact. Therefore, I have nothing but sympathy for how people behave – and nothing but laughter to console them with.

Laughter is my religion, Mrs Poole. In the manner of most religions, I admit that my laughter is pretty desperate. I want to tell you a little story to illustrate what I mean. The story takes place in Bombay, India, where many people starve to death every day; but not all the people in Bombay are starving.

Among the nonstarving population of Bombay, India, there was a wedding, and a party was thrown in honor of the bride and groom. Some of the wedding guests brought elephants to the party. They weren't really conscious of showing off, they were just using the elephants for transportation. Although that may strike us as a big-shot way to travel around, I don't think these wedding guests saw themselves that way. Most of them were probably not directly responsible for the vast numbers of their fellow Indians who were starving all around them; most of them were just calling 'time out' from their own problems, and the problems of

the world, to celebrate the wedding of a friend. But if *you* were
a member of the starving Indians, and you hobbled past that
wedding party and saw all those elephants parked outside, you
probably would have felt some disgruntlement.

Furthermore, some of the revelers at the wedding got drunk
and began feeding beer to their elephant. They emptied an ice
bucket and filled it with beer, and they went tittering out to the
parking lot and fed their hot elephant the whole bucket. The
elephant liked it. So the revelers gave him several more buckets of
beer.

Who knows how beer will affect an elephant? These people
meant no harm, they were just having fun – and chances are fairly
good that the rest of their lives weren't one hundred percent fun.
They probably needed this party. But the people were also being
stupid and irresponsible.

If one of those many starving Indians had dragged himself
through the parking lot and seen these drunken wedding guests
filling up an elephant with beer, I'll bet he would have felt
resentful. But I hope you see I am not making *fun* of anyone.

What happens next is that the drunken revelers are asked
to *leave* the party because their behavior with their elephant
is obnoxious to the other wedding guests. No one can blame
the other guests for feeling this way; some of them may have
actually thought that they were preventing things from getting
'out of hand,' although people have never been very successful at
preventing this.

Huffy and brave with beer, the revelers struggled up on
their elephant and veered away from the parking lot – a large
exhibition of happiness, surely – bumping into a few other
elephants and things, because the revelers' elephant plowed
from side to side in a lumbering wooze, bleary and bloated with
buckets of beer. His trunk lashed back and forth like a badly
fastened artificial limb. The great beast was so unsteady that he
struck an electric utility pole, shearing it cleanly and bringing
down the live wires on his massive head – which killed him, and
the wedding guests who were riding him, instantly.

Mrs Poole, please believe me: I don't think that's 'funny.' But along comes one of those starving Indians. He sees all the wedding guests mourning the death of their friends, and their friends' elephant; much wailing, rending of fine clothes, spilling of good food and drink. The first thing he does is to take the opportunity to slip into the wedding while the guests are distracted and steal a little of the good food and drink for his starving family. The second thing he does is start to laugh himself sick about the manner in which the revelers disposed of themselves and their elephant. Alongside death by starvation, this method of enormous dying must seem funny, or at least quick, to the undernourished Indian. But the wedding guests don't see it that way. It is already a tragedy to them; they are already talking about 'this tragic event,' and although they could perhaps forgive the presence of a 'mangy beggar' at their party – and even have tolerated his stealing their food – they cannot forgive him for *laughing* at their dead friends and their dead friends' elephant.

The wedding guests – outraged at the beggar's behavior (at his *laughter,* not his thievery and not his rags) – drown him in one of the beer buckets that the late revelers used to water their elephant. They construe this to represent 'justice.' We see that the story is about the class struggle – and, of course, 'serious,' after all. But I like to consider it a comedy about a natural disaster: they are just people rather foolishly attempting to 'take charge' of a situation whose complexity is beyond them – a situation composed of eternal and trivial parts. After all, with something as large as an elephant, it could have been much worse.

I hope, Mrs Poole, that I have made what I mean clearer to you. In any case, I thank you for taking the time to write to me, because I appreciate hearing from my audience – even critically.

> Yours truly,
> 'Shithead'

Garp was an excessive man. He made everything baroque, he believed in exaggeration; his fiction was also extremist. Garp never forgot his failure with Mrs Poole; she worried him, often, and her reply to his pompous letter must have upset him further.

Dear Mr Garp,
[Mrs Poole replied]
   I never thought you would take the trouble to write me a letter.
You must be a sick man. I can see by your letter that you believe
in yourself, and I guess that's good. But the things you say are
mostly garbage and nonsense to me, and I don't want you to
try to explain anything to me again, because it is boring and an
insult to my intelligence.

                                          Yours,
                                          Irene Poole

Garp was, like his beliefs, self-contradictory. He was very
generous with other people, but he was horribly impatient.
He set his own standards for how much of his time and
patience everyone deserved. He could be painstakingly
sweet, until he decided he'd been sweet enough. Then he
turned and came roaring back the other way.

Dear Irene:
[Garp wrote to Mrs Poole]
   You should either stop trying to read books, or you should try
a lot harder.

Dear Shithead,
[wrote Irene Poole]
   My husband says that if you write to me again, he'll beat your
brains to a pulp.

                                          Very sincerely,
                                          Mrs Fitz Poole

Dear Fitzy & Irene:
[Garp shot right back]
   Fuck you.

Thus was his sense of humor lost, and his sympathy taken
from the world.
   In 'The Pension Grillparzer' Garp had somehow struck the

chord of comedy (on the one hand) and compassion (on the other). The story did not belittle the *people* in the story – either with forced cuteness or with any other exaggeration rationalized as necessary for making a point. Neither did the story sentimentalize the people, or otherwise cheapen their sadness.

But the balance of this power in storytelling felt lost to Garp now. His first novel, *Procrastination* – in his opinion – suffered from the pretentious weight of all that fascist history he had taken no real part in. His second novel suffered his failure at imagining *enough* – that is, he felt he had not imagined far enough beyond his own fairly ordinary experience. *Second Wind of the Cuckold* came off rather coldly to him; it seemed just another 'real' but rather common experience.

In fact, it seemed to Garp now that he was too full of his own lucky life (with Helen and their children). He felt he was in danger of limiting his ability as a writer in a fairly usual way: writing, essentially, about himself. Yet when he looked very far outside himself, Garp saw there only the invitation to pretention. His imagination was failing him – 'his sense a dim rushlight.' When anyone asked him how his writing was coming, he managed only a short, cruel imitation of poor Alice Fletcher.

'I've *thtopped*,' Garp said.

9

The Eternal Husband

In the Yellow Pages of Garp's phone directory, Marriage was listed near Lumber. After Lumber came Machine Shops, Mail Order Houses, Manholes, Maple Sugar, and Marine Equipment; then came Marriage and Family Counselors. Garp was looking for Lumber when he discovered Marriage; he had some innocent questions to ask about two-by-fours when Marriage caught his eye and raised more interesting and disturbing questions. Garp had never realized, for example, that there were more marriage counselors than lumberyards. But this surely depends on where you live, he thought. In the country, wouldn't people have more to do with lumber?

Garp had been married nearly eleven years; in that time he had found little use for lumber, still less for counsel. It was not for personal problems that Garp took an interest in the long list of names in the Yellow Pages; it was because Garp spent a lot of time trying to imagine what it would be like to have a job.

There was the Christian Counseling Center and the Community Pastoral Counseling Service; Garp imagined hearty ministers with their dry, fleshy hands constantly rubbing together. They spoke round, moist sentences, like soap bubbles, saying things like, 'We have no illusions that the Church can be of very much assistance to individual problems, such as your own. Individuals must seek individual solutions, they must retain their individuality;

however, it *is* our experience that many people have *iden-tified* their own special individuality *in* the church.'

There sat the baffled couple who had hoped to discuss the simultaneous orgasm – myth or reality?

Garp noticed that members of the clergy went in for counseling; there was a Lutheran Social Service, there was a Reverend Dwayne Kuntz (who was 'certified') and a Louise Nagle who was an 'All Souls Minister' associated with something called the United States Bureau of Marriage & Family Counselors (who had 'certified' her). Garp took a pencil and drew little zeroes beside the names of the marriage counselors with religious affiliations. They would all offer fairly optimistic counsel, Garp believed.

He was less sure of the point of view of the counselors with more 'scientific' training; he was less sure of the training, too. One was a 'certified clinical psychologist,' another simply followed his name with 'M.A., Clinical'; Garp knew that these things could mean anything, and that they could also mean nothing. A graduate student in sociology, a former business major. One said 'B.S.' – perhaps in Botany. One was a Ph.D. – in marriage? One was a 'Doctor' – but a medical doctor or a Doctor of Philosophy? At marriage counseling, who would be better? One specialized in 'group therapy'; someone, perhaps less ambitious, promised only 'psychological evaluation.'

Garp selected two favorites. The first was Dr O. Rothrock – 'self-esteem workshop; bank cards accepted.'

The second was M. Neff – 'by appointment only.' There was just a phone number after M. Neff's name. No qualifications, or supreme arrogance? Perhaps both. If *I* needed anybody, Garp thought, I would try M. Neff first. Dr O. Rothrock with his bank cards and his self-esteem workshop was clearly a charlatan. But M. Neff was serious; M. Neff had a vision, Garp could tell.

Garp wandered a bit past Marriage in the Yellow Pages. He came to Masonry, Maternity Apparel, and Mat Refinishing (only one listing, an out-of-town, Steering phone number:

Garp's father-in-law, Ernie Holm, refinished wrestling mats as a slightly profitable hobby. Garp hadn't been thinking about his old coach; he passed over Mat Refinishing to Mattresses without recognizing Ernie's name). Then came Mausoleums and Meat Cutting Equipment – 'See Saws.' That was enough. The world was too complicated. Garp wandered back to Marriage.

Then Duncan came home from school. Garp's older son was now ten years old; he was a tall boy with Helen Garp's bony, delicate face and her oval yellow-brown eyes. Helen had skin of a light-oak color and Duncan had her wonderful skin, too. From Garp he had gotten his nervousness, his stubbornness, his moods of black self-pity.

'Dad?' he said. 'Can I spend the night at Ralph's? It's very important.'

'What?' Garp said. 'No. When?'

'Have you been reading the phone book again?' Duncan asked his father. Whenever Garp read a phone book, Duncan knew, it was like trying to wake him up from a nap. He read the phone book often, for names. Garp got the names of his characters out of the phone book; when his writing was stuck, he read the phone book for more names; he revised the names of his characters over and over again. When Garp traveled, the first thing he looked for in the motel room was the phone book; he usually stole it.

'Dad?' Duncan said; he assumed his father was in his phone book trance, living the lives of his fictional people. Garp had actually forgotten that he had nonfiction business with the phone book today; he had forgotten about the lumber and was thinking only about the audacity of M. Neff and what it would be like to *be* a marriage counselor. 'Dad!' Duncan said. 'If I don't call Ralph back before supper, his mother won't let me come over.'

'Ralph?' said Garp. 'Ralph isn't here.' Duncan tipped his fine jaw up and rolled his eyes; it was a gesture Helen had, too, and Duncan had her same lovely throat.

'Ralph is at *his* house,' Duncan said, 'and I am at *my* house

and I would like to go spend the night at Ralph's house –
with Ralph.'

'Not on a school night,' Garp said.

'It's Friday,' Duncan said. 'Jesus.'

'Don't swear, Duncan,' Garp said. 'When your mother
comes home from work, you can ask her.' He was stalling, he
knew; Garp was suspicious of Ralph – worse, he was afraid
for Duncan to spend the night at Ralph's house, although
Duncan had done it before. Ralph was an older boy whom
Garp distrusted; also, Garp didn't like Ralph's mother – she
went out in the evening and left the boys alone (Duncan
had admitted that). Helen had once referred to Ralph's
mother as 'slatternly,' a word that had always intrigued
Garp (and a look, in women, that had its appeal to him).
Ralph's father didn't live at home, so the 'slatternly' look
of Ralph's mother was enhanced by her status as a woman
alone.

'I *can't* wait for Mom to get home,' Duncan said. 'Ralph's
mother says she has to know before supper, or I can't come
over.' Supper was Garp's responsibility and the idea of it distracted him; he wondered what time it was. Duncan seemed
to come home from school at no special time.

'Why not ask Ralph to spend the night here?' Garp said.
A familiar ploy. Ralph usually spent the night with Duncan,
thus sparing Garp his anxiety about the carelessness of *Mrs*
Ralph (he could never remember Ralph's last name).

'Ralph *always* spends the night here,' Duncan said. 'I want
to stay *there*.' And do *what*? Garp wondered. Drink, smoke
dope, torture the pets, spy on the sloppy lovemaking of Mrs
Ralph? But Garp knew that Duncan was ten years old and
very sane – very careful. The two boys probably enjoyed
being alone in a house where Garp wasn't smiling over
them, asking them if there was anything they wanted.

'Why not call Mrs Ralph and ask her if you can wait until
your mother comes home before you say whether you'll
come or not?' Garp asked.

'Jesus, "*Mrs* Ralph"!' Duncan groaned. 'Mom is just going

to say, "It's all right with *me*. Ask your father." That's what she always says.'

Smart kid, Garp thought. He was trapped. Short of blurting out that he was terrified Mrs Ralph would kill them all by burning them up in the night when her cigarette, with which she slept, set fire to her hair, Garp had nothing more he *could* say. 'Okay, go ahead,' he said, sulkily. He didn't even know if Ralph's mother smoked. He simply disliked her, on sight, and he suspected Ralph – for no better reason than that the child was older than Duncan and therefore, Garp imagined, capable of corrupting Duncan in terrible ways.

Garp suspected most people to whom his wife and children were drawn; he had an urgent need to protect the few people he loved from what he imagined 'everyone else' was like. Poor Mrs Ralph was not the only victim perhaps slandered by his paranoid assumptions. I should get out more, Garp thought. If I had a job, he thought – a thought he had every day, and rethought every day, since he wasn't writing.

There was almost no job in the world that appealed to Garp, and certainly nothing he was qualified for; he was qualified, he knew, for very little. He could write; *when* he was writing, he believed he wrote very well. But one reason he thought about getting a job was that he felt he needed to know more about other people; he wanted to get over his distrust of them. A job would at least force him to come into contact – and if he weren't forced to be with other people, Garp would stay home.

It was for his writing, in the beginning, that he had never taken the idea of a job seriously. Now it was for his writing that he was thinking he needed a job. I am running out of people I can imagine, he thought, but perhaps it was really that there had never been many people he *liked*; and he hadn't written anything he liked in too many years.

'I'm going now!' Duncan called to him, and Garp stopped dreaming. The boy was wearing a bright orange rucksack on his back; a yellow sleeping bag was rolled and tied under the pack. Garp had chosen them both, for visibility.

'I'll give you a ride,' Garp said, but Duncan rolled his eyes again.

'Mom has the car, Dad,' he said, 'and she's still at work.'

Of course; Garp grinned foolishly. Then he saw that Duncan was going to take his bicycle and he called out the door to him. 'Why don't you *walk*, Duncan?'

'Why?' Duncan said, exasperated.

So your spine won't be severed when a car driven by a crazed teenager, or a drunken man suffering a heart attack, swipes you off the street, Garp thought – and your wonderful, warm chest is cracked against the curbstone, your special skull split open when you land on the sidewalk, and some asshole wraps you in an old rug as if you were somebody's pet discovered in the gutter. Then the dolts from the suburbs come out and guess who owns it ('That green and white house on the corner of Elm and Dodge, I think'). Then someone drives you home, rings the bell and says to me, 'Uh, sorry'; and pointing to the spillage in the bloody backseat, asks, 'Is it yours?' But all Garp said was, 'Oh, go ahead, Duncan, *take* the bike. Just be careful!'

He watched Duncan cross the street, pedal up the next block, look before he turned (*Good boy; note the careful hand signal – but perhaps this is only for my benefit*). It was a safe suburb of a small, safe city; comfortable green plots, one-family houses – mostly university families, with an occasional big house broken into apartments for graduate students. Ralph's mother, for example, appeared certain to be a graduate student forever, though she had a whole house to herself – and although she was older than Garp. Her former husband taught one of the sciences and presumably paid her tuition. Garp remembered that Helen had been told the man was living with a student.

Mrs Ralph is probably a perfectly good person, Garp thought; she has a child, and she no doubt loves him. She is no doubt serious about wanting to do something with her

life. If she were just more *careful!* Garp thought. You must be
careful; people didn't realize. It's so easy to blow everything,
he thought.

'Hello!' someone said, or he *thought* someone said. He
looked around, but whoever had spoken to him was gone
– or was never there. He realized he was barefoot (his feet
were cold; it was an early spring day), standing on the
sidewalk in front of his house, a phone book in his hand.
He would have liked to go on imagining M. Neff and the
business of marriage counseling, but he knew it was late
– he had to prepare the evening meal and he hadn't even
been shopping. A block away he could hear the hum of the
engines that powered the big freezers in the supermarket
(that was why they had moved into this neighborhood – so
that Garp could walk to the store and shop while Helen took
the car to work. Also, they were nearer to a park for him to
run in). There were fans on the back of the supermarket and
Garp could hear them sucking the still air out of the aisles
and blowing faint food smells over the block. Garp liked it.
He had a cook's heart.

He spent his day writing (or trying to write), running, and
cooking. He got up early and fixed breakfast for himself
and the children; nobody was home for lunch and Garp
never ate that meal; he fixed dinner for his family every
night. It was a ritual he loved, but the ambition of his
cooking was controlled by how good a day he'd had writing,
and how good a run he'd had. If the writing went poorly, he
took it out on himself with a long, hard run; or, sometimes,
a bad day with his writing would exhaust him so much that
he could barely run a mile; then he tried to save the day with
a splendid meal.

Helen could never tell what sort of day Garp had
experienced by what he cooked for them; something special
might mean a celebration, or it might mean that the food
was the *only* thing that had gone well, that the cooking was
the only labor keeping Garp from despair. 'If you are careful,'
Garp wrote, 'if you use good ingredients, and you don't

take any shortcuts, then you can usually cook something very good. Sometimes it is the only worthwhile product you can salvage from a day: what you make to eat. With writing, I find, you can have all the right ingredients, give plenty of time and care, and still get nothing. Also true of love. Cooking, therefore, can keep a person who tries hard sane.'

He went into the house and looked for a pair of shoes. About the only shoes he owned were running shoes – many pairs. They were in different phases of being broken in. Garp and his children wore clean but rumpled clothes; Helen was a smart dresser, and although Garp did her laundry, he refused to iron anything. Helen did her own ironing, and an occasional shirt for Garp; ironing was the only task of conventional housewifery that Garp rejected. The cooking, the kids, the basic laundry, the cleaning up – he did them. The cooking, expertly; the kids, a little tensely but conscientiously; the cleaning up, a little compulsively. He swore at errant clothes, dishes, and toys, but he left nothing lie; he was a maniac for picking things up. Some mornings, before he sat down to write, he raced over the house with a vacuum cleaner, or he cleaned the oven. The house never looked untidy, was never dirty, but there was always a certain haste to the neatness of it. Garp threw a lot of things away and the house was always missing things. For months at a time he would allow most of the light bulbs to burn out, unreplaced, until Helen would realize that they were living in almost total darkness, huddled around the two lamps that worked. Or when he remembered the lights, he forgot the soap and the toothpaste.

Helen brought certain touches to the house, too, but Garp took no responsibilities for these: plants, for example; either Helen remembered them, or they died. When Garp saw that one appeared to be drooping, or was the slightest bit pale, he would whisk it out of the house and into the trash. Days later, Helen might ask, 'Where is the red arronzo?'

'That foul thing,' Garp would remark. 'It had some disease.

I saw worms on it. I caught it dropping its little spines all over the floor.'

Thus Garp functioned at housekeeping.

In the house Garp found his yellow running shoes and put them on. He put the phone book away in a cabinet where he kept the heavy cooking gear (he stashed phone books all over the house – then would tear the house down to find the one he wanted). He put some olive oil in a cast-iron skillet; he chopped an onion while he waited for the oil to get hot. It was late to be starting supper; he hadn't even gone shopping. A standard tomato sauce, a little pasta, a fresh green salad, a loaf of his good bread. That way he could go to the market after he started the sauce and he'd only need to shop for greens. He hurried the chopping (now some fresh basil) but it was important not to throw anything into the skillet until the oil was just right, very hot but not smoking. There are some things about cooking, like writing, that you don't hurry, Garp knew, and he never hurried them.

When the phone rang, it made him so angry that he threw a handful of onions into the skillet and burned himself with the spattering oil. 'Shit!' he cried; he kicked the cabinet beside the stove, snapping the little hinge on the cabinet door; a phone book slid out and he stared at it. He put all the onions and the fresh basil into the oil and lowered the flame. He ran his hand under cold water, and, reaching off-balance, wincing at the pain of the burn, he picked up the phone in his other hand.

(Those fakers, Garp thought. What qualifications *could* there be for marriage counseling? No doubt, he thought, it is one more thing that those simplistic shrinks claim expertise in.)

'You caught me right in the fucking middle of something,' he snapped to the phone; he eyed the onions wilting in the hot oil. There was no one who could be calling whom he feared he might offend; this was one of several advantages of being unemployed. His editor, John Wolf, would only remark that Garp's manner of answering the phone simply confirmed his notion of Garp's vulgarity. Helen was used to how he answered the phone; and if the call were for Helen, her friends and colleagues already pictured Garp as rather bearish. If it were Ernie Holm, Garp would experience a momentary twinge; the coach always apologized too much, which embarrassed Garp. If it were his mother, Garp knew, she would holler back at him, 'Another lie! You're *never* in the middle of anything. You live on the fringes.' (Garp hoped it *wasn't* Jenny.) At the moment, there was no other woman who would have called him. Only if it were the day-care center, reporting an accident to little Walt; only if it were Duncan, calling to say that the zipper on his sleeping bag was broken, or that he'd just broken his leg, would Garp feel guilty for his bullying voice. One's children certainly have a right to catch one in the middle of something – they usually do.

'Right in the middle of *what*, darling?' Helen asked him. 'Right in the middle of *whom*? I hope she's nice.'

Helen's voice on the phone had a quality of sexual teasing in it; this always surprised Garp – how she sounded – because Helen was not like that, she was not even flirtatious. Though he found her, privately, very arousing, there was nothing of the sexy come-on about her dress or her habits in the outer world. Yet on the telephone she sounded bawdy to him, and always had.

'I've burned myself,' he said, dramatically. 'The oil is too hot and the onions are scorching. What the fuck is it?'

'My poor man,' she said, still teasing him. 'You didn't leave any message with Pam.' Pam was the English Department secretary; Garp struggled to think what message he was supposed to have left with her. 'Are you burned badly?' Helen asked him.

'No.' He sulked. '*What* message?'

'The two-by-fours,' said Helen. *Lumber*, Garp remembered. He was going to call the lumberyards to price some two-by-fours cut to size; Helen would pick them up on her way home from school. He remembered now that the marriage counseling had distracted him from the lumberyards.

'I forgot,' he said. Helen, he knew, would have an alternative plan; she had known this much before she even made the phone call.

'Call them now,' Helen said, 'and I'll call you back when I get to the day-care center. Then I'll go pick up the two-by-fours with Walt. He likes lumberyards.' Walt was now five; Garp's second son was in this day-care or preschool place – whatever it was, its aura of general irresponsibility gave Garp some of his most exciting nightmares.

'Well, all right,' Garp said. 'I'll start calling now.' He was worried about his tomato sauce, and he hated hanging up on a conversation with Helen when he was in a state so clearly preoccupied and dull. 'I've found an interesting job,' he told her, relishing her silence. But she wasn't silent long.

'You're a writer, darling,' Helen told him. 'You *have* an interesting job.' Sometimes it panicked Garp that Helen seemed to want him to stay at home and 'just write' – because that made the domestic situation the most comfortable for her. But it was comfortable for him, too; it was what he thought he wanted.

'The onions need stirring,' he said, cutting her off. 'And my burn hurts,' he added.

'I'll try to call back when you're in the middle of something,' Helen said, brightly teasing him, that vampish laughter barely contained in her saucy voice; it both aroused him and made him furious.

He stirred the onions and mashed half a dozen tomatoes into the hot oil; then he added pepper, salt, oregano. He called only the lumberyard whose address was closest to Walt's day-care center; Helen was too meticulous about some things – comparing the prices of everything, though he admired her for it. Wood was wood, Garp reasoned; the best place to have the damn two-by-fours cut to size was the nearest place.

A *marriage* counselor! Garp thought again, dissolving a

tablespoon of tomato paste in a cup of warm water and adding this to his sauce. Why are all the serious jobs done by quacks? What could be more serious than marriage counseling? Yet he imagined a marriage counselor was somewhat lower on a scale of trust than a chiropractor. In the way that many doctors scorned chiropractors, would psychiatrists sneer at marriage counselors? There was no one Garp tended to sneer at as much as he sneered at psychiatrists – those dangerous simplifiers, those thieves of a person's complexity. To Garp, psychiatrists were the despicable end of all those who couldn't clean up their own messes.

The psychiatrist approached the mess without proper respect for the mess, Garp thought. The psychiatrist's objective was to clear the head; it was Garp's opinion that this was usually accomplished (*when* it was accomplished) by throwing away all the messy things. That is the simplest way to clean up, Garp knew. The trick is to *use* the mess – to make the messy things work for you. 'That's easy for a *writer* to say,' Helen had told him. 'Artists *can* "use" a mess; most people can't, and they just don't want messes. I know *I* don't. What a psychiatrist you'd be! What would you do if a poor man who had no use for his mess came to you, and he just wanted his mess to go away? I suppose you'd advise him to *write* about it?' Garp remembered this conversation about psychiatry and it made him glum; he knew he oversimplified the things that made him angry, but he was convinced that psychiatry oversimplified everything.

When the phone rang, he said, 'The lumberyard off Springfield Avenue. That's close to you.'

'I know where it is,' Helen said. 'Is that the only place you called?'

'Wood is wood,' Garp said. 'Two-by-fours are two-by-fours. Go to Springfield Avenue and they'll have them ready.'

'*What* interesting job have you found?' Helen asked him; he knew she would have been thinking about it.

'Marriage counseling,' Garp said; his tomato sauce bubbled – the kitchen filled with its rich fumes. Helen maintained a respectful silence on her end of the phone. Garp knew she would find it difficult to ask, this time, what qualifications he thought he had for such a thing.

'You're a writer,' she told him.

'Perfect qualifications for the job,' Garp said. 'Years spent pondering the morass of human relationships; hours spent divining what it is that people have in common. The failure of love,' Garp droned on, 'the complexity of compromise, the need for compassion.'

'So *write* about it,' Helen said. 'What more do you want?' She knew perfectly well what was coming next.

'Art doesn't help anyone,' Garp said. 'People can't really use it: they can't eat it, it won't shelter or clothe them – and if they're sick, it won't make them well.' This, Helen knew, was Garp's thesis on the basic uselessness of art; he rejected the idea that art was of any social value whatsoever – that it could be, that it should be. The two things mustn't be confused, he thought: there was art, and there was helping people. Here he was, fumbling at both – his mother's son, after all. But, true to his thesis, he saw art and social responsibility as two distinct acts. The messes came when certain jerks attempted to combine these fields. Garp would be irritated all his life by his belief that literature was a luxury item; he desired for it to be more basic – yet he hated it, when it was.

'I'll go get the two-by-fours now,' Helen said.

'And if the peculiarities of my art weren't qualification enough,' Garp said, 'I have, as you know, been married myself.' He paused. 'I've had children.' He paused again. 'I've had a variety of marriage-related experiences – we both have.'

'Springfield Avenue?' Helen said. 'I'll be home soon.'

'I have more than enough experience for the job,' he insisted. 'I've known financial dependency, I've experienced infidelity.'

'Good for you,' Helen said. She hung up.

But Garp thought: Maybe marriage counseling is a charlatan field even if a genuine and qualified person is giving the advice. He replaced the phone on the hook. He knew he could advertise himself in the Yellow Pages most successfully – even without lying.

MARRIAGE PHILOSOPHY
& FAMILY ADVICE –
T. S. GARP

author of *Procrastination* and *Second Wind of the Cuckold*

Why add that they were novels? They sounded, Garp realized, like marriage-counsel manuals.

But would he see his poor patients at home or in an office?

Garp took a green pepper and propped it in the center of the gas burner; he turned up the flame and the pepper began to burn. When it was black all over, Garp would let it cool, then scrape off all the charred skin. Inside would be a roasted pepper, very sweet, and he would slice it and let it marinate in oil and vinegar and a little marjoram. That would be his dressing for the salad. But the main reason he liked to make dressing this way was that the roasting pepper made the kitchen smell so good.

He turned the pepper with a pair of tongs. When the pepper was charred, Garp snatched it up with the tongs and flipped it into the sink. The pepper hissed at him. 'Talk all you want to,' Garp told it. 'You don't have much time left.'

He was distracted. Usually he liked to stop thinking about other things while he cooked – in fact, he forced himself to. But he was suffering a crisis of confidence about marriage counseling.

'You're suffering a crisis of confidence about your *writing*,' Helen told him, walking into the kitchen with even more than her usual authority – the freshly cut two-by-fours slung over and under her arm like matching shotguns.

Walt said, 'Daddy burned something.'

'It was a pepper and Daddy *meant* to,' Garp said.

'Every time you can't write you do something stupid,' Helen said. 'Though I'll confess this is a better idea for a diversion than your last diversion.'

Garp had expected her to be ready, but he was surprised that she was *so* ready. What Helen called his last 'diversion' from his stalled writing had been a babysitter.

Garp drove a wooden spoon deep into his tomato sauce. He flinched as some fool took the corner by the house with a roaring downshift and a squeal of tires that cut through Garp with the sound of a struck cat. He looked instinctively for Walt, who was right there – safe in the kitchen.

Helen said, 'Where's Duncan?' She moved to the door but Garp cut in front of her.

'Duncan went to Ralph's,' he said; he was not worried, *this* time, that the speeding car meant Duncan had been hit, but it was Garp's habit to chase down speeding cars. He had properly bullied every fast driver in the neighborhood. The streets around Garp's house were cut in squares, bordered every block by stop signs; Garp could usually catch up to a car, on foot, provided that the car obeyed the stop signs.

He raced down the street after the sound of the car. Sometimes, if the car was going really fast, Garp would need three or four stop signs to catch up to it. Once he sprinted five blocks and was so out of breath when he caught up to the offending car that the driver was sure there'd been a murder in the neighborhood and Garp was either trying to report it or had done it himself.

Most drivers were impressed with Garp, and even if they swore about him later, they were polite and apologetic to his face, assuring him they would not speed in the neighborhood again. It was clear to them that Garp was in good physical shape. Most of them were high school kids who were easily embarrassed – caught hot-rodding around with their girlfriends, or leaving little smoking-rubber stains in front of their girlfriends' houses. Garp was not such a fool as to imagine that he changed their ways; all he hoped to do was make them speed somewhere else.

The present offender turned out to be a woman (Garp saw her earrings glinting, and the bracelets on her arm, as he ran up to her from behind). She was just ready to pull away from a stop sign when Garp rapped the wooden spoon on her window, startling her. The spoon, dribbling tomato sauce, looked at a glance as if it had been dipped in blood.

Garp waited for her to roll down her window, and was already phrasing his opening remarks ('I'm sorry I startled you, but I wanted to ask you a personal favor . . .') when he recognized that the woman was Ralph's mother – the notorious Mrs Ralph. Duncan and Ralph were not with her; she was alone, and it was obvious that she had been crying.

'Yes, what is it?' she said. Garp couldn't tell if she recognized him as Duncan's father, or not.

'I'm sorry I startled you,' Garp began. He stopped. What else could he say to her? Smeary-faced, fresh from a fight with her ex-husband or a lover, the poor woman looked to be suffering her approaching middle age like the flu; her body looked rumpled with misery, her eyes were red and vague. 'I'm sorry,' Garp mumbled; he was sorry for her whole life. How could he tell her that all he wanted was for her to slow down?

'What is it?' she asked him.

'I'm Duncan's father,' Garp said.

'I *know* you are,' she said. 'I'm Ralph's mother.'

'I know,' he said; he smiled.

'Duncan's father meets Ralph's mother,' she said, caustically. Then she burst into tears. Her face flopped forward and struck the horn. She sat up straight, suddenly hitting Garp's hand, resting on her rolled-down window; his fingers opened and he dropped the long-handled spoon into her lap. They both stared at it; the tomato sauce produced a stain on her wrinkled beige dress.

'You must think I'm a rotten mother,' Mrs Ralph said. Garp, ever-conscious of safety, reached across her knees and turned off the ignition. He decided to leave the spoon in her lap. It was Garp's curse to be unable to conceal his feelings from people, even from strangers; if he thought contemptuous thoughts about you, somehow you *knew*.

'I don't know anything about what kind of mother you are,' Garp told her. 'I think Ralph's a nice boy.'

'He can be a real shit,' she said.

'Perhaps you'd rather Duncan not stay with you tonight?' Garp asked – Garp *hoped*. To Garp, she didn't appear to know that Duncan *was* spending the night with Ralph. She looked at the spoon in her lap. 'It's tomato sauce,' Garp said. To his surprise, Mrs Ralph picked up the spoon and licked it.

'You're a cook?' she asked.

'Yes, I like to cook,' Garp said.

'It's very good,' Mrs Ralph told him, handing him his spoon. 'I should have gotten one like you – some muscular little prick who likes to cook.'

Garp counted in his head to five; then he said, 'I'd be glad to go pick up the boys. They could spend the night with us, if you'd like to be alone.'

'Alone!' she cried. 'I'm *usually* alone. I *like* having the boys with me. And *they* like it, too,' she said. 'Do you know why?' Mrs Ralph looked at him wickedly.

'Why?' Garp said.

'They like to watch me take a bath,' she said. 'There's a crack in the door. Isn't it sweet that Ralph likes to show off his old mother to his friends?'

'Yes,' Garp said.

'You don't approve, do you, Mr Garp?' she asked him. 'You don't approve of me at all.'

'I'm sorry you're so unhappy,' Garp said. On the seat beside her in her messy car was a paperback of Dostoevsky's *The Eternal Husband*; Garp remembered that Mrs Ralph was going to school. 'What are you majoring in?' he asked her, stupidly. He recalled she was a never-ending graduate student; her problem was probably a thesis that wouldn't come.

Mrs Ralph shook her head. 'You really keep your nose

clean, don't you?' she asked Garp. 'How long have you been married?'

'Almost eleven years,' Garp said. Mrs Ralph looked more or less indifferent; Mrs Ralph had been married for twelve.

'Your kid's safe with me,' she said, as if she were suddenly irritated with him, and as if she were reading his mind with utter accuracy. 'Don't worry, I'm quite harmless – with children,' she added. 'And I don't smoke in bed.'

'I'm sure it's good for the boys to watch you take a bath,' Garp told her, then felt immediately embarrassed for saying it, though it was one of the few things he'd told her that he meant.

'I don't know,' she said. 'It didn't seem to do much good for my husband, and *he* watched me for years.' She looked up at Garp, whose mouth hurt from all his forced smiles. Just touch her cheek, or pat her hand, he thought; at least *say* something. But Garp was clumsy at being kind, and he didn't flirt.

'Well, husbands *are* funny,' he mumbled. Garp the marriage counselor, full of advice. 'I don't think many of them know what they want.'

Mrs Ralph laughed bitterly. 'My husband found a nineteen-year-old *cunt*,' she said. 'He seems to want *her*.'

'I'm sorry,' Garp told her. The marriage counselor is the I'm-sorry man, like a doctor with bad luck – the one who gets to diagnose all the terminal cases.

'You're a writer,' Mrs Ralph said to him, accusingly; she waved her copy of *The Eternal Husband* at him. 'What do you think of this?'

'It's a wonderful story,' Garp said. It was fortunately a book he remembered – neatly complicated, full of perverse and human contradiction.

'I think it's a *sick* story,' Mrs Ralph told him. 'I'd like to know what's so special about Dostoevsky.'

'Well,' Garp said, 'his characters are so complex, psychologically and emotionally; and the situations are so ambiguous.'

'His women are *less* than objects,' Mrs Ralph said, 'they don't even have any *shape*. They're just ideas that men talk about and play with.' She threw the book out the window at Garp; it hit his chest and fell by the curb. She clenched her fists in her lap, staring at the stain on her dress, which marked her crotch with a tomato-sauce bull's-eye. 'Boy, that's me all over,' she said, staring at the spot.

'I'm sorry,' Garp said again. 'It may leave a permanent stain.'

'Everything leaves a stain!' Mrs Ralph cried out. A laughter so witless escaped her that it frightened Garp. He didn't say anything and she said to him, 'I'll bet you think that all I need is a good *lay*.'

To be fair, Garp rarely thought this of people, but when Mrs Ralph mentioned it, he *did* think that, in *her* case, this oversimple solution might apply.

'And I'll bet you think I'd let *you* do it,' she said, glaring at him. Garp, in fact, *did* think so.

'No, I don't think you would,' he said.

'Yes, you think I would *love* to,' Mrs Ralph said.

Garp hung his head. 'No,' he said.

'Well, in *your* case,' she said, 'I just *might*.' He looked at her and she gave him an evil grin. 'It might make you a little less smug,' she told him.

'You don't know me well enough to talk to me like this,' Garp said.

'I know that you're *smug*,' Mrs Ralph said. 'You think you're so superior.' True, Garp knew; he *was* superior. He would make a lousy marriage counselor, he now knew.

'Please drive carefully,' Garp said; he pushed himself away from her car. 'If there's anything I can do, please call.'

'Like if I need a good *lover*?' Mrs Ralph asked him, nastily.

'No, not that,' Garp said.

'Why did you stop me?' she asked him.

'Because I thought you were driving too fast,' he said.

'I think you're a pompous fart,' she told him.

'I think you're an irresponsible slob,' Garp told her. She cried out as if she were stabbed.

'Look, I'm sorry,' he said (again), 'but I'll just come pick up Duncan.'

'No, *please*,' she said. 'I can look after him, I really *want* to. He'll be all right – I'll look after him like he was my own!' This didn't truly comfort Garp. 'I'm not *that* much of a slob – with *kids*,' she added; she managed an alarmingly attractive smile.

'I'm sorry,' Garp said – his litany.

'So am I,' said Mrs Ralph. As if the matter were resolved between them, she started her car and drove past the stop sign and through the intersection without looking. She drove away – slowly, but more or less in the middle of the road – and Garp waved his wooden spoon after her.

Then he picked up *The Eternal Husband* and walked home.

10

The Dog in the Alley,
the Child in the Sky

'We've got to get Duncan out of that mad woman's house,'
Garp told Helen.

'Well, you do it,' Helen said. 'You're the one who's
worried.'

'You should have seen how she drove,' Garp said.

'Well,' said Helen, 'presumably Duncan isn't going to be
riding around with her.'

'She may take the boys out for a pizza,' Garp said. 'I'm
sure she can't cook.'

Helen was looking at *The Eternal Husband*. She said, 'It's
a strange book for a woman to give to another woman's
husband.'

'She didn't give it to me, Helen. She *threw* it at me.'

'It's a wonderful story,' Helen said.

'She said it was just *sick*,' Garp said, despairingly. 'She
thought it was unfair to women.'

Helen looked puzzled. 'I wouldn't say that was even an
issue,' she said.

'Of course it isn't!' Garp yelled. 'This woman is an idiot!
My mother would love her.'

'Oh, poor Jenny,' Helen said. 'Don't start on her.'

'Finish your pasta, Walt,' Garp said.

'Up your wazoo,' Walt said.

'Nice talk,' Garp said. 'Walt, I don't *have* a wazoo.'

'Yes, you do,' Walt said.

'He doesn't know what it means,' Helen said. 'I'm not sure what it means, either.'

'Five years old,' Garp said. 'It's not nice to say that to people,' Garp told Walt.

'He heard it from Duncan, I'm sure,' Helen said.

'Well, Duncan gets it from Ralph,' Garp said, 'who no doubt gets it from his goddamn mother!'

'Watch your own language,' Helen said. 'Walt could as easily have gotten his "wazoo" from you.'

'Not from me, he couldn't have,' Garp declared. '*I'm* not sure what it means, either. I never use that word.'

'You use plenty just like it,' Helen said.

'Walt, eat your pasta,' Garp said.

'Calm down,' Helen said.

Garp eyed Walt's uneaten pasta as if it were a personal insult. 'Why do I bother?' he said. 'The child eats nothing.'

They finished their meal in silence. Helen knew Garp was thinking up a story to tell Walt after dinner. She knew Garp did this to calm himself whenever he was worried about the children – as if the act of imagining a good story for children was a way to keep children safe forever.

With the children Garp was instinctively generous, loyal as an animal, the most affectionate of fathers; he understood Duncan and Walt deeply and separately. Yet, Helen felt sure, he saw nothing of how his anxiety for the children made the children anxious – tense, even immature. On the one hand he treated them as grown-ups, but on the other hand he was so protective of them that he was not allowing them to grow up. He did not accept that Duncan was ten, that Walt was five; sometimes the children seemed fixed, as three-year-olds, in his mind.

Helen listened to the story Garp made up for Walt with her usual interest and concern. Like many of the stories Garp told the children, it began as a story for the children and ended up as a story Garp seemed to have made up for Garp. You would think that the children of a writer would have more stories read to them than other children, but Garp preferred that his children listen only to *his* stories.

'There was a dog,' Garp said.

'What kind of dog?' said Walt.

'A big German shepherd dog,' said Garp.

'What was his name?' Walt asked.

'He didn't have a name,' Garp said. 'He lived in a city in Germany, after the war.'

'What war?' said Walt.

'World War Two,' Garp said.

'Oh sure,' Walt said.

'The dog had been in the war,' Garp said. 'He had been a guard dog, so he was very fierce and very smart.'

'Very *mean*,' said Walt.

'No,' Garp said, 'he wasn't mean and he wasn't nice, or sometimes he was both. He was whatever his master trained him to be, because he was trained to do whatever his master told him to do.'

'How did he know who his master was?' Walt asked.

'I don't know,' Garp said. 'After the war, he got a new master. This master owned a café in the city; you could get coffee and tea and drinks there, and read the newspapers. At night the master would leave one light on, inside the café, so that you could look in the windows and see all the wiped-off tables with the chairs upside-down on the table tops. The floor was swept clean, and the big dog paced back and forth across the floor every night. He was like a lion in his cage at the zoo, he was never still. Sometimes people would see him in there and they'd knock on the window to get his attention. The dog would just stare at them – he wouldn't bark, or even growl. He'd just stop pacing and stare, until whoever it was went away. You had the feeling that if you stayed too long, the dog might jump through the window at you. But he never did; he never did anything, in fact, because no one ever broke into that café at night. It was enough just having the dog there; the dog didn't have to *do* anything.'